NIGHT

TRAIN

TO

MOTHER

Ronit Lentin

CLEIS
PRESS

Ɐ Ʌ Y 7523

Originally published in 1989 in Ireland by Attic Press,
44 East Essex Street, Dublin 2 Ireland.

Published in the United States by Cleis Press,
P.O. Box 8933, Pittsburgh, Pennsylvania 15221, and
P.O. Box 14684, San Francisco, California 94114.

Printed in the United States.
Cover design: Cecilia Brunazzi
Cover photograph: C. Oscar Gaiter, Bistritsa
Typesetting: CaliCo Graphics
Logo art: Juana Alicia

First Edition.
10 9 8 7 6 5 4 3 2 1

Library of Congress Cataloging-in-Publication Data

Lentin, Ronit.
  Night train to Mother :
  a novel / by Ronit Lentin. — 1st U.S. ed.
    p. cm.
  Summary: From 1895 to 1984, members of four generations
of women in a Jewish family journey from Romania to Israel
and back again.
    ISBN: 0-939416-32-8 : $24.95 —
    ISBN: 0-939416-33-6 (pbk.) : $9.95
    [1. Jews—Fiction.]   I. Title.
PR9510.9.L46N54 1990
823—dc20
[Fic]   90-1316
                                   CIP
                                   AC

Israeli-born RONIT LENTIN has lived in Ireland for the last 19
years. She has written as a freelance writer-journalist for most
of Ireland's daily and Sunday newspapers. She has published
two novels; *Stone of Claims* (1976) and *Like a Blindman* (1978). In
1979 Ronit Lentin won second prize for 'Friends', a radio play
which was broadcast by Israeli and Irish Radio. Her first English
language novella, *Tea with Mrs. Klein* was published in 1985. Her
non-fiction work includes *Who is Minding the Children*, co-
authored with Geraldine Niland (1980) and *Conversations with
Palestinian Women* (1981).

To Lia
To Louis
Always

USSR

Chernovtsy ●

Suceava
Gura Humorlui ● ●
Cirlibaba ● ● Vatra Dornei
Bistritsa ●

ROMANIA

©Bucharest

CONTENTS

Glossary

Alav ha shalom — may he rest in peace
Aleha ha shalom — may she rest in peace
Baruch ha shem — blessed be His (the Lord's) name
Buchtels — small yeasty cheese cakes
Challah — plaited white bread, used for Sabbath and holidays
Chuppah — wedding canopy
Conditions — marriage contract, signed between fathers of bride and groom before the wedding. It's said that once signed, the marriage must go ahead
Ciorba — Romanian for a very thick, chunky soup
Doddi zach ve adom etc — verses from the Song of Song, describing courting but according to biblical interpretations, really meant to describe the love between the Lord and Israel
Doamna — Mrs in Romanian
Domnul — Mr in Romanian
Eretz Israel — the land of Israel
Eshte Romaneshte — In the 1950s used mockingly in Israel against immigrants from Romania
Gemarra — the second part of the Talmud, providing commentary on the Mishna, the first part
Gefüllte Fish — stuffed fish, usually sweet water fish, and a renowned Jewish delicacy
Gnädige Frau — honoured lady, an Austrian expression
Goyim — gentiles
Hamotsi — literally, he who brings forth, and short for the blessing on the bread, said by Jews whenever bread is partaken
Hamsin — 'Fifty' in Arabic and the name for a Mistral-like wind blowing from the desert which is said to afflict Israel 50 days a year
Hanukah — literally, inauguration — the name of a Jewish holiday celebrating the victory of the Jews over the Greeks
Hassid — literally righteous — member of a religious sect at the head of which there is a Rebbe who runs a court
Heder — Hebrew word for 'room', refers to the one room school where Jewish male children studied religion and scriptures
Kaddish — literally, magnified and sanctified be his great name — said by the graveside, a prayer for the dead
Kinderlach — Yiddish word for 'children'
Lokshen — noodles
Mamaliga — cornmeal bread, eaten hot or cold with cheese or cream, a Romanian speciality

Mamser — literally, bastard, in Hebrew

Mazel tov — 'Good luck' in Hebrew, meaning congratulations and used throughout the Jewish world

Matza/matzo — unleavened bread, eaten in passover to commemorate the exodus from Egypt when the Israelites didn't have time to wait for their bread to leaven

Melamed — A teacher. Used for religious teachers teaching children scriptures and the law

Meshugenner — Yiddish for crazy

Miquva — A reservoir — denotes ritual communal bath where Jews go to purify themselves

Mitzva — command, religious duty, obligation

Nu — literally 'well' in Russian, but used in Yiddish meaning well, come along, so

Oma — grandmother

Opa — grandfather

Ostjude — Eastern Jew — used contemptuously by central European Jews about the less affluent eastern European Jews

Pessach — Passover in Hebrew

Propination — a licence to sell spirits

Rebbe — a Hassidic Rabbi

Reb — a title one Jew addresses another Jew by, especially if he values him as a scholar

Schmalz — lard in German

Schwarzer — literally 'blacks', used by Israeli European Jews to describe Jews from Arab countries

Shabbat — Sabbath in Hebrew

Shadchan — matchmaker

Shidduch — match

Shiksa — gentile woman

Talmud — books of commentaries on the Torah written by learned Rabbis and compiled about 375-500 AD

Torah — the books of Moses in Hebrew

Totul pentru Tară — literally, 'all for the fatherland' in Romanian — the slogan of the Iron Guard fascist party

Trăsură — carriage in Romanian

Tsena U Reena — literally, 'come and see' in Hebrew — the name of a special prayer book for women

Tsores — Yiddish for troubles

Tuică — plum brandy in Romanian

Verfluchte Kommunisten — Cursed communists in German/Yiddish

Yimach Shemam — May their name be struck off

Yishuv — Settlement, meaning the establishment settlers in Palestine before the state of Israel.

Ruth 1984

When did the journey begin?

Did it begin when you asked grandfather Mendel to draw family trees? You were only eight or nine and he sat, patient, and put down Hirsches and Laxes, Hellers and Königs and your father's Goldmans on pieces of paper he tore out of his account ledgers.

Or did it begin when he took you by the hand and brought you to Zamenhof synagogue in Tel Aviv, a place where he was an important man, where people took notice of him and therefore of you?

Or when Oma Rosa made masses of food, urging you to eat, always more and more? Eat maminka, eat mein Kind, put some flesh on your skinny bones, get stronger, a real sabra, not a pale little girl from there. But Oma, you protested, it's too much, I am full already. But she stood over you, watching your every mouthful.

Did it begin on the slopes of Mount Carmel, in a field full of grey rocks and yellow thorns where you had escaped and sat holding your knees obstinately because you didn't like the woman from there who was visiting them? And later on, when they found you, white with worry, father slapped you across the face, a hard, angry slap.

Or when you sat on grandma Tattu's bony knee and had your photograph taken, she all white and stern-looking and you a squirming two-year-old, wriggling to get away from the musty smell and her arthritic hands holding you too tightly?

Did the journey begin when going to Tel Aviv was long and boring and when arriving was only when you reached Oma and grandfather's shady avenue where the sandy ground was hard on knees and elbows which scraped when you fell?

Or with the eternal arguments between mother and Oma? Why do it this way, why not like this and let me wash up already, you never let anyone do anything and sit down now, I am doing it. Guilt was fostered like this. Two hard-working women, the men sitting while they worked. And as you grew up and they argued and worked, you were made feel more guilty for not offering to help. They were good at fostering guilt, Oma and mother. They knew the tune from early childhood when your best was never enough.

Did the journey begin with being told by grandfather Mendel never, but never to think about God in the water closet and then, for years, thinking only of God when you peed and did the other thing? And being told off, softly but very sternly, that writing on Shabbat was forbidden, something good children never did because He saw everything. And then writing only at home, on the slopes of the mountain, so grandfather's beautiful features wouldn't crumple in anger. And the eternal guilt.

Did it begin on Saturday afternoons, when Oma and grandfather's families gathered in the two rooms which had a heavy glass door between them and where you slept behind the glass door, always hearing her moan and shout in her sleep, particularly in later years, when he was not there to listen?

They came, strange people, the women wearing dark lipstick, always kissing you, making red or purple marks on reluctant cheeks. And the men wearing dark suits when no one else did. And smelling of other places. Not musty like grandma Tattu but a there smell. And speaking no Hebrew or if they did, you couldn't understand it. It was heavy with thick accents, the Hebrew of people who came from there. There was Tante Hetti, limping, fat, her eyes small and unsmiling and Tante Hanna, already stooped, her serious face grimaced with pain. They all spoke German. You got to understand because father and mother spoke it to each other, but not to you. To you they spoke Hebrew. They wanted you to grow up here, not share a there language which many school mates said was a Nazi language.

It could have begun when great-grandmother Dora came to live with them. She scared you, sitting on the veranda where lizards climbed the pebbly wall, hiccupping endlessly and asking every hour is it already one? Is it already two? Her toothless mouth fixed in eternal expressionless pain in her wrinkled pale face framed by hair, even whiter than grandma Tattu's, pulled back in a tight bun, making her head look small, like the scalped heads you had read about in Karl May's cowboys and Indians books.

When did the journey begin? When did you first know that love was a word from novels and dictionaries, a word no one talked of? Only Oma said it from time to time when she hugged you too tight, pressing you to her big bosom, her sweat trickling down her body, arrested by sweat pads, carefully sewn on to the summer dresses Grosstante Hetti made for her? When did you learn that Oma and grandfather did not hug and that mother and father did not hug but that they never fought before you children? And when Oma said that word, you recoiled. Her attention overwhelming, you wanted her older, remoter, like other children's grandmothers who didn't interfere.

When did you learn that grandfather Mendel didn't do very much when he went to town, joking with you when you begged him not to go? He then brought back little chocolaty sweets

11

covered in tiny coloured things and sugared almonds in brown paper bags. One for you and one for Avner and one for Yossi when he stayed. He allowed you to run your thin fingers along his large, veined hands, the softness of which you will never forget as he sat with his fat Polish partner in the third room, speaking fast in Yiddish which no-one spoke at home.

When did you learn that Mendel Heller, the big businessman from Dorna and Czernowitz, broke his heart in the land of his dreams? That promises from political colleagues came to nothing and business was not business though he never said a word against this cruel land? When did you realise that Mendel and Rosa belonged to a lost generation? That they could never forgive themselves for escaping in time and leaving their families behind? That they couldn't live with the guilt?

Till her dying day, you heard Rosa cry in her sleep for the parents she had left behind. When her mother came, broken, old, there was not much left of beautiful, strong Dora. And Rosa continued to cry, shedding tears she couldn't shed while awake.

When did the journey begin?

When was the first time you remember being told about there? Was it Grossonkel Shmaya or Grosstante Hanna who first spoke about there and when they saw you listening, stopped talking and instead started eating Oma's cheese buchtels or spooning strawberry confiture they washed down with iced water?

The word Dorna rang golden on their lips but other words, Tate, Grossmutter, Transnistria, Tod, were only whispers. Lost and poor, until the reparation money started coming, they replayed a solitary board game in Oma's glass-panelled room, passing the code words cautiously, hoping their Israeli-born grandchildren wouldn't pick up their clues.

Hard to remember when you first realised the past was always bad. The goyim, the troubles, the endless moves, the camp, the sick stomachs. They all had sick stomachs. From the goose schmalz they had been fed as children so that they wouldn't catch TB like Dora's poor sister-in-law Rosa. And from the camp.

All the while when they talked opaquely of there, grandmother Dora sat alone, older than her seventy-odd years. Her mouth hollow when she smiled one of her rare smiles. She hiccupped continuously and never spoke to the children, scaring you, she and the lizards on the wall. Rosa spoke to her without gentleness and the others shook her hand when they came and before they left. When she died you stopped thinking about her,

12

but your brother wept.

Oma Rosa ruled these gatherings, urging them to eat, talking a shade louder than the others. Grosstante Hanna sat quietly but from time to time said something which put Rosa in her place. You must always be right, you heard Rosa hiss, more than once. Grosstante Hetti, when she came from Haifa, was also quiet, looking at Rosa with what you thought was envy. Rosa's family was in the minority compared with Mendel's large family but with the years the balance changed as Mendel's family died off. You grew up and left home and then left the country and every so often mother would write and tell you who died.

When did the journey begin? Was there ever a time when you didn't journey, searching mother's hand, gasping for air, your asthmatic bronchials rasping to her reassuring voice? You were too thin, too ill, not eating enough, not sleeping enough, standing obstinately shaking your cot sides for nights on end, never secure in the knowledge.

You could have been a child from there, but they did all they could so you would be a child from here, a strong, earth-smelling sabra. The children at school mocked your skinny body and you developed an acid tongue in reply.

You could have been a child from there, but mother, golden-haired Carla, who had been too European for father's pioneering friends (she paints her lips, they whispered behind her back when he first introduced her to them), and father, for whom there had been nothing but a vague, distant childhood there, feared for your ability to withstand. Did they, secretly, think you wouldn't have survived had you been born there?

Father said, I want you to grow up not fearing the anti-semites. And he also said, when I was a child in Vienna, we often had to eat potato peels and chicken skins (you said yuk). You, my sabra, father said, must eat and be strong. He showed you the country, talked of art and of music and of queueing up to see Kaiser Franz-Josef in Vienna where grandma Tattu and grandpa went when they left Bucovina. And of his youth in Jerusalem, a new immigrant in a society of sabras, mocking his otherness already then. But he never spoke of there. Poor lost father. He wanted to give his children a gift of the free Jewish land, but your brother Avner and you ended leaving it. Replaying their fate. Your exile.

The others averted their gaze when you listened in while they talked of there. You listened avidly to their frail voices as if your life depended on the knowledge. You wanted to know but they wanted to forget. And couldn't.

13

And mother said I hated it there, this is where I belong. Oma was not quite so certain. When you made her talk, she embellished the past with small details. We weren't uneducated, you know, she would write in the long letters you made her write. We studied much more than just Torah and Yiddish. Or she would write about what she thought made picturesque reading. Mother was more ruthless but she too decorated her stories with tales of ice skating and coffee houses.

All the rest you had to fill in for yourself. The longings, the searching for true love, the perpetuation of women looking for acceptance and men yearning for power which eludes.

Then there were the empty pains of a generation which thought it was coming to a promised land and found itself in a harsh climate, struggling to make sense of the eternal rifts, the bureaucracy, the wars, the hopes for their children, the realisation that the children had to live their own pangs of separation, make their own journeys.

Where did the journey begin? Was there ever a time when you didn't feel Dora and Rosa, Hetti and Tattu and Carla were you? Was there ever a time you weren't journeying to connect the here and the there, the now and the then, love and other words?

* * *

You don't know when the journey began. But one day you are in Bucharest airport arguing with a fat official about visas and dollars. Something you wanted to do for years. Put pictures where only words had been.

It hadn't been easy. Whenever you mentioned it to mother, she shuddered. Why go there when there are so many places? I wouldn't go there for anything. And then one year she said she would come. The only way I'd go back is with you. But she didn't come and you had to go alone.

Romania? You must be going to the Black Sea, friends say.

Bucovina? The fat official laughs, calling a colleague to share the joke. There is no place of that name. Vatra Dornei? Yes, but it's in the county of Suceava. Suceava, he repeats, remember, not Bucovina. And you worry there will be nothing to find. Not even the name.

Contemporary Romania rears its head. Visas, foreign currency, transport to town for the price of a packet of Kent. Later you learn you can get everything here, from an appointment with the doctor to a kilo of meat the butcher would otherwise not sell, for a packet of Kent. "Saint Kent" they call it here.

Poverty and deprivation hit as soon as daylight fades. Streets, hotel rooms, public buildings are all under-lit. Bucharest is ghost city, slave to the energy crisis. Jokes about Bucharest tough winters: close the window, the street will get cold. There is something chilling about it even in June.

Money exchange is constantly on offer. The greed for foreign currency incredible. The official exchange rate is nearly 20 lei per pound. Waiters offer 40 and later you will get 58 lei per pound ending up with too much money and little to spend it on.

Bucharest. Here mother, Herbert, Oma and grandfather waited for their Turkish transit visas in the cold winter of 1940-1. They lived not far from where you are now, off the Calea Victoriei, a broad street, its beautiful buildings ageing but still elegant. The Paris of the East they called Bucharest.

Your first night. Think of Carla here alone, 19 years of age, waiting for her parents and brother in a small pension off the Calea in the middle of the war and stop being scared. There is an unshaven man slouching outside the room in Muntenia, a shabby city centre hotel. Is he a secret agent, a randy local preying on innocent female tourists or simply a tired Romanian, resting on the conveniently placed armchair? You'll never know. You turn the key to the room. You wouldn't have got very far if you had to flee the fascist Iron Guard, you think, your heart pounding.

In the morning you wake early. It's Sunday and the streets below are crowded with strollers, buying flowers, the only commodity never in short supply here. You leave the room carefully but the man is gone.

Bucharest in the morning is softer, less menacing. This is going to be a total journey, right to the centre. For years you had probed, questioning Carla, Rosa, Hanna, Hetti, about there. I am here now, mother, you want to scream. I am on my way.

Marshall is an elderly American Jew. Angry at a young official who is helping you to book a night train ticket to Vatra Dornei because he expects the same service you'd get in America. He agitates, gesticulating and in the commotion you meet.

He has been here for a while to find a wife. He takes you to see Jewish Bucharest, where Jews still live under the auspices of Rabbi Moshe Rosen, His Pestilence, as he is ironically called by the few Jews who still inhabit Bucovina, once a major Jewish centre, today a land without Jews.

The Jewish museum. Your first meeting with Transnistria. Yellow stars they had to make themselves and bars of rein jüdisches Fett. Later Mimi will say that after years in the camp without soap, she washed herself in RJF soap. She had

15

nightmares for years afterwards. Eighty per cent of the Jews exiled to Transnistria did not return — like Menashe and Anschel they died of hunger, cold, typhoid, depression. Death without annihilation.

You are starting to connect. Slowly. Jewish Romania has disappeared by and large. The remainder is kept alive only by US dollars brought into this beleaguered state by Rabbi Rosen. Every Jew allowed to leave has his hard currency price.

The Coral Synagogue, a beautiful pink building in the centre of Bucharest, is full this Sunday morning. Talmud Torah, choir practice, lively debates about the rights and wrongs of immigration to Israel.

Yet Jewish Bucharest has the sadness of people living on borrowed time. You meet several who have already got a visa to Israel but cannot work until they leave and haven't enough funds to travel. For others Israel has never been a possibility which is why they didn't leave with the rest of Romanian Jewry of whom only 15,000 remain in Bucharest and several thousands scattered throughout the country.

Marshall takes you to meet a former Lebanese minister. As you sit with him, his second wife, a shy, beautiful daughter and her moustachioed Falangist fiancé eating tabouleh on the second-floor landing of the sleazy Hotel Opera, changing sterling travellers' cheques into lei, you feel in the centre of a Balkan drama. Was this how Carla felt during those long 1940 winter months calling daily at the Turkish embassy?

Marshall envies your journey. You hate him talking about it in those sentimental, American-Jewish terms but allow him to see you to the dark Gara de Nord where your night train awaits.

You sit up all night with two couples just back from the Soviet Union, chattering about the gold they purchased. They will sell it at great profit. In Romania gold is at a premium. You will be constantly approached for your two wedding rings, one yours and the other Rosa's, inscribed, "Mendel, 31.12.1919", her wedding day.

The dawn lights familiar place names, appearing through the wet green fields like pictures in a family album. Gura Humorlui, father's birthplace. Frasin, where Mendel and his brothers set up the family timber business. Cimpulung and finally, in the grey morning light, Vatra Dornei, mother's birthplace and your destination.

The railway station, a charming Bucovinian style white and yellow building, looks disappointing in the grey morning light. Your first encounter with this magical town, about which you have made Rosa and Carla talk for hours, is a fiasco. You lie on

16

your hotel bed in a square sparse room, its large curtainless window looking onto the town hall clock tower, playing every hour on the hour a tune by Romania's national composer Ciprian Porumbescu, sobbing your heart out. What are you doing here, why have you come, two weeks alone on the eastern outskirts of the once flourishing Austro-Hungarian Empire in a hotel room with no hot water? Why this obsession with journeys into a past which doesn't seem to exist? Why the need to connect with the part of you which is Dora, Rosa, Hetti, Carla?

It takes a sleep, a short walk and a meeting with Helena, mother's school friend, and her husband Siegmund to fix the sights of Dorna in your head and get it into focus. Helena and Siegmund are two of forty-two Jews in a town which was once mostly Jewish.

They met in Mogilev, Transnistria and married when he was discharged from the Red Army after the war. He then worked in the local timber company, once a Heller enterprise, today the nationalised Dorna Foresta, and during Stalin's time was tried for sabotage with a group of local Jews in a show trial. He was found not guilty but in a subsequent case, although nothing was proven, was sentenced to prison.

Helena, whose voice and tone remind you of Rosa, dead now almost five years, has harboured bitterness all her married life. Others received money from abroad to get themselves out of prison, we had no one, she says. To this day Siegmund has to pay a third of his meagre pension to cover his fine, 58 million lei in all, a sum no ordinary citizen can dream of repaying. They have no children. First there was the trial, then his imprisonment. Helena had several abortions and when he left prison, she could not conceive. They are still in love, two solitary, dignified figures, spending their days dreaming of food, always dreaming of food, bartering, dealing, concocting their next meal.

How lucky you were, Carla, to have left this place, where a mere rumour of lemons arriving in town sends shivers of delight down your school friend's spine. Costica, a young farmer from the mountains, works their vegetable patch which they have to cultivate, by governmental decree, in return for half the crops. Every morning Helena makes your breakfast and Siegmund brings fresh radishes and scallions to go with the hard cow's milk cheese Helena makes in hanging muslin bags, as they used to do since Dora's days.

A famous spa, frequented by many tourists, Vatra Dornei lacks the greyness prevailing in Ceaucescu's Romania. It has all the charm and natural beauty of Bucovina, always a frontier

17

region and a symbol connected with the struggle for Romanian national freedom. Its name was initially used to designate the beech (buk) forests covering its mountain peaks. The traveller, journeying, like you, through its picturesque villages and from hairpin curve to hairpin curve on its wooded mountains, will, say the guide books, forever cherish the image of the soft green hills, ivory citadel walls, the natural elegance and the honey-coloured light which enwraps Bucovina in a golden halo.

Dorna itself, situated between the mountains where the Dorna stream flows into the Bistritsa river, is one of the most picturesque towns in this otherwise grey country. Every day, after breakfast and a bath Siegmund heats for you with precious timber, you walk into the little town centre. Six Martie Street is a pedestrianised shopping street with little to buy. A woman in a red jacket and white trousers sticks out in the greyness. Down the road is Hellergasse, today Dobreanu Gherea street, named after a Jewish writer. In consideration?

Here is Carla's first home, named after her, Villa Carla. Today it's a tenement, housing several families. You glimpse poverty, unmade beds covered with grey blankets. In the yard, surrounded by the glass veranda, an old woman. You manage to explain your mother once lived here and she allows you to take photographs, declining, in the generosity of the poor, an offer of a tip.

You love the street. You can see Onkels Faivel and Shmaya and grandfather Mendel hurrying home from the family bank, the family sawmill, the family hotel, to be greeted by the aromas of their wives' cooking. The children, all of an age, studying together in the Heder Mendel organised for them, sharing French and English tutors after school, running up the mountain to pick blueberries late in summer. You can see Carla and Helena coming home from school in their thick black stockings, having to speak Romanian, their mother tongue, German, forbidden by nationalist and anti-semitic school mistresses.

You stroll with Helena up the mountain to the Jewish cemetery. Here is a tombstone for the RJF soap and the desecrated Torah books. Helena sighs at her parents' graves, looking down towards the beautiful valley. I love it here, she says, but in the years after Siegmund's trial I made myself ill. Now we try to forget. When we have, we eat, when we don't we don't. Life under a dictator is tough, she whispers, looking around at the wild flowers, to make sure nobody hears.

You were lucky, Carla, to have got out of this place, where your school friend is scared the militzia has seen her with your daughter, where people live in constant fear.

The old synagogue, once a formidable temple opposite the Lycee, lies empty, a store house for ritual vessels guarded by a gruff old Jew, embarrassed by your visit.

You walk to the banks of the Dorna stream, where Dorna Foresta, once Mendel's sawmill, still stacks timber as it did in his days. You walk in the park, by the casino, where Mendel took Rosa when they first met here after the first war.

Why do you feel so good here? Why does it feel like home? It is nothing like the Israel of your childhood, the Israel you have since left. But somehow it feels right, despite the harshness of the present. The journey is beginning to have a sense of destination.

Gura Humorlui, father's birthplace, is another story. Not a spa town, there are no tourists here, there is little charm. Father's cousin, an ageing piano teacher who spends his days in bed surrounded by photographs of days gone by, tells how ashamed grandma Tattu had been when she discovered, at 45, she was pregnant with father. They left for Vienna and later, having followed her scholarly but utterly unworldly husband to the dusty Jerusalem of the mid-twenties, she was to spend the later part of her life shunted from daughter-in-law to daughter-in-law, penniless, her only asset a carved silver candlestick which now stands in your living room, a million light years from her dreams.

Another cousin, Mimi, whose husband is regional doctor and therefore one of the favoured citizens in this corrupt society, lives in style in her parents' large glass-encased house. They too met in Mogilev, Transnistria and live in its shadow, like all its survivors.

On the way back from visiting father's cousin, you meet three elderly Jews returning from Shabbat morning service. With 24 Jews, there isn't even a prayer quorum in Gura Humorlui. The local cemetery is overgrown and the synagogue is but a tiny room.

Bucovina is a land without Jews. Those who stayed had to because of sick parents, trials or illness. They are ageing fast. A year after your visit, Mimi and her husband would leave for Israel and father's cousin would die, leaving just 21 Jews in Gura Humorlui.

Then there is Friedrich Ausländer, the old advocate. Once an officer in the Kaiser's army and never a very religious Jew, he is an isolated relic of old times. About Jews like him Anschel said to Dora that only assimilated Jews who don't care for their Torah served in the goyim's army. Anschel died in Transnistria, his

Gemarra books on his lap and Fritz Ausländer survived to live in abject poverty, alone in a roomful of old, dusty lawbooks, dreaming of the last days of the Empire. Dear, dear, Onkel Frit. z.

Another night train takes you to Czernowitz, today Chernovtzy in southern Ukraine. It takes a lot of bureaucracy and considerable bribing simply to buy a train ticket here. Romania is a most wonderfully corrupt society. The golden rule seems to be never buy anything without bribing if you can buy it with a bribe.

Mimi and her husband take you to the railway station in Suceava, a large county town at which the Sofia-Moscow train stops. The summer night is pitch black and they are worried about driving in the dark so they leave you to wait for your train which leaves at ten.

The station's waiting room is crowded with peasants, children, chickens, baggage. Was this how they waited for the trains to take them to Transnistria? Under-lit, with layers of dirt accumulated for years, the scene is that of a refugee transit camp. Half asleep, people jump up from their benches as trains pull into the station. Finally you are almost alone with an elderly Jew from Düsseldorf whose incredible name is Hitler.

Why should I change my father's name? His name is all I have after he died in the camp, he smiles toothlessly before he staggers to his train, dragging his suitcase, on his way to Tel Aviv, to see his Israeli grandchildren.

A young man approaches. The station is almost deserted now. His talk of exchanging lei for dollars sounds unreal here. His is the face of contemporary Romania. An engineer and part-time taxi driver, speculator and hustler. Though you politely reject his advances, he sees you, very courteously, to your approaching train, making sure you get on safely.

Did anyone make sure you got on safely, Hetti? Did anyone see you off, Dora? Trains carry a strong emotional association with death here and you are now on another one, journeying towards another unknown.

At three in the morning the train stops at Vadul Siret to change tracks. Alone on a stationary night train between Romania and the Soviet Union, with no one speaking a language you understand. Bureaucrats come and go, asking for papers, visas, money, each obliquely looking for his pound of flesh. You bribe no one, uncomfortable with this corruption. You would have given them a lei or two had you travelled here forty-odd years ago. And Helena's voice: give them something, don't be so moralistic, this is how this society works.

The bureaucratic nightmare ends, no bribes, no victims.

Soviet officials find nothing among your papers, not even the one address you had hidden. Romanian officials succeed in confiscating all your Romanian money, promising to return it all when you come back. Two cultures, one greedy, the other suspicious, controlling. The train travels on towards another, greyer dawn.

Were you scared, Hetti, when you travelled alone with Yossi back from the camp southwards to Dorna, then Bucharest, then Israel? Were you all alone in the Displaced Persons camps, the transit camps, with a pale, thin child who refused to be comforted by his lame mother? Trains bring you in contact with Carla on her solitary journey to Bucharest. With Hetti and Hanna on their hopeful journey to the south. With Dora, beautiful Dora, on her last journey, old before her time, away from her devastated home, away from her Anschel's roughly-dug grave.

It is on this train, between Suceava and Czernowitz that you, true sabra mother and father had worked so hard to nurture, start getting in touch with there. Why should Jews have a state? Germans have a state, as do Romanians and Poles. Jews have an eternal diaspora, you think as the train chugs on through the dawn.

Arriving at Czernowitz, that cosmopolitan centre where village girl Dora had come to buy her engagement outfits with her mother-in-law Helen Lax and her dear friend, ailing Rosa, is another anti-climax. The Austrian style station is painted white and yellow. Your guide, polite, modern, efficient Vladimir picks you up.

It is here that mother stood watching over the family linen and crystal, you want to say to him. Here she and her parents took the last train to freedom.

But you don't. You exchange civilities and he takes you to Hotel Bucovina, the only tourist hotel in Chernovtsy, a large building on the broad Lenin avenue. An empty sensation of fear takes over from the old sabra arrogance of nobody is going to tell me what to do and where to do it.

What would you like to do in our city, Vladimir asks courteously, not really awaiting a reply. Just roam around, just walk, you say. My people came from here, you know. You smile and your jaws ache.

First you walk to the Ringplatz. Now a large statue of Vladimir Illich Lenin stands in the middle, surrounded by bright red wreaths. Flowers everywhere, beautifully tidy. Der Schwarze Adler at one end of the Platz, painted light green, now town hall. Which of Der Schwarze Adler's large rectangular

21

windows did Dora look out of in her first bewildering visit to the big city? At what dining hall did Mendel treat Hetti and Menashe to their wedding drink?

You spend the next three days walking up and down Herrengasse, today Olga Koblianska street, pedestrianised, full of shoppers. Visualising young Carla with her student friends sipping eternal cups of coffee. You enter a coffee house but there are no cakes, only watery coffee and thick rolls. In the crowded streets you shut your eyes, trying to see Hetti and Menashe walking after a movement meeting in the deep snow. Which corner did you turn, Hetti? Where did you first lie with your Menashe?

The street is full of courtyards. You peep into several. Was this where Rosa and Mendel's apartment was? What grace this city must have had, what a glorious past. Even today, the stuccoed stones have the faded charm of an ageing beauty.

You are alone and the city envelops you. You will not find our type of Jew there, mother had warned. They were all taken away. The Jews of today are new arrivals, Russian Jews. You hear Yiddish in the street. Your people never spoke Yiddish. There is something Russian about the two men conversing in Yiddish in the middle of Herrengasse. Definitely not our people.

Our people? What are you? Where do you come from? They tried to make a sabra out of you, but here you are part of the story. This is my place, mother.

You visit the university where David Greifer wanted to study but could not because of the first war. It's a lovely red and gold brick building, busy with end of year students who don't look twice in your direction. Only the guard tells you not to walk on the grass. By order.

On your last day a young man approaches you in a book shop. Yevrei (Jew), he says. Me too, you say enthusiastically. His name is Boris and he invites you to walk with him. Life is not bad, he says, only it's hard to be a Jew. He takes you for a ride to his factory where he exchanges a large sum of money for some spare parts. You have the feeling you are witnessing an illicit deal but you ask no questions. He takes you to see the Jewish cemetery, vandalised the previous year. You can find no family graves, the cemetery is overgrown, its synagogue in ruins. Look there, across the road, Boris says, at the Russian cemetery. How tidy it is.

The synagogue is a tiny building in a small side street. The big temple had long since been turned into a cinema. Chernovtsy in southern Ukraine lives on. It may have many Jews, but your Czernowitz is dead. A deserted Jewish graveyard.

Boris drives you back into town. Later they will tell you he must have been sent by the KGB to check you out, hence the money deal. All this for you, you wonder, in this Jewish desert?

The night train back to Suceava is easier to take. When searched copiously, you can laugh in their faces. What do you take me for, a criminal? The searcher and the two men who oversee him smile back, very polite.

Coming back to Gura Humorlui and Dorna is like coming home. It feels like you have never left Dorna, like Carla had never left it. Yet every waking moment you bless her for not having stayed behind like Helena who, childless, wakes every morning dreaming of food.

1

Dora 1895

Küss die Hand. Herr Klipper slid past her as she carried a bucket of frothy milk from the yard. His shiny pate almost covered with the velvet yarmulka. Gnädige Frau, he bowed to mother as he came out of father's mouldy book-lined study. Dora lifted her face. Saw him grabbing father's hand with both his fat-fingered hands, walking backwards to his one-horse cart.

Mother came, wiping her hands on her apron, from the kitchen. "Nu, Shulem", Dora heard her ask, "did you do business?"

"Hush, Rivka, hush. I shall go back to my studies and later we'll talk," father said.

Later they talked. Whispering. Little point asking mother about the matchmaker's visit. Giving the eldest daughter to another man in marriage was men's business.

Herr Klipper called on other days. Always bowing and scraping. His lips narrowing in a sly smile when he saw her.

Before Pessach father summoned her to his study. A rare occasion. Girls were not encouraged to glimpse the holy books.

"You are coming of age." he opened. "It is time for you to marry.

"Herr Klipper has been working hard to come up with a young man suitable for Shulem Hirsch's daughter. You know of our Viznicher origins. And my scholarship. It was so highly thought of that your mother's father took me from the yeshiva at eighteen to marry your mother. Unfortunately, my financial standing is not so high. Had my father not lost all his fortunes, I may not have had to dirty my hands with money-lending and land transactions. But what to do? A man has to live and this is the will of God. You are a smart girl," father paused.

The first compliment he had ever paid her. "You could marry a scholar and run a business for him if only I had the money to set you up as my father-in-law set me up. But what to do and I have no capital?"

Father paused again and looked into Dora's dark blue eyes. "So Herr Klipper came up with the perfect match. A man whose scholarship is as deep as his father's pocket. What do you say, little one?"

Dora said nothing.

"You are not saying much, little one. You are not asking who the young man is. But I shall tell you. His father, Yacob Lax, is a rich landowner with much forest acreage and an inn at the edge of the village of Putila Kaselitsa. The son, Anschel, is nineteen and a Talmudist. And the father is coming to look us up before the holidays."

Don't ask father about the young man's scholarship. Young

girls, he would say, should not busy their little heads with Talmudic matters. Strictly for men and boys. Girls were for helping their mothers and women for being the help against their husbands. And more than anything else, for giving birth.

Dora asked nothing. Shulem returned to his studies. She returned to her duties. Hanging the milk in muslin bags to make curd cheese. Baking challahs for shabbat. Helping with her young brothers, Duvid and Shmuel. At night she was allowed to read her prayer book, Tsena U Reena, a special prayer book for women.

Two mornings a week she and her younger sister Sara took lessons with old Herr Abraham, a Czernowitzer who taught German reading and writing and some arithmetic. Enough for housekeeping. Herr Abraham's assistant, a nervous young man, ran Heder for her brothers and some other boys. Twice a week he took the girls for Hebrew reading, to be able to find your way around the Siddur.

Dora did not ask why her brothers spent every afternoon doing history, geography, science, bookkeeping, German, arithmetic. They were boys and that was why.

Dora took to brooding about the impending visit by her intended father-in-law. Soon after her talk with father, mother and the German maid started polishing silver and copper, washing linen, scrubbing hard until the white hurt your eyes when hung on the line, stretching between two large trees in the yard, as the watery spring sun endeavoured to dry them, fighting the fading winter grey.

Windows and floors shined, cushions mended, rugs beaten violently. Three fat farm hens slaughtered and plucked. On the day of Herr Lax's arrival, a large cauldron of chicken soup simmered on the range. Filling the house with a comforting aroma. Home-made lokshen, heaped on a platter beside the stove, ready to be popped into the soup.

The house shining with Rosenthal plates on mahogany dressers, washed and carefully dried. Lace table cloths and curtains white and sparkling.

Dora had ironed her good dress as mother had bid. On the morning of Herr Lax's arrival, she dressed slowly, combed her long brown hair and sat with mother waiting in the glass-panelled veranda.

Herr Yacob Lax was a big man, his white beard long and bushy. Dora saw from her seat on the porch his black-coated body descend a carriage, his voice bidding the coachman water the horses.

Never before had she heard a Jew behave like the local

landowners she saw when she went to buy produce at the town market. Water the horse, Costia, they would order, their waxed moustaches glistening, sending shivers down her spine, fear mingled with fascination. Forbidden thoughts.

Father went out to greet the guest: "Welcome, Reb Yacob". He led Herr Lax to his study without introducing him to the waiting women. Dora felt a surge of excitement. Being discussed, bartered and handed over was adult stuff.

As the men came out for the meal mother had worked to perfect, father introduced his wife and children. "Gnädige Frau. I am delighted to make your acquaintance." Herr Lax's German was impeccable, to Dora's eternal relief. No Ostjude he. A sideways glance into his face: she liked the kindly gaze under the knitted eyebrows.

After the meal, as Dora helped the German carry dishes into the kitchen, father and Herr Lax withdrew again into father's study. She was not to know everything had already been agreed upon that evening. Herr Lax left the dowry to father's discretion, offering a parallel sum, slightly smaller. Not seemly for a groom's father to give more than the bride's. He also offered the young couple board and lodging for the rest of their married life.

Then the men came out of the study. Herr Lax's eyes rested on her face. Dora knew she had been sealed and delivered.

At the heavily-laced window Dora watched father ascend onto Herr Lax's carriage. A visit to the local Rebbe's court to obtain his blessing to the match. Dora wished her intended to be as imposing as his father. At the same time feeling for father, who she knew was poorer, less powerful outside his home realm. I don't want another man to tell me what to do, she thought. But mother's voice, saying, a man knows best, when you grow up, you'll understand, kept breaking through.

The men returned from the Rebbe glowing. Father smiled at mother, saying, "it is done". "Blessed be the Lord," mother replied, rushing past him to order the German to have the water ready for the evening tea. They supped that night on milchige savouries and cakes, Dora's cheesecake held high for Herr Lax to appreciate her domesticity. A coveted, if unconsulted jewel in her father's crown.

In the morning, they lined up to bid Herr Lax farewell. He addressed her for the first time since his arrival. "Good day, Fräulein Hirsch," said his strong, deep voice. "I take it that you and I shall meet again."

Pessach, always extra work for the girls, saw a sober, less childish Dora. Mother was grooming her for her future role as

28

Hausfrau. Recipes entered into in great detail. Unlike the past, when she was but a silent and reluctant observer.

Together they cleaned cupboards of all traces of bread and wheat flour. They tied cutlery onto long strings, ready to be plunged into boiling water the German had placed in a pot on a fire in the yard. Special Pessach crockery taken out of the summer larder, cleaned and placed over fresh sheets of white paper. Pots and pans, kept separately all year round for the week ahead, brought out and their copper bottoms polished so you could see your face in them.

Under mother's watchful eye, Dora baked potato flour cakes, using no forbidden flour. She made egg and matzo flour pancakes and sliced them into long golden snakes, ready to accompany the matzo meal kneidls in the eternal chicken soup.

A late crop of potatoes, dug out by the yardsman, stored ready to make hundreds of potato cakes. Huge boxes of matzos, bought by the local community from Czernowitz, were stored in the clean larder and fresh butter churned in the special Pessach churn which had not been in contact with leavened bread or wheaten flour throughout the year.

Dress rehearsal. Her last Pessach as a young girl. Next year she will be engaged to be married.

Dora sat at father's table, listening and not listening to the story of the exodus of the children of Israel from slavery to redemption. Soon she too will be released from the slavery of being a girl child in a small town in the eastern part of the Austro-Hungarian Empire to become a full member of the sorority of women married according to the law of Moses and Israel.

There was as much polishing and scrubbing in preparation for the first visit by Dora Hirsch's intended with his father and brother. Dora eyed herself stealthily in the oval mirror mother kept inside her wardrobe. Clothes were washed, starched and coal ironed. Hair washed and brushed. Her younger sister Sara argued endlessly as to what suited best, what accentuated best the dark blue eyes and light brown long hair. Not the modest thoughts becoming of the daughter of a Hassidic scholar. But father, preoccupied with his studies, was not to know.

Unlike his brother Berl, who could not take his eyes off their red-haired German, Anschel Lax was all modesty and good manners. During their first mid-day meal, he displayed his Talmudic brilliance when father quizzed him. The authority he lacked in dealing with mundane matters like ordering coachmen, which Berl, sounding like their father, took over, Anschel had in discussing fine points of Gemarra. But Dora could not help feeling disappointed that he was more like her father than like his.

No one had yet asked her if she wanted to marry this shy, sharp-witted Talmudist. After the meal, the men withdrew to father's study and Dora was summoned to mother's large, white bedroom.

Mother sat on the big wooden rocker in the corner, motioning Dora to sit on the handloomed bedspread, criss-crossed in Romanian embroidery with red and white diamond shapes, the only splash of colour in this white room.

"You know, child, that your father and Herr Lax had agreed you will marry young Herr Anschel," mother started.

"No one had said anything to me," Dora whispered, searching mother's eyes for traces of doubt.

"The time has not yet come, my dear girl, when young women are asked by their fathers whom they want to marry," mother said, severe, returning an unblinking look. "Right now, they are signing the conditions. Herr Klipper, who has worked so hard to secure this excellent shidduch, is also present."

Mother paused, looking over Dora's head for traces of dusty air in the distant sunshine. "You know what conditions are like. Conditions cannot be broken, come what may. So there you are."

Rivka Hirsch noticed her daughter frown and added, more gently, "Don't have fears, child. Anschel Lax is a good man. He will look after you. Marriage is only frightening when you look at it from the outside. Once you are married, things run themselves. All you have to do is be an obedient wife."

"But mother," Dora could not find the words.

"Yes, child, what is it that has you so worried?"

"Do you learn to love your husband?"

"Love? You can love a good man if you put your mind to it. Marriage is not what they tell you in those cheap novelettes the servants read. It is give and take. Compromise. You are a good girl. You come from good Hassidic stock. Anschel is a good man. Comes from good Hassidic stock. And he is an excellent scholar. I heard your father say so. And he has enough money to look after you. What more can a Jewish girl want? Let the goyim worry about love. It will come with time."

Dora sneaked a look at mother as she was speaking her lines, an actress reciting a well-rehearsed part. Mother's face was sealed to her and there was no telling if she was saying the truth. Was she happy in her marriage to father, who spent every free moment in his book-lined room, chanting Torah portions and pondering over his worn Gemarra tomes? Who read German only when he had to and a newspaper only in the water closet in the yard? Who watched every penny for household expenses but who gave generously to charity in his Rebbe's court?

Dora had never detected any sign of discontent. Mother was always in accordance with her strong-willed husband.

Perhaps this was love.

"Nu, what do you say, Dorale?" Mother smiled for the first time since they entered the white bedroom. "When we come out of this room we shall tell the others, Sara, Duvid, Shmuel. And next month you go to Putila Kaselitsa with your father to meet Herr Anschel's mother and family. Then we shall have the engagement party."

"Yes, mother," was all she could manage. She had never been out of Cirlibaba. The prospect of a journey filled her with awe.

Dora and Rivka left the white room as the men were leaving the study, Herr Klipper in front, his face beaming. Later on, he will dance at Dora and Anschel's wedding. Now he looked like a man who had concluded an important business deal. He bowed slightly towards mother, then towards Dora. As a religious Jew he knew he was not to shake the hands of women not related to him. "Mazel tov," he grinned. "Mazel tov," mother replied.

"Must pay him," Dora heard mother whisper to father during the meal which followed. "We must pay the shadchan, get him off our back." Herr Klipper was busy emptying Schnaps glasses with Berl, Dora's future brother-in-law

Dora observed Anschel surreptitiously during the meal. His table manners were perfect, as were his long, transparent hands. His beard was thin and his dark eyes shone under a tall forehead. Despite an apparent shyness, his movements were resolute. There would be no arguing with him, Dora was thinking. The two did not talk and Anschel remained polite, distant.

Dora felt no attraction. No revulsion. He is to be my husband. This dark stranger with the long white hands. This shy scholar is going to be my husband.

A whole new wardrobe for the trip to Putila Kaselitsa. Frau Katz was summoned to the house and material mother had bought from a travelling draper, in case it was needed one day, was taken out of the bedroom hamper and made into a light grey suit. A long flared skirt down to her buttoned ankle boots and a lace-collared thick linen blouse, complete with a feathered hat and a travelling cape, made Dora look less like the village girl she was. Or so she thought, catching stolen glimpses of herself in the window of the room she shared with Sara.

"Must make a good impression on the womenfolk," mother said to father, who shrugged and turned away. Dora plumped her hair around her head in the halo style, fashionable on the outskirts of the Empire that year.

Dora, father and mother, whose curiosity about how the rich Laxes lived did not allow her to stay behind, made the day-long journey in the carriage Herr Lax had sent for them. Pine forest followed pine-covered mountain peak as the carriage wound its way up and down, through fir trees amidst wooden farmhouses.

The shady afternoon was turning darker as their carriage drew up outside the Laxes' house opposite Putila's Catholic church. "Why opposite the church?" mother hissed. "Never mind, woman," father said firmly. "The Laxes are good Jews. What matters what is opposite their house?"

Dora was struck by the dark wood furniture, obviously more expensive than their own locally-made dressers and tables. The hall, swept by the evening sun, was where the Hirsches now stood, their wraps taken by a maid, the likes of whose manners Dora had never seen.

"Must be Viennese, this girl," mother whispered as soon as the girl turned her back with their wraps on her extended arm, having curtsied and promised to tell Frau Lax who was eagerly awaiting her honoured guests. "Her German is perfect."

"Yes, but can she speak Yiddish?" father said in an unusual burst of humour.

"Never mind you and your Yiddish. Since when do shikses speak Yiddish?"

Helen Lax, who welcomed them with many words and little warmth, matched the Viennese style of her house more than her husband and sons had. The Laxes were good Jews but there was not much of Jewish Bucovina about Helen. A fully-fledged Austrian, as she stressed at every opportunity, Frau Lax found it hard to hide her thinly-disguised contempt towards her elder son's intended and her family.

Dora had never seen mother in such awe. Helen Lax commanded not only respect. As she eyed her future mother-in-law's carefully tailored clothes, Dora felt her own new elegance pale by comparison.

The first half hour the Hirsches spent in Frau Lax's company, father fidgeting with his tsitsit, sitting nervously on the edge of the chintz sofa, waiting impatiently for Yacob Lax's return from his rounds with his two sons, was awful. But Dora made the acquaintance of Anschel's young sister, seventeen-year-old Rosa, a strangely pale girl, her white face framing deep black eyes.

The girls chatted brightly, breaking the stilted silence, which came to an end with the arrival of Herr Lax, whose white beard and black caftan were in complete contrast with his wife's composed cosmopolitan manners. Herr Lax brought with him a hearty welcome for the Hirsches who had been beginning to feel that they and the planned wedding were not wanted here.

"Why have you chosen such a dull girl for our first born?" Helen questioned Yacob later that night, after they had all dined on a table laden with Czech crystal and German crockery.

"Dora Hirsch is a decent girl, Hindel," Yacob said using his wife's Jewish name, infuriating her. "Her father is a good Hassid. There was no one more suitable within a radius of a thousand kilometres, my dear." He said this firmly. He had grown used to his wife's bitter criticism over the years.

A descendant from a wealthy Viennese Jewish family, Helen Lax had never got used to living out of town when her father's circumstances worsened. When she was married off to Yacob Lax, she promised herself she would keep a proper Viennese home in this godforsaken village. She always had a well-trained Saxon maid who kept the establishment ticking over as Helen ran the family's prosperous inn. Being the richest family in the area, respected by Jews and gentiles, made precious little difference.

Dora spent most of her time with Rosa. They walked in the forest, picking wild flowers and field strawberries and laughing. Anschel, whose studies and work took him away for most of the day, took time off and was very attentive. On the third day of their visit, Dora and Anschel were allowed a short walk in the village high street, with the mothers walking a respectable distance behind.

Dora liked what she saw. He was not boastful like his mother, nor was he strong and insistent like his father. His was a quiet determination. He told her of his plans to study and at the same time go into his father's business here in Putila Kaselitsa once he was safely out of the reach of the recruiting officer.

Not that he planned to serve, he explained calmly. No God-fearing Jew who could afford to buy his way out did. Only those officer types who preferred fencing at university fraternities to the Talmud, young men who rejected God and his eternal law, went into the goyim's army.

Dora was stunned. She was getting used to the idea of marrying this pale scholar, whose gaze now rested on her face, wrinkled with uncertainty.

"Does that mean you will be gone for some years now?" Her voice was small, trying not to show her disappointment.

"No, Fräulein Hirsch. There are ways. If you know who to pay. These worries are not for women." She could not help marvelling at his confidence. At nineteen he seemed far more mature than her own seventeen years.

They rejoined their mothers, who, relieved of the need to continue their strained conversation, eyed them curiously. The four walked to the house, saying little, target to the probing glances from behind curtained windows, as the villagers speculated on the Laxes' guests, a rare occasion in a village where most non-Jews were peasants or artisans, living in wooden houses with wells in the yard, geese and chickens running across muddy roads more often than strange humans.

That night, before she kissed mother goodnight, Dora asked father about the army. "We shall talk about it when we return home," he said.

She had a growing feeling she had no control over her life. First they found her a husband without asking and now that she was getting fond of him, they were telling her she could not marry him until the Kaiser allowed.

Dora and Rosa cried and kissed as they said goodbye and swore to write every week. As the Hirsches drove home, Dora kept having visions of Anschel's uniformed body, decorated with the Kaiser Cross, like those gentile soldiers she had seen back home strolling like peacocks for the local girls to see, lying dead on the ground. No one told her what those ways of getting Jewish men out of service were.

In the next months she corresponded regularly with Rosa and Anschel. Anschel started his letters with "My dear Fräulein Hirsch" and signed himself, "Your fond Anschel Lax." Dora wrote to "Dear Herr Lax", signing herself "hearty greetings, Dora Hirsch."

Anschel wrote mainly about his studies and about the Rebbe's court, where he was becoming a prodigy. Never about the army. Dora wrote about her daily life, not asking about the army. "He will write when he has something to report," was what father said. Rosa wrote chatty letters, telling her new friend about Berl's succession of girlfriends, how he infuriated their parents, about Anschel's affection for her and about her own undying friendship.

Once or twice Dora lingered by mother in the kitchen, trying to talk about her uncertain future. "You mustn't worry, child," mother would say. "Once conditions are signed, there is always a wedding. No one dares break conditions."

Dora was not sure she wanted this wedding to go ahead before she understood about love. Talking to her sister Sara was no use — Sara was five years younger. She wrote to Rosa asking if she thought her brother loved her. Rosa answered cheerfully that of course he did and not to be such a silly girl. She could not take it any further. Rosa, after all, was Anschel's sister.

Still as she went marketing, she lingered, watching the peasants court. There was such freedom in their ways. The men were dressed in dirty white tunics and tight cotton white trousers over which they wore leather jerkins embroidered in strong colours. Their cheeks red with drink and the strong sun, they were chasing the women whose tightly tied headscarves revealed strands of abundant hair, thick and curly, sometimes peppered with fresh hay.

Shouting to each other, with open sexual gestures, there was nothing about these young peasants to remind Dora of the pale, careful manners of young Jewish men and women she knew. Their laughter, mirth, even abandon, made her feel strangely lonely, something stirring in her rigid body.

In moments like these, sometimes stealthy, because she was not allowed into the market without having business there, Dora imagined herself standing amongst the peasants, laughing and throwing her head back at the men. She then imagined Anschel, correct, logical, mature, and a sense of shame at her lusty thoughts made her turn on her heels and run back to the house, her heart pounding under her rounded breasts.

The summer drew to a close and the mountain air sharpened on the green peaks of Bucovina. Anschel Lax wrote to Dora Hirsch. "My dear Fräulein Hirsch. I have paid my first visit to the recruiting officer in Czernowitz. My father paid the required sum to Herr Dorner, who, for a consideration, passed the commission to the regional command, recommending in his careful copperplate German, to delay my mobilisation. I received a document delaying my army service for another year. Take heart, dear Fräulein, we have only two more years to wait. In the meantime, I shall visit your honourable father next month, before the winter sets in. My sister Rosa sends her love and friendship as do all here. Your fond Anschel Lax."

After the visit, Dora Hirsch wrote to Anschel Lax. "Dear Anschel, (I allow myself to call you Anschel although we are not yet man and wife). Your visit was a pleasant time in Cirlibaba. All here were happy with your company. Father never stops praising your knowledge of the Gemarra and our Rebbe was said to have been more than pleased with your scholarship. I am happy you are a scholar. Scholarly men, mother says, make good husbands. I hope you have a good winter. Bucovina winters can be so cold and damp. We have taken out the feather beds and aired them and are almost ready for the snow. I hope to learn to ski this winter. It may be my last before the wedding. When are

35

you going next to Czernowitz to pay the recruiting officer? Hearty greetings to your respected family and to you, Dora Hirsch."

Helen Lax insisted on having the engagement party in her house. "This is the least we can do, dear Yacob, to show these country Jews what stylish people do when their first born gets married," she said sternly.

She wrote to Dora offering her the services of her Czernowitz tailor as an engagement present. Dora begged mother to let her accept the invitation to go to Czernowitz. "She is trying to show us off," mother complained, "as if I cannot supply you with good enough clothes for her grand party." But father intervened and persuaded mother to let Dora go. Rosa was also coming. She wouldn't have to spend a week alone with Frau Lax.

Helen Lax hired two rooms in Der Schwarze Adler Hotel, the most elegant in town, right on the Ringplatz. At a sharp angle was Herrengasse, which, Helen Lax explained, was as good as any in Vienna and even Paris. In its shops were riches the likes of which Dora had never seen.

Helen Lax called on her tailor, Herr Friedmann, on the first morning. Dora had been too excited to sleep and she and Rosa whispered until the small hours of the morning. Rosa, who had been here several times before, coached her friend through cosmopolitan Czernowitz. "Most businesses here are in Jewish hands," she said to the incredulous Dora, as the girls followed Helen to Herr Friedmann's Herrengasse shop.

Herr Friedmann's shop was decorated with the most exquisite pictures of costumes from the capitals of Europe.

"I am here to see Herr Friedmann. Tell him Frau Lax is waiting," Helen addressed the shop assistant, a young man in a stiff collared dark suit.

"Gnädige Frau," the assistant said, leaving the three women to wait for the couturier.

"Herr Friedmann is the most respected master of his craft, girls," Helen said, looking above their heads to anticipate the tailor's entrance. "He makes clothes for the best in the land."

Herr Friedmann let them wait for some time. When he did enter, he was all apologies. "Had to oversee the cutting of a costume, Küss die Hand, Frau . . ."

"Frau Lax. Lax, Herr Friedmann, from Putila," Helen said.

"Of course, dear Frau Lax. And these must be your daughters." He looked at Dora and Rosa, his gaze somewhat bored, Dora thought.

"No, Herr Friedmann. This here is my daughter Rosa and the other young lady is my future daughter-in-law. I have come to

36

choose costumes for her engagement to my son."

"Congratulations, dear ladies," the tailor was not using the Jewish Mazel tov, thus displaying his move from a mere Jew to a metropolitan couturier.

He spread before them drawings of what he said were the latest fashions from Paris and Vienna. He even produced one drawing of a suit from London, mumbling "very chic" every time anybody looked at it.

Frau Lax was far from the important customer she had made herself sound when she talked of Herr Friedmann to the girls. While always courteous, his demeanour did not disguise his lack of respect for that lady from the eastern outskirts of the Empire. Helen, on the other hand, remained insensitive to the innuendos and proceeded to select her outfits. Rosa and Dora deliberated and finally settled on one suit, an English model, one dress and one travelling outfit each, different yet similar enough to celebrate their friendship.

Far from being a country mouse, when it came to the choice of colour and style, Dora knew what she wanted, having leafed carefully through Herr Friedmann's catalogues and listened to his advice. There was no trying to dissuade her. Helen Lax had to admit, grudgingly, that Dora had chosen well.

When not looking at materials and patterns or going for fittings, Helen and Rosa took Dora to see the Golden Residenz, where the best of Bucovinian architecture housed the Kaiser's representative. They strolled along Herrengasse, sipping strong coffee in coffeehouses along the street, which, day or night, was teeming with elegant men and women, going about their business, oblivious to the excitement their mere existence kindled in Dora's heart.

One evening, Helen took the girls to see a visiting company do a ponderous German play about love and death at the local theatre. Dora's first visit to the theatre. How she loved the sighs and asides on the lit-up stage. Helen and Rosa made her promise to keep their visit a secret. "Father would not be too happy if he knew that his wife, his daughter and his future daughter-in-law visited the theatre with all the goyim," Rosa said. "His orthodoxy prohibits it, but mother longs for the pleasures of culture, don't you, mother?"

"Yes," Helen sighed. "All the things that were denied me when I was forced out of my beloved Vienna."

Later that night, Rosa whispered Helen's story in their room. "Mother's grandfather was a rich man but when his son, my grandfather, came into the business, things went wrong. When mother was sixteen and preparing to start looking for a match amongst the eligibles of Vienna's Jewish society, her father heard that his ships, loaded with spices from the east, had been lost at sea. This was everything he had owned — he was hoping to make a fortune with the spices."

Rosa's clear eyes looked into the darkened distance of their hotel bedroom, trying to conjure her grandfather's despair in her mind's eye. "He managed at the last moment to sell his house and get out of Vienna, chased by his creditors."

Rosa paused and sighed. "Mother will never forgive her father for depositing his family in Bucovina and going away to seek his fortune, never to return. She and her sisters had to find matches, aided by community funds. There was no dowry, no trousseau. Grandmother barely managed to keep body and soul together, working as housekeeper to the local Jewish landowner, whose wife had died in childbirth.

"After one hundred rabbis had declared her an agunah — a woman whose husband disappeared without trace in the lands of the sea — she married her employer. It had been a long struggle but she had some good years with her husband before she died several years ago."

"And your grandfather?" Dora asked, bewildered.

"He never returned. We don't know whether he is alive or dead. From time to time mother speaks of her swine of a father but I do believe she would love to see him again." Rosa sighed once again.

"She was lucky to marry father," Rosa continued. "His father was taken with her good looks and class and her mother's reputation, that of a tsadika — a just and virtuous woman, whose life was hard but who managed to give her daughters not only a good Jewish upbringing but also much Viennese culture.

"Father had money and mother was restored to the grandeur she keeps telling us she had been accustomed to. But if you ask me, this style is nought but a distant fantasy. And the price — living in the country — is high. If you ask me whether she is happy, my answer would have to be no. She is forever complaining of her lot. She hated being buried, as she calls it, in Putila, which, she says, is no more than a godforsaken hole, not even a town. She has little patience with father's orthodox friends, his involvement with the Rebbe. She would like him to move here to Czernowitz or another big city and start again. But father would not hear of it. He makes a good living. He has his Rebbe whom he always consults about every transaction and move. He is influential in Putila. So when she has a chance to grab some city life, she always does it, although I dare say she wasn't taken much to the theatre before they left Vienna when she was only sixteen." Rosa sighed and breathed slowly, as if with great effort.

Before their visit ended, Helen Lax took the girls to Hauptstrasse 16, to have their photographs taken by Herr Rosenbach, at his modern studio for photography and painting. Dora, who by now was less bewildered by the city, was asked to sit down by a round walnut table, laying her elbow on an open book by which lay a bunch of dried roses.

Herr Leo Rosenbach and his young assistant, stern looking in a pince-nez, asked her to look dreamily into the distance. The assistant threw beads around her neck to accentuate the lace collar of her new ivory blouse. Herr Rosenbach jumped behind a large box standing on a tripod, covered his head with a black cloth and shouted, smile now. Dora smiled, trying to look dreamily into the distance, as a big burst of light exploded from the box, making her jump in her seat.

Rosa, who had already had her photograph taken on a previous visit to the city, angled her head at the camera, licking her lips to give them a sheen, looking sideways as the light exploded. Helen came next, sticking her broad chin up and staring at the camera. When Herr Rosenbach's assistant tried to arrange her suit collar, she slapped his hand lightly, barely concealing her contempt. She did not smile at Herr Rosenbach's camera but looked stern and determined, straight ahead.

There were two photographs in Oma's bundle. One had two smiling young women, holding each other affectionately, the other an austere older woman, circling with an opulent arm the shoulders of a young girl, both looking unhappy in this forced display of affection.

Her first visit to a big city made Dora start to believe that married life was going to be joyous. She could not wait for the engagement party. She was becoming an adult at last.

Dora returned from Czernowitz and there was no sign of snow on the peaks surrounding Cirlibaba and the trees started donning their green robes. She sang every morning and in the evenings unwrapped her new outfits, fingering them lovingly. Once or twice she tried them on in the room she shared with Sara who eyed her with envy.

She was still not sure about love, but becoming an adult was making up for the uncertainty. She was looking forward to meeting Anschel and testing her feelings towards him. What she really wanted was for her heart to flutter, a word she heard from their German when she told her of her liaison with a young soldier who served in the Kaiser's army, no one knew for how long.

Mother called her into her room. She fished in her wooden box and took out a gold bracelet adorned with a small ruby and two diamonds. "My mother aleha ha shalom, got this bracelet from my father alav ha shalom, when they got engaged. When she died, she left it for me to give to you when you got engaged," she said unsmilingly.

As Dora fingered the delicate piece of jewellery, mother added, "and when your daughter gets engaged, you pass it on to her."

She moved to hug Dora, holding her tight against her soft large breasts. She smelt of fresh soap, her head scarf slipping to reveal her beautiful brown hair. To Dora she seemed the most beautiful woman on earth that moment.

"Thank you, mama," she whispered. She knew the ritual of passing jewellery from mother to daughter was one way of initiating Jewish daughters into womanhood.

Yacob Lax arranged for the Hirsches to stay in an empty house which he had purchased some months ago. There was no Jewish hotel and not enough room in his own house, even he had to agree, for six Hirsches and for Shulem's elderly parents.

Anschel had another year before he was completely free of the military threat and no Jew married before he was free. Dora knew of young Jews who could not afford the bribes and had to join the Kaiser's army. Not that all poor Jews had to join up. Bribes paid by rich Jews often exempted the poor. Another indirect taxation levied only from Jews.

She could not understand why her benevolent Kaiser Franz-Josef, who in 1849 gave his Empire a liberal constitution granting equality to all his people, insisted on taking young Jews into his army, where they ran the risk of not being able to keep their religion. It was he, after all, who granted Jews permission to move about and purchase land. But for the Hungarian revolution and the riots against the Jews who fought side by side with Hungarian nationals, life for the Empire's two million Jews had not been bad, if the Kaiser could only keep the Vienna anti-semites at bay, she had heard father say.

Before the party Dora spoke to Anschel about her fears but he assured her that his man in Czernowitz was reliable. He had a cousin who was an infantry officer, Anschel said. "He is intent on succeeding in this Austro-Hungarian Empire of ours," Anschel said mockingly. "Forgetting his Judaism, never praying, living like a goy."

Dora was startled. She had never heard Anschel mock before. "I wonder what good all this will do him when they come again for the Jews," Anschel was saying. "All we need is another local revolution. Look at Hungary. The Jews there are still paying that million florins for their part in the revolution. So much more than the goyim."

Dora listened but the flutter the German talked about when describing her meetings with her young soldier was missing. Anschel had rigid views and Dora could not help feeling she was being squashed, just like she felt in her father's house.

One morning as she was sitting with Rosa on the Laxes' glass-encased veranda, she was alarmed to see a pang of pain pass her friend's pale face.

"What is it, Rosa?"

"It's nothing, Dora, don't worry."

"But something pained you. I could see."

"It's only my lungs, nothing much." Rosa was now drained of colour, her pale face burning as if in great pain.

Dora's hand caressed her friend's face. Her forehead was red hot and she withdrew her hand, shocked. "You are ill, little one. Let me call your mother."

"Don't. Let me sit in peace with you. Mother will only fuss and call the doctor and the silly old man will want to send me to the sanatorium once again."

"The sanatorium?" Dora knew what this meant.

"Yes," Rosa whispered. "I have had tuberculosis for some time. I haven't much time left."

Dora opened her mouth to say something but Rosa hushed her. "Don't, Dora. Let me enjoy your party and then I will go to the sanatorium."

"But why didn't you tell me?" Angry that no one else had said anything.

"What was the use?" Rosa sounded tired now. "I wanted you to be my friend. I didn't want you too to fuss over me, like all the others. Really wishing I'd die and release them."

That night Dora shivered under the feather blanket. She knew she was to live with her in-laws and having Rosa there was the only comfort. Now, with Rosa so ill, she could not face the prospect of moving in with her stern mother-in-law and kind but distant father-in-law.

She spent every free moment with Rosa now, avoiding the others. Once or twice she caught Berl's gaze on her face, making her blush. He moved his eyes slowly down her body, grinning very slightly.

She wasn't quite sure what that flutter the German was talking about was, but she knew she didn't trust herself with her future brother-in-law. She tried to talk about it to Rosa, but could not bring herself to say the words. She had a constant

41

feeling of drowning.

As Helen promised, the party was a grand affair. Every middle-class Jew from the area was there and the food resembled what Dora had only eaten at the Jewish restaurants in Czernowitz.

There were large chickens, boiled to perfection and eaten with tiny new potatoes from the Laxes' gardens. There was roast veal, sliced thinly and eaten with red currant sauce. There was stuffed carp, sweet gefüllte fish and fresh trout caught that day in the local river. There were home made breads and cakes, soft and crisp potato cakes covered with freshly picked pungent dill. There were field mushrooms, cooked in oil until their sharp aroma filled the house.

To end with, there were forest berries, just ripened in the early summer sun. Tiny alpine strawberries, red succulent loganberries, blackcurrants, all heaped together and covered with a dusting of sugar.

The Rebbe came with his disciples for whom it was a rare chance to eat a festive meal, the likes of which they never got in their yeshiva and for which they had to be invited out by kindly burghers seeking matches for their daughters. Rebbe Itzhak Hager, an imposing man, who smoked endless foul-smelling cigars, ate little and pushed his plates aside to have two or three disciples lick it hungrily, as was the custom.

After the meal, Reb Itzik, as he was fondly known, blessed the meal and there was much singing. The disciples danced in unending circles, holding white handkerchiefs in the air, waving them above their heads while the women sat and watched.

Not allowed to join in, Dora sat between her mother and Rosa, looking on at her own engagement party in which she did not partake. Anschel first sat opposite her, his face serene, as if absorbed in some Talmudic riddle, his eyes rarely focusing on her face. Then, pulled by the singing, he rose to join the dancers.

Before the guests arrived, he had given her a diamond ring and a gold chain as engagement presents. She did not feel moved. Anschel did not touch her hand or look into her eyes. "It won't be long now, Dora. Another year and we shall be man and wife." It was the first time he used her first name. Dora thought this to be a sign of affection.

"What is the matter, Fräulein Dora?" she heard a voice behind her. Hissing. "Are you not enjoying yourself?"

She turned and saw Berl squatting behind her chair, smiling. "I am enjoying myself perfectly," she said.

"I would have asked you to dance with the groom's brother, but I am afraid this is not that kind of gathering, much to

42

mother's chagrin," said his hissing voice.

Dora noticed she had not seen Helen anywhere since the dancing began. "She was thinking in terms of a Viennese danse de salon," Berl said, "but father went and asked Reb Itzik and shattered her plans. Poor mama, she tries so hard to convince herself she isn't stuck in Putila."

Berl said this and Dora thought poor Helen indeed, but said nothing. By the time she looked in mother's direction to ascertain she hadn't heard the exchange, Berl was gone. Rivka was clapping in time to the singing and the kleismer band. Reb Itzik's disciples were now joined by Yacob Lax, Shulem Hirsch, Anschel and his brothers Yossel and Faivel and by her own little brothers, Duvid and Shmuel, dancing in rings, waving kerchiefs high above their heads.

The dancing intensified and Dora whispered to Rosa, "Why don't we get out of here, little one?" The two left their seats, moving towards the kitchen, where the servants were washing dishes and cleaning up.

"I heard that brother of mine," Rosa started without warning. "I want you to be careful. He is an evil soul. I often pray for him to stop being so evil."

"Why? What does he do?"

"I wrote to you, didn't I, of his women. Berl cannot resist new conquests. Have you read the legend of Don Juan?"

Dora was blank. Her education did not include secular literature.

"Sometimes I ask our Lord to let me die and make him good in return," Rosa whispered. "All the others are so good. He is the only evil soul. And mother loves him so. Much more than she loves any of us."

"If the Lord has any compassion, he won't let you die, whether it makes your brother better or not. You are a good girl, you must not die." Dora's voice was breaking, tears stinging her eyes.

"You will be careful, won't you, Dora?" her friend was saying. "You are marrying a tsadik. Anschel is a good man and he will be good to you."

The two girls clasped hands in the kitchen, looking and not looking at the noisy servants. He will be good to me, Dora tried to think, yet she found it difficult to conjure Anschel's face behind her shut lids.

"Let's get back now. You should be there, Dora, not in the kitchen with me." Rosa led her friend back into the singing crowds who by now were becoming hoarse, their faces shining with perspiration. Across the room, Dora saw Helen, leaning on

43

an open window. Berl was whispering something in her ear and Helen was laughing.

Before the Hirsches left for Cirlibaba, Rosa gave Dora a lace collar she had made for her. "Dear Dora. Do remember to be careful and remember me also, your loving friend and sister, Rosa," said a neat little note attached to the intricate lace. Dora kissed Rosa and said, "Promise me you will get better, little one. I want you to be maid of honour at my wedding."

"I will, Dora, I will. The three of us will again go to Czernowitz to buy your wedding dress," Rosa said, her face pale under a forced smile.

Dora waved to her long after she could not see her clearly in the distance as the carriage took her back home. She feared this was the last time she was to see her friend. Parting from Anschel was not painful by comparison.

The following winter was longer and colder. The snow covered the slated roofs and still Dora did not learn to ski. She spent her days embroidering her trousseau, ornate Ds on stiff white linen pillowcases, and making button-holes in the covers of her feather blankets.

Every week she wrote to Rosa at her sanatorium in Czernowitz. Every week Rosa wrote to her as her health deteriorated. Anschel, who knew of her love for Rosa, tried to keep her informed, as Rosa never wrote about her health, only about other patients and theatre shows which visited the sanatorium.

"Dear Dora," he wrote before Hanuka. "I have been studying at Reb Itzik Hager's court for three months now and preparing for a rabbinical degree which will not harm even if it won't help. Father is preparing me to take an active part in the business. I have been on some of his rounds, monitoring rents and collecting money owed from the peasants. The news from Rosa's doctors is not good.

"She is coughing most of the time and they aren't even sure she will be able to come to the wedding. I do hope she can be your maid of honour as you both planned. Berl takes care of the inn most days now that mother is busy preparing for the wedding and for our living here with them. She has been buying things for our part of the house. Father buries himself in the business. I am never quite sure if he is glad of my scholarship. At times I think he wishes me to become more involved in the business, like Berl. From time to time he says, when your bride joins you, you will have to provide for her. I will always provide for you. I only wish my eyes were not giving me such trouble. I have been, for the last time, to visit the recruiting officer and paid the right amount into the right hands. Next summer, God willing, the long wait will be over and we shall be properly married, man and wife at long last. Regards to your respected family, your fond fiancé, Anschel Lax."

When Dora dutifully replied to Anschel's letters, she did not write about her classes at Baron Mantz's mansion. Having lost his fortunes gambling, the baron, who, people were saying, was not a real baron at all, wanted to improve the local population by arranging classes for embroidery and dressmaking for women. The local Rebbe approved saying, it doesn't do a pretty woman any harm to be a skilled dressmaker, so Shulem allowed Dora to participate with some other Jewish women.

"You never know, you may have to use these skills one day," mother said. "I know many a woman who finances her husband by taking in sewing. Not that I think that your Anschel will let you do this, but you never know. Look at poor Frau Dauber. When he was alive, her husband never dreamt of letting her take in dressmaking. But since his death she has to. And what would we all do without her?"

Dora had asked Helen to arrange for her to receive catalogues from Czernowitz for Frau Dauber to copy a wedding gown for her. Rosa's illness made another trip to Czernowitz out of the question, Helen wrote. Mother said Rosa had nothing to do with it. This is Helen Lax all over, she said, her mouth curling downwards bitterly. The wedding is not her responsibility, so why help?

With mother's approval, Dora chose a broderie anglaise stiff collared gown with puffed sleeves, pinched waist and a full skirt, which she saw in one of Herr Friedmann's catalogues, which he kindly agreed to lend her. Frau Dauber arranged for the fabric to be sent from Czernowitz and spent long hours cutting the complex shape, filling her workroom with yards of summery cotton.

The wedding was to be on Tuesday, the day God said twice that it was good, July the first. There was no sign of Rosa leaving her sanatorium. Dora wrote to her every second day now, describing her dress, her veil, the flowers she was planning, the food. Rosa wrote short letters, not saying much and ending each letter with hopes to be with Dora and Anschel on the day.

One cloudless day, Dora returned from Baron Mantz to find another of Rosa's letters. "My dearest Dora," it began. "I must tell you I am very sick. Every day I fade a little. The doctor says I must not travel by train or by carriage. I cough blood every day now. I know, dear friend, I have not much time to live. I am happy you and Anschel will be married. I know you will make him happy and I hope he too will bring you happiness. If only he remembers there is more to life than his books. Don't cry on my grave, sing for me. I loved life and am happy to go. And don't forget to come and see me on your way back from your honeymoon. There is no more to say but that I love you dearly."

She would have to be married without Rosa. Anschel alone was never enough. Now there was only Berl.

Dora tried on her dress and was dazzled at how metropolitan she looked. As she looked into the window to catch her reflection, she tried to evoke Anschel whose face was fading. She then conjured Rosa, laughing, chatting, and tears welled in her eyes.

She did not share her mother's worries about the food, wondering will the wedding be good enough for her in-laws. "Don't worry, mother," she said, meaning don't humiliate yourself, there is nothing wrong with us. "We have come a long way since your own parents came to Cirlibaba from Galizia, when grandfather took father into his business."

It's not that different from father looking for a scholar for me, she wanted to say to mother. The only difference is money and you always said money is not important.

But as mother's face twitched with anxiety, Dora knew money was important. Otherwise, why would father commission Herr Klipper to seek both money and scholarship for her? Money, she recalled father saying over the years, never harmed a good girl. She took mother in her arms, repeating only, "There is nothing to worry about, mother, it will be a beautiful wedding." And all the while wishing it was mother taking her in her arms, rocking her and saying, don't worry, child, I'll look after you even when you go away to live in Putila.

But mother, preoccupied with her own worries, rushed off to oversee yet another pot of chicken soup, yet another crop of freshly dug potatoes, yet another starching, stretching, ironing.

Guests were staying all over town since there was no Jewish hotel in Cirlibaba, and friends and relatives were asked to house the Laxes and their extensive family. Cirlibaba became festival town. Even the peasants seemed to celebrate.

Dora's last visit to the market as a single woman two days before her wedding did not fill her with the same jealousy as before. There were still sexual overtones between the young peasants but she distanced herself from their mirth. Soon I too will have this, she told herself, believing and not believing.

The Laxes sent her a coach full of wedding presents. There were copper pots, silver dishes, china and cutlery. There were personalised silver toiletry sets, feather blankets, woollen blankets, linen towels. "Why bother to send it all here if it goes back to Putila after the wedding?" Mother's bitter words. "Only to show us up again, that's why. As if to say we cannot give you enough." Mother turned her head to conceal her angry tears.

With the toiletry sets, there was a bone box with the inscription "For Dora Lax". Dora stared for a long time, not grasping it was meant for her. Soon her father's name will become her husband's. Where am I in all this, she thought.

Inside the box lay the most perfect string of pearls with a diamond clasp. Who is it from, Dora wondered. There was no signature.

The coach was followed by another, carrying the Laxes' luggage, all four trunks of it. Finally, on the eve of the wedding, the Laxes appeared too. As their carriage rolled into the back yard, Dora could make out Rosa's pale face, peeping from the blankets wrapping her frail body. She ran towards her, waving wildly, shouting, "Rosa, you came after all," barely greeting Anschel or the rest of her future family. She hugged Rosa long after she had been carried by Faivel and Berl into the Hirsches' warm kitchen, where a hot cup of tea with much fresh milk was made for her at Dora's insistence.

She was not allowed to see Anschel until the wedding as was the custom. He departed with his parents and brothers to the house they were staying at but Rosa stayed to sleep for the last time in Dora's old room.

Dora left Rosa sleeping, her head light and pale on the white pillow, to go to the miquva where she submerged herself in the calm murky water of the communal bath, repeating the blessings after the bewigged supervisor who cut her nails almost to the bone, looking on sternly. Dora pleaded with mother to let her keep her long hair which now floated above her in the water. Mother slipped the supervisor some money and the woman grunted angrily but accepted the bribe leaving Dora's hair long. From tomorrow her hair will always be covered. Tomorrow, she was thinking, I shall not be the same.

That night she sat with Rosa who talked in a dull, unchanging voice about the sanatorium. "Some days I haven't got the energy to get out of bed," she said slowly. "You spend your days lying in bed or sitting on the veranda, wrapped up like an old woman, thinking and not thinking."

"But are they looking after you, little one? You are looking so tired."

"Yes, they are looking after me," Rosa sighed. "They are doing the best they can. Only I, I have no energy."

Dora sat by her bed until Rosa fell into a troubled sleep,

murmuring several times during the night words which sounded like shouts.

In the morning she woke up to the sun pouring through the shutters in narrow strips to see Rosa looking at her. She felt like screaming. Her face must have been distorted because Rosa looked at her and asked, "What is it, little bride? Are you in pain?"

She was not in pain, Dora thought and yet she was. "I am alright, Rosa," she whispered. Then the shout came through her. She was unable to stop it. "No, I am not," she said, her voice terrible in her ears.

"What is the matter, little bride? Are you not happy to get married? Don't you love my brother?"

"Love? What is love, Rosa? I have been trying to understand it for these last three years." She regretted this as soon as the words came out. "No, Rosa, I didn't mean it. It isn't important."

"Yes, you did. And it is important."

"But how important can it be when you cannot break conditions? Once you are engaged, you have to get married. Or so mother says. And I don't even know that I wanted to get engaged." She paused, then added fast, "You know, the flutter, the excitement a woman is supposed to feel. I don't feel a thing."

And I don't want you to die, she thought, but didn't say it.

"And you are not sure about moving in to live with us. Is that it too?" Rosa said.

"Yes," Dora whispered. "Living there without you. It all seems so frightening."

"Poor little bride." Rosa's smile was comforting. "I'll get better soon and we'll all live as one happy family."

But you are dying, Dora wanted to scream, and I am to be left with Anschel, whom I don't know. And Berl, who frightens me. And Helen, who likes no one.

But she didn't scream. Instead she smiled at her friend and said brightly, "I am now going to get you a good country breakfast to make you stronger. If you eat well, you will soon get better and come to live with us in Putila." Her voice sounded falsely gay as she rushed out of the room, tears clogging her throat.

She was fasting on the day of her wedding as was the custom. Her stomach reeled as she watched Rosa pick at her food but she urged her to eat. Ministering to Rosa's pain was easier than thinking of her own.

Rosa was too weak to help her dress. Sara came in to braid her long hair and decorate it with flowers. The last day her hair would be on view. The three girls were sitting in Dora's room, waiting for the time, much of the commotion about the house escaping them. From time to time mother rushed into their haven, collapsing into a chair and heaving a silent sigh. From time to time too, her brothers burst in, reporting excitedly of more presents sent in by local townspeople.

Dora felt out of it all. What she really wanted was to sit quietly by Rosa and will her friend back to good health, but all she could do was wait.

The time approached and Sara dressed her sister with care. Anschel was not to see her until the ceremony. Just before the canopy was set, Helen came into the room, adorned with lace and sequins.

"You do look beautiful," she said severely. "Anschel asked me to give you this," she smiled and gave Dora a little box with an oval black ring with a diamond in the centre. "It belonged to my mother, aleha ha shalom and I promised it to Anschel once he found a bride."

"Thank you, Frau Lax," Dora said, not aware whether she should already address her future mother-in-law as mother in the third person, the correct form once she was married. "I now have a piece of jewellery from your mother and one from my own maternal grandmother."

And to herself she thought that now she was truly fixed into the family tree, like a gem sunk in gold.

The canopy was erected outside Shulem Hirsch's house and the local Rebbe, the famous Viznitz tsadik, Reb Aharon Hager, brother of the Laxes' Reb Itzik, clad in black silk and a fur streiml, married Dora and Anschel.

As Anschel was saying, his voice loud and clear for all the gathered guests to hear, "You are hereby betrothed to me according to the law of Moses and Israel," Dora caught Berl's eyes on her face from the far corner of the canopy where he was holding one of the poles. Under her veil she lowered her eyelids and concentrated on the ceremony. A gold band, inscribed Anschel, 1.7.1898, was slipped onto her finger. She lifted her veil and sipped from the sweet wine and heard, as in a daze, a glass breaking under Anschel's foot and the crowd shouting mazel tov, mazel tov. Someone, Anschel perhaps, lifted her veil and kissed her lightly on her lips, which she pursed, responding.

Years later she would try to recall the rest of the wedding party when food and drink poured generously. She would sit on the veranda in her daughter's Tel Aviv apartment trying to recall Helen Lax sitting at the bridal table chatting to the local dignitaries and mother's anxious look, or even Rosa's little body slouched wearily in the armchair brought specially from the sitting room to make her comfortable. Things she heard Sara talk about years later. But she could not.

During her years in the camp she couldn't remember sitting at her father's table on this day, the happiest day in a woman's life, and thinking only that tomorrow she would not have to bring in the milk. She couldn't remember the hassidim dancing and the special trays laid out in the yard for the peasants who looked on at the canopy, silent, almost menacing. She couldn't remember surreptitiously looking for Berl, who was nowhere to be seen, to ask him if he knew who had sent the pearls.

She could not remember much about her wedding night either. There was a hazy memory of lying in her parents' double bed beside Anschel, whose long white nightshirt looked strangely virginal. She remembered knowing she had to do something, make this night different to all other nights but falling into a heavy, disturbed sleep and waking, alarmed by the bright morning sun in her parents' white bedroom, to see Anschel, standing beside the bed, his phylacteries spiralling around his hairless arm and high forehead, murmuring the morning prayer. She woke up as a married woman and this voice was chanting in a low whisper: "blessed be the Lord that hath not made me a woman" and she mumbled, automatically, joining in the prayer, "blessed be He that hath made me according to his will."

Parting with Rosa was as hard as parting with her parents. Once again she had the feeling she would not see Rosa again. Rosa tried to chat cheerfully as she was carried onto her father's coach, wrapped in warm blankets despite the July heat. But seeing her pale face and big circled eyes, Dora had a pang of certainty of Rosa's imminent death. I'll write, was all she could manage as the coach drove off.

Later, Dora and Anschel got into another carriage which took them to the station on their way to Karlsbad. Mother wept openly when they made their farewells. It was the first time Dora saw mother cry. She knew she was crying because she was not coming back. From Karlsbad the couple was to return to Putila. Dora felt no great sorrow and no great joy watching her family waving in the dusty distance.

In Karlsbad Dora and Anschel Lax stayed in a small kosher pension and took the water every day. Anschel spent time each day with his books and while he was studying, Dora took lengthy mud baths with other Jewish women who came to Karlsbad to lose weight or get rid of their rheumatism.

The complete rest and relaxation allowed Dora to ask Anschel about his eyes. When she suggested shyly that his failing eyesight could have got him exemption from army service without bribes, he laughed lightly and said his eyesight had nothing to do with it. Anyway, he added softly, "this was all in the past now that we are man and wife at last."

That night he lay beside her in his white nightshirt and caressed her hair. "We should," he whispered, "it's a mitzva."

"Yes, I know," she whispered back, bashfully letting him lead her slowly, his hands moving lightly along her rigid body, his bearded face touching hers, closing soft lips on hers, but all she felt was a dull pain when he penetrated her, skin barely touching skin, both remaining in their night clothes, pulled above their waists.

Dora was not used to resting. Apart from her stay in Czernowitz with Helen, she had always risen at dawn, bringing in the milk, making bread and cheese, helping mother with the younger children, studying for some hours with the family melamed.

Now she had the day to herself. She began to enjoy the idleness, the chat with the older women from places as far apart as Prague and Linz. Unlike Helen Lax's conversation, mainly clothes, food and etiquette, these women spoke politics. She got involved in such conversations for the first time here. At home only men spoke politics. From time to time she would hear her parents discuss anti-semitism, but in Cirlibaba, where Jews were comfortably off, ruling over the local peasants who were tacitly hostile but not dangerous, anti-semitism seemed far away.

Now, up to her neck in mud and listening to her newly-found acquaintances, Dora learnt of the growing anti-semitism in Vienna, that capital city she had heard spoken of for its splendour. She learnt that after the emancipation the number of Jews in the capital doubled, worrying the Viennese who saw the Jews succeed in the professions but particularly in commerce. Frau Altmann, a stout woman whose sister lived in Vienna, told the mud-covered gathering of the open hostility of her sister's neighbours who had blamed the Jews for the economic slump.

"They are saying we are half Asian," said Frau Altmann, shrugging her fat shoulders, "only because we came from Galicia. What do you say to that?" The women gasped. The mere thought of being thought of as Asian was to these women anti-semitism in its embodiment. Frau Altmann told her captive audience of the Viennese anti-semitic associations, imported from Berlin.

"They keep using Professor Rohling's writings to prove we are pagans and anti-Christs, although everyone knows that Rohling's argument has been proven wrong at the Tisa Aesler trial," she said to the incredulous women.

51

That night Dora questioned Anschel about what she had heard. At first, he tried to dissuade her from asking, saying all this was no matter for women. But Dora had just heard other women, all respectable matrons from big cities, discuss political matters and insisted she wanted to know.

Sighing, Anschel told her about the Tisa Aesler trial where a Jewish child testified against his own father, saying his father killed a Christian child for ritual purposes. "The priest Professor August Rohling published another of his anti-semitic publications, trying to prove the blood plot was right," Anschel explained.

"To prove Rohling was an anti-semite," Anschel continued, "Reichstag member Dr Yoseph Bloch, also a rabbi to the Florisdorf congregation near Vienna, took Rohling to court, having published articles in the Wiener Allgemeine Zeitung, proving Rohling's lack of knowledge in Talmudic literature. Dr. Bloch, one of the brave Jews of our generation, promised Rohling three thousand florins if he could read one page from the Talmud and translate it into German."

Anschel got carried away with the story. "Instead of answering the challenge, Rohling said he was prepared to swear under oath that his quotations from Talmudic literature proving that religious crimes were rampant amongst Jews, were authentic."

"But did he know anything about the Talmud?" Dora was fascinated. Her first real experience of adult conversation, about real life, not at all like the small-town sneering behind waxed moustaches and sweet insincere smiles she had known in her home town.

"Hard to tell. He may have known something, not much," Anschel said. "Bloch published in the papers an accusation against Rohling who was prepared to swear a false oath, to force Rohling to take him to court and thus expose his ignorance. Professor Rohling did sue him. It took some time because Dr Bloch was a member of the Reichstag with parliamentary immunity but by 1884 the Reichstag gave permission to take him to court.

"In court, experts testified that Rohling's so-called scientific works were bound in ignorance and self-deception. When he saw he could not escape a verdict against him, Professor Rohling withdrew his complaint against Dr Bloch. By now most people had realised he was nothing but an impostor, but the seeds of anti-semitism were sown and in the 1891 elections, the anti-semites voted twelve deputies into the Reichstag. The worst of these were Schnerer, Prince Lichtenstein and Schneider."

"But we are quite safe in Bucovina, aren't we, Anschel?" Dora was frightened.

"I hope so, little one." Anschel sounded so grown up when he said this. "But now with the election of Karl Lüger, the biggest anti-semite of all, as the Mayor of Vienna, things are not improving.

"So far, the Kaiser has not ratified his election and last year, after Lüger was elected for the third time, he met the Kaiser and they agreed Lüger should not take up his post to keep the peace. It was a complete fiasco, though. Instead of Lüger, the mayor was the anti-semite bookseller Strobach. Lüger was his deputy but in fact, he ruled the City Council with Strobach a figurehead only."

Talking like this with Anschel made Dora more comfortable in this new marriage. She still spent much of her time with the women in the mud baths while Anschel was studying, but in the evenings and during the meals, they talked at length, seriously, discovering the pleasures of companionship. Even bed times were less pressured now. Anschel was getting less bashful and Dora took to closing her eyes, allowing herself to be guided further. Once or twice she thought she sensed what she came to call the flutter, as her body responded to Anschel's.

When her period came and she was not permitted to her husband according to the purity laws of her religion, she came to miss their nightly love-making. Anschel slept in another bed during her menstrual period, observing the strict dictum forbidding him to touch an impure woman. Dora sat in an easy chair by the mud baths during her exile, talking to the women and wondering if they too were exiled from their husbands' beds.

The month swept by. Dora had acquired a glow from the health-giving mud baths and the nightly love-making. By the end of their stay, Anschel suggested shyly that Dora buy herself some clothes and hats at the spa shop, where model costumes from Vienna and Prague were sold to the rich matrons who frequented the spa.

The train ride back to Bucovina was long. Stepping out of the spa atmosphere and speeding through the night, in a first-class wagon lit, Dora felt a pang of regret.

Visiting Rosa's sanatorium in Czernowitz was their last stop before taking the coach Yacob had sent for them. Rosa looked small and pale, lying in a white bed with only deep silence for company, saying little but smiling sadly with her big black eyes.

Waiting for the carriage at the Schwarze Adler hurled Dora towards an unknown adulthood, different from that acquired

53

with her new grown-up clothes and pleasures.

Anschel prayed silently as the carriage negotiated peak after peak while Dora kept repeating to herself there was no need to fear her new life. Seeing the imposing white front of the Lax family house did nothing to dispel her unease. The carriage ground to a halt on the gravel outside the front door and, as the coachman stepped outside to lower the step for her, Dora saw Berl grinning towards her.

"Welcome home, Frau Lax," said his smile. "Had a nice time at Karlsbad?"

"Yes, thank you Berl." Dora was careful to use the familiar term, attempting to put him in his place.

"You are more beautiful than ever. What a welcome addition to our dull household."

He led her, slightly touching her elbow, into the house, Anschel lagging behind.

There was much formal greeting, dry pecking on cheeks, much polite enquiry after her health and honeymoon. There was much chat about Rosa's state of health, then everything quietened down and Dora was left with her mother-in-law, poised at the edge of an armchair, looking her over curiously.

"Any news, child?" Helen asked anxiously, her eagle eyes scrutinising Dora's body. Dora was unsure what the question meant and Frau Lax had to repeat it in more explicit terms. "Are you expecting yet, dear?"

Dora burst out laughing. So this was what it was about, producing an heir to the Lax throne. "What are you laughing about, Dora Lax?" said the older woman's stern voice. "Have I said something funny?"

"I am sorry, mother, if I offended her," Dora was addressing her mother-in-law in the third person, as she had heard her own parents address their in-laws. "Mother has said nothing funny. I am sorry."

"No need to be, child. All I wanted to know was if you and my son are getting on well. That's all."

Dora looked at the other woman's face and to her surprise saw a frank, clear gaze back. "Yes, we are, mother, very well. I had a very nice time at Karlsbad, thank you."

"I am relieved to hear that." Helen Lax sounded as if their little tête-à-tête was coming to an end. But there was more to come. "I want to show you your rooms," she said in the tone of a hotel manageress taking a new guest to her room for the first time. "I was hoping Anschel would help Herr Lax by running the inn," she added as the two women ascended the stairs. "His health has not been too good recently. I would like him to take things a bit easier but he wouldn't hear of it. If Anschel offered to take the load off his father's shoulders, Herr Lax would get a chance to rest."

"Yes, mother, I am sure Anschel will do his best to help," Dora said. "I could help you around the house." She paused and when no answer came, she added, speaking too fast, "I have always helped my own mother. In the house and the yard."

"I am sure you did, child," there was a hint of the old contempt in her mother-in-law's voice. "But we have enough help around the house."

She was shown to a bedroom, large and roomy. The large double windows let in much light through the handmade curtains, patterns of peacock laced in. There was a double bed in the centre, a little round table in dark wood covered with a fine embroidered tablecloth and two deep armchairs on both sides. There was a washstand with a china jug and bowl.

"The maid would bring you hot water in the morning," Frau Lax was saying as Dora surveyed the double wardrobe.

"And there is a small room for Anschel to study in and another small room for when you have your first child."

She paused, awaiting a reaction. When Dora said nothing, she added, "you will, of course, take your meals with us."

"Thank you, mother, this is all very nice," Dora said. But there is nowhere here for me, she was thinking. No place for me.

The inn was cold and musty as Berl was showing Anschel around. He had been working here as his father looked after the family's land leasing business.

"It has been in our family for three generations," Berl said, only half boastfully, never quite serious. "We were the first Jews in this region of Bucovina to be granted a spirit licence. The Laxes, you know, are a very important family in this little village of Putila Kaselitsa," he said, mockingly.

Dora was not looking at her brother-in-law as he was speaking, knowing his gaze was glued to her body. Anschel, oblivious to his wife's discomfort, said angrily to his younger brother, "Cut the chat, Berl, and tell me where things are. I would like to start as soon as possible so you can join father on his rounds. Mother and I have been worried about his health. I would like you to lighten his burden."

Berl shot his brother a quick glance, chuckled to himself and continued, unabashed, "Jews, you know, can be anything they want in this part of the world. Anything, that is, apart from Lord Mayor or Prefect."

"What nonsense you speak at times, Berl," Anschel cut him short. "You know as well as I do that anti-semitism is raising its ugly head all over the Empire. And you know that emancipation is only on paper, not in reality."

"I beg to differ, brother." Berl sounded serious for once. "This is our Empire. Our Kaiser loves us. Look how lenient his officials have been in the matter of mobilising you into the Imperial army."

"This is just a matter of greasing the appropriate palms. Nothing to do with the Kaiser's benevolence."

"That is as may be. The fact remains that a Jew can be a tinsmith or a high-ranking officer or even an inn-keeper in Bucovina, which is not how things stand in Poland or Russia."

"You are right there, Berl. Things are not quite so good for our brethren in Poland or Russia," Anschel said. "But why don't you start showing me things around here?"

It was the first time Dora heard Anschel sound impatient, but Berl continued chatting and gesticulating as he showed them the bottles, the stored spirits, the barrels, the ledgers, the list of credit customers, not to be added to, the glasses. The inn was furnished in highly polished wood with a wide counter and small stools around coarse square tables. Everywhere there was a musty smell of old dust mingled with beeswax.

She was lost in thought when Berl said, directly to her, Anschel having stooped over the counter, checking the ledger, "You, at least, won't have to work here. Lucky lady."

"I have worked every day God gave since I was five," she said without thinking, surprised at her own anger. "Tidying the house, sweeping the yard, hanging clothes, folding them for the German to coal iron. When I was older I went marketing, haggling over prices. I am well used to trading and better used to hard work."

"Pity a pretty lady like you had to work so hard." Something in Berl's voice was making her feel naked. "Don't you like pearls?" he added suddenly.

Dora gasped. So this was where the pearls came from. She opened her mouth to speak, but Berl hushed her. "Say nothing, Frau Lax. It was no more than a bad joke, giving you grandmother's pearls without telling you they had always been meant for the wife of the first Lax son who was to marry."

"I don't understand what it is that you want of me, brother Berl," Dora tried to speak as sternly as she could. "The pearls are lovely and I have often worn them in Karlsbad, you'll be glad to know. Now, if you'll excuse me."

Berl smiled and bowed to kiss her hand, tickling the back of her palm with his black moustache. Then, not saying another word, he joined his brother.

That night before she said her prayers, Dora quizzed Anschel about the inn. "I hadn't expected to be asked to operate the inn," Anschel said. "Berl must have tired of it. He probably wants to be back on the road, where he can womanise freely."

"But what about your studies?"

"Someone has to take care of the inn now that Berl is backing out. If we let it go, another Jew may never get the concession and we would lose much of our financial influence in the village. As for my studies, I shall have to find time. I shall rise a little earlier and go to bed a little later. Time must be found for the word of the Lord."

Dora shrugged and sighed lightly. The first of many sighs. "And time must also be found for the mitzva of being fruitful and multiplying," Anschel said earnestly. There was no sensuality in his voice, only a sense of urgency as he started unbuttoning his nightshirt, not looking at her body as his hands moved swiftly down her belly. The flutter wasn't there that night but Dora closed her eyes, telling herself this was what she got married for as the thudding of his penetration filled her with warmth.

Anschel started rising at dawn, praying and then studying for an hour before breakfast. Dora rose to serve his breakfast which the cook had prepared. He then made for the inn to oversee stocks and do the bookkeeping before he opened at noon.

Some nights he did not come home until midnight. Other days he left at dusk, leaving his helper, the one-eyed Shimon Lepler, to lock up. Thursdays he left early to go to the public bath preparing for the Sabbath and on Fridays he did not open at all. Sunday was the big day. The inn was full of red-faced peasants, soldiers and craftsmen in one corner and officers and burghers in the other, all getting pleasantly drunk, shouting to Anschel to fill their glasses while he looked soberly on.

Dora spent many hours on her own. She was not used to having so much time. If this was married life, she wondered why her mother and aunts were always grumbling. Helen allowed her to partake in cooking for the Sabbath once she discovered how well Dora baked and how well praised her breads and cakes were. But there was no heavy work to do, no marketing.

She wrote many letters to her parents whom she missed greatly and to Rosa, whose letters grew shorter. Everybody was busy except her. Helen had her home to run and her women friends to impress with clothes she periodically bought from Herr Friedmann in Czernowitz. When Dora joined Helen and her friends for afternoon coffee, a Viennese custom just taking root at the edges of the Empire, she found their conversations trite in comparison with the conversation of the women she had met in Karlsbad. Anschel had the inn and his studies, which left little time for her. Yacob, whose good-natured talk she always enjoyed, was away during the week on his rounds or with his Rebbe. Berl spent most of his week on the road with his father and Dora found herself missing his company, despite the unease she felt when he was around. Even little Yossel and Faivel were at the Yeshiva and came home only for the High Holidays.

Before Rosh Hashana, Anschel travelled with his father to visit Reb Itzik. Dora expected him to return glowing with the Rebbe's light but instead he addressed her sternly in their bedroom that night. "The Rebbe asked me if there was any sign of children yet," he said directly.

"And what did you say?" Dora asked.

"What could I say?" Anschel's voice sounded desperate. "We are married two months and no sign yet."

"Everyone seems anxious for me to produce a child as soon as possible. I received a letter from mother asking me the same question. And your mother too. The first thing she wanted to know when we returned from Karlsbad."

"Are you surprised, my dear?" Anschel softened somewhat. "This is the purpose of marriage. The Lord said it was our duty to be fruitful and multiply and God willing, we shall soon have a son of our own."

Dora said nothing and surrendered to his renewed efforts that night, wondering why he had said son when what she wanted was a daughter. Marriage was turning out to be duller than she had envisaged. There was nothing adult about living in someone else's house, eating someone else's food, feeling dispensable.

When the high holidays arrived homesickness was alleviated only by Yacob Lax as he led his family through the blessings just like her father used to do year in, year out. Dora dipped a piece of apple in honey, wishing herself and her new family a sweet year.

"May this house be filled again with the laughter of children," Yacob added softly when all the blessings were done and everyone looked at Dora whose lowered eyelids they took for modesty, not guessing at her rising anger.

She knew she was pregnant soon after Hanukah. Snow covered everything as Dora staggered, vomiting, from one morning to the next. Overjoyed, Anschel had sent for a fox coat from Czernowitz, "to keep my little family warm." Her parents communicated their delight and Helen spent hours with the local seamstress making Dora a series of warm maternity frocks for the cold winter ahead.

Her breasts tender and her back aching, Dora continued to feel nauseated until the mountain snows started melting. Her pregnancy, which made everybody else around her so happy, filled her with awe. Like Eve, I am carrying children in sorrow, she thought. But what have I done to deserve it? I have tempted no one, I haven't been disobedient. If anything, this had been all decided for me.

She tried to write some of this to Rosa, but her friend's short reply brought no solace. "When my life ebbs away," she wrote, "there will be another soul to take my place. Make sure you look after yourself. Get plenty of rest and eat well as your loving friend is thinking of you."

Pessach came and Dora's figure was rotund, showing her pregnancy to the full. She thanked the Lord that the nausea had stopped as she helped Helen prepare for the Seder meal. Had she not been pregnant, she and Anschel would have travelled to Cirlibaba to spend the holiday with her parents.

When the men came back from temple, Helen's elegant table welcomed them. Yacob blessed the wine, the men washed their hands with water the women carried in for them in china bowls. He then gave each participant a bit of parsley dipped in salt water, halved the middle matza on the table and reminded them of the Children of Israel's enslavement in Egypt.

"Why is this night different from all other nights?" Faivel, the youngest, chanted four times. "Because we were slaves to Pharoah in Egypt and the Lord our God brought us forth from there with a mighty hand and an outstretched arm," Yacob chanted in reply. The family proceeded with the service, relating the going out of Egypt, taking turns reading the old story, and Dora kept thinking of her own enslavement, here in this elegant house, away from family and friends, imprisoned in her own body.

After the meal she and Helen had prepared, at the blessing on the third cup of wine, the youngsters were sent to open the door for Elijah the prophet. Yacob called loudly, "Pour out thy wrath upon the heathen that have not known thee and upon the kingdoms that have not called upon thy name. For they have devoured Yacob and laid waste his dwelling place."

As he was reading, the young boys came running in shouting, "there is a stranger at the door, there is a stranger at the door."

Yacob looked annoyed to have to interrupt the ceremony. "What is it, Faivel?" he asked impatiently.

"There is a man at the door. Says he has a telegram for you." Faivel looked excited and disturbed.

"Show him into the kitchen," Yacob said. "We must not

interrupt our seder. You deal with it, Berl."

Berl went out as Yacob continued calling out the Lord's wrath upon Israel's enemies. No one pointed out to the boys that Elijah the prophet must have been for a visit and sipped from the large silver cup laid out for him at the centre of the table as was the custom year after year. They were too old to believe it. When Berl came in, Dora knew his tidings from the way he looked in her direction.

"What is it, Berl?" Helen urged him.

"I am afraid it is Rosa," Berl said softly, putting his hand on his mother's shoulder but not taking his eyes off Dora's face.

"No," Dora heard herself scream. Her screams pierced the house long after Anschel had led her gently to their bedroom, sitting quietly by her as she sobbed herself to sleep.

Rosa was to be buried on the night after the second day of Pessach. Because of the holiness of the day, her family could not be present, but Yacob and Helen interrupted the customary Shiva, seven days of mourning, to travel to Czernowitz to view the freshly-dug grave and say the appropriate prayers. Dora stayed in bed for the whole week, barely able to touch her food, staring for long hours out the window through which the spring sun sent pale rays to dance on her bedroom walls, while in the living room, quorums of ten men prayed for her dead friend three times each day.

When Helen and Yacob returned with Rosa's belongings, Helen came into Dora's room. "There was a letter by her bed, saying goodbye to us all and asking for certain things to be given to certain people," she said. "This box is for you."

Dora tried to smile at her mother-in-law as she took the wooden box, but her tears welled and she was unable to speak. To her surprise, Helen, who up until then seemed to keep her courage, started crying softly. "I shall miss her. I shall miss my little girl," she sobbed. Dora put out her arm and hugged Helen and the two women cried together.

When Helen left the room, Dora opened the box where she found her own letters tied in a silk ribbon, some lace handkerchiefs, a golden locket with a piece of Rosa's black hair and a letter.

"My dear friend," she read and cried. "As I lie dying here in my quiet room, I think of you in my family home. I know you are alone and I know how much you miss your own parents. Life with the Laxes cannot be easy, with mother's big town graces, father's preoccupation with his religion and Berl's taciturn advances. I also know that the love between you and Anschel is not what you had hoped for. I did not want to talk to you before.

There was nothing we could do and I had hoped I would return home and keep you company. Now that I know I am dying — the doctors are trying to hide it from me, but I feel the end is near — I want you to know that I know you are not happy. There is no point dreaming of things getting better one day. There is little chance of that. We are what we are and unless you find in yourself the peace of mind to accept what you have, you will never find happiness. I have accepted that I am to die, never having loved any man. I want you to promise me one thing. Try and find your own way of doing things. Don't always live as others want you to. There isn't much time and we have but one chance.

"And pray for me, dear Dora. Your loving sister, Rosa."

By the time Dora had read the letter twice, she knew she was not going to stay and have her baby in this house. Soon after Pessach she told Anschel she had to visit her parents. Anschel, who had been worried about her deep mourning at Rosa's death, agreed to let her make the day-long coach journey despite her condition.

When a letter arrived some weeks later saying Dora was not coming back to live in Putila Kaselitsa and that if Anschel wanted to be with her when their child was born, he was to join her at her parents' home in Cirlibaba, Anschel's first reaction was anger. He had been far too busy to notice Dora's loneliness at his parents' house and now he could not understand what brought on such a letter.

To his surprise, his father did not share his anger at what he saw as Dora's rebellion. "The poor girl had a hard time with us here." Yacob said quietly.

"But father, a woman's duty is to be by her husband's side," Anschel protested.

"She does not say she does not want to be by your side, son," Yacob said patiently. "There are times in a man's life when he has to listen to his wife. I have often thought of the cruel fate which took your mother away from the metropolis to this little village. I know she has not been happy here and I would like your Dora to be happier. She is a good woman and she is carrying your child."

Anschel shrugged. There was no arguing with his father, who could see, already then, that his son was not cut out to lead his wife through the cycle of life. Yacob preempted his son's worries about the inn by saying he had already decided to sell.

"Times are changing for the Empire Jews," he said firmly. "Things will never be as they used to be before Lüger and the anti-semites took over in Vienna. I have heard talk of pogroms in

Russia and Poland and the first to be hurt are Jews who own conspicuous properties like our inn. I was going to sell it within the year but with you moving to Cirlibaba, I'd better start looking for a buyer right now."

Anschel sought his mother's help but Helen, her contempt for her daughter-in-law's family apart, also said her son's place was by his young wife when she was having their first child. "It may not be for long, son. After she has her child, you may come back here," she said. Anschel smiled hopefully. He was not to know he would never return.

His parents urged him not to delay so as to spend the last months of Dora's pregnancy with her. Anschel packed all his books scrupulously and at Dora's request, had the maid put their linen, the trousseau she had so carefully embroidered at Baron Mantz during the years she awaited the wedding, and her wedding gifts, into tea chests and hampers. When the time came to leave, he loaded everything onto two carriages and, with his heart heavy, bid farewell to his childhood village.

In July 1899 Dora gave birth to a daughter whom she talked Anschel into calling Rosa. Anschel added the Jewish Reisale and Dora's joy made up for his disappointment that his first was not a boy.

Anschel spent the first few months studying and making frequent visits to Shulem Hirsch's Rebbe for lessons and discussions of the Talmud. Shulem and he spent night after night unravelling complex Talmudic questions in Shulem's book-lined study. The fact that his son-in-law's reputation as a sharp scholar and a devout hassid was growing in the Rebbe's court, made up for Shulem's financial worries with the addition to his household.

During the day, Anschel helped his father-in law with his money-lending business which barely stretched now to feed Dora and himself. Dora nursed her baby and continued to help her mother with the house and the yard, but life was far from affluent. She found herself missing Helen's well-to-do household where there was no scraping and making do.

Yacob Lax, who knew the situation from previous visits to Cirlibaba, wrote to Anschel offering to buy him some property in the vicinity. "After all," he wrote, "I agreed to give you and your young wife board and lodging for life. Things have turned out not as I planned and you are living away from us. But the sale of the inn freed some money and I would like to make things easier for you and Dora. I shall come to visit in a few weeks and we shall settle the matter."

Anschel, who was enjoying his scholarly status and his light business duties, greeted his father's offer with little enthusiasm. Property would mean having to divert more time away from his studies. Dora, on the other hand, restless after the birth, recalled her father's dream of her running a business for a scholarly husband.

"You are such an excellent scholar, you should continue your studies," she said when the letter arrived.

"But you are a woman," Anschel said. "Women cannot do business with strange men."

"I am a woman but you are a scholar," she replied softly. "What is a higher mitzva for a Jewish wife than to enable her husband to study the Lord's word?"

"I will not dream of it," Anschel snapped, but Dora said quickly, "There are many Jewish women who marry men for their scholarship. When my father told me about you, he spoke of your Talmudic brain. He said he wished he could offer me a business to run so that you could study. Luckily, your father can look after us financially. I caused you to move from your father's house and now the least I can do is to help you pursue your studies with the property your good father is offering to buy for you. You can go out to meet clients but let me do the paperwork. You know my poor father's business can barely keep his own family."

When Anschel continued to dither, Dora wrote to the Rebbe asking his advice. The Rebbe's reply, that it was indeed a Jewish woman's duty to enable her scholarly husband to pursue his studies, convinced Anschel.

Yacob Lax bought three fields and a small forest, registering them in Anschel's name. He also bought them a little house right beside Shulem's house where they had been residing. The pale green house had two stories, the bottom for winter and the top for summer, with a special room for guests.

While Anschel studied and the wet nurse Dora had hired nursed her little Rosa-Reisale, who was becoming plumper than her dead aunt had ever been, Dora started looking after the Lax property. Anschel had made the initial contacts, letting the fields to local peasants and the forest to a sawmill against a certain percentage of its profits, providing it was worked to the full. It was up to Dora to ensure that this was done. She visited the sawmill once a week, overseeing the cutting and the floating of the planks down the Bistritsa and Cirlibaba rivers to neighbouring towns.

As waybills piled up from far-away places like Varna, Czernowitz and even Bucharest in Romania, Dora collected the percentages, feeling strange pangs of excitement. Anschel continued to help Shulem in his money-lending rounds but Dora looked after the books, straightening Shulem's crumpled IOUs and reminding the men as to who owed what for how long.

She still helped her mother cooking and baking but she now had her own German to clean and wash and look after Rosa when she had to be out in the sawmill. For her visits she had bought a small two-horse carriage driven by the son of the Hirsches' German maid.

She still did most of the marketing for mother and for herself but now she had her own carriage, she no longer eyed the courting peasants with sensuous envy. I am a businesswoman, she muttered to herself, her dark blue eyes closed as Anschel fulfilled the mitzva of being fruitful and multiplying during the period each month when she was permitted to her husband. He wanted a son, she knew, but if there was ever a flutter, it came from her new sense of power, not from Anschel's long fingers on her rounded breasts.

2

Rosa 1914

The screams kept invading her. Holding more fear than Rosa had ever experienced. They are here, they are here. The words came through the noise. Rumours about the fall of Czernowitz to Brussilov. But it wasn't until troops were sighted on the hills surrounding the forest that the silent screams began.

In the house beyond theirs, at the edge of the town, a peasant woman was expecting a child. Her anguished voice mingled with the screams.

The German maid came in and curtsied. "The Cossacks are here," she told mother. "The poor woman won't make it in time. It's her first."

"Bring her in and prepare a feather bed in the back kitchen," mother said briefly. The German kissed Dora's hand.

"Go now," Dora pushed her away. She turned to Rosa and chided, "Don't just stand there like a kleismer and stare. Help me deliver the wretched woman."

The German returned, supporting the peasant. Her flesh bulging under her embroidered clothes, stiff with black muck, her gait heavy, not helped by heavy boots, covered in dried cow's dung. Still odorous.

"God bless you, lady," she turned to Dora who didn't look her in the eye.

"Come now, come," Dora kept saying. Coldly.

Rosa felt a surge of sympathy for the peasant, whose husband, the German had said, had been mobilised by the Kaiser. She extended her hand to help the stumbling woman.

"I have such a pain," the woman whispered hoarsely.

The birth was short as first births go, Dora said later. To Rosa it seemed endless. The peasant screamed. Cursed her husband and her maker. Writhed and kept calling for her mother in heaven. All alone in the world, Rosa kept thinking.

And throughout the birth, the silent screams. When the bloodied head appeared between the young woman's legs, Rosa was mesmerised by a particularly piercing voice outside. A male voice, in sharp contrast to the high female voices.

Inside Dora and the German urged the woman to push harder. Her breathing became more regular, less anguished. Then Dora declared, "It's a little girl you have, woman," and the peaceful expression on the peasant's face changed to one of despair.

"He'll kill me," she sobbed. "He said before going to war he wanted a son. What am I to do?"

"Don't be stupid, woman," Dora's voice held no compassion. "It's a healthy baby. And you will have more."

She left the room, bidding Rosa to follow. To the German she said, "You can tend to her for a while. As long as you don't neglect your duties."

She didn't stay to listen to the peasant's blessings. Washed her hands carefully with carbolic soap, reserved for dealing with the yard's animals, wiped her hands on her starched apron and said to Rosa, "Well, Rosl, you have now witnessed your first birth. Women pain much in order to have their children. Never forget."

As the screams persisted, Trajan, their coachman, burst into the house and said the Russians were hiding in the forest. "They raped three peasants on their way to milk, lady," he said, out of breath.

"Stop it, man," Dora said. "Get hold of yourself. These rumours always circulate at times of war."

Rosa followed Trajan to the stable. "Is it true about the rape?" she asked, trying to sound as adult as she could.

"So they say, Fräulein Rosa." He averted his gaze from her eager face. "The women were returning from Valea Stinei. They had just milked their cows and the soldiers pounced on them."

He stopped, realising he was talking to his mistress' young daughter. "Excuse me, Fräulein Rosa. I must be getting back to the horses."

Rosa was not sure what rape was. The image of menstrual blood mixed with milk, dirty red on muddy white, coupled with the screams in her head for a long time.

That night, Rosa heard mother talk to father about leaving Cirlibaba. "We'll have to move on, Anschel," she said, her measured voice not revealing the fear she had been surrounded by that day with Germans, peasants and townspeople running in and out, panic-stricken, while father sat in his room, reading the small print of his Gemarra.

Rosa had often heard him say that Jews are always on the move. Wars bring us bad luck. No matter who wins, we are always the losers. But now, looking suddenly small, he looked at mother and said, "But where to, Dora?"

"To Bistritsa," Dora said unhesitatingly.

"Golden Bistritsa?" Rosa asked excitedly. "I heard people say someone had once found gold there."

"Don't be silly, Rosl. You mustn't believe in rumours." Mother sounded tired.

Father said, "I am sure you have worked it all out, Dora. You must be right."

"There has been no business for ages, Anschel. The sawmill cannot be worked with Russian troops all over the forest and the tenants won't pay up. It is time to save our skins."

"But where will we live there, mother?" Rosa asked.

"Leave it be, Reisale," father said softly. "The Lord will provide." He got up from the kitchen table and went into his room.

Dora sighed and called after him. "We shall leave first thing Sunday morning. So, if there is anyone still owing, can you collect tomorrow and Thursday?"

"Yes, yes." Father's voice echoed wearily from amongst the ancient books.

"And write to tell your parents we are going," Dora called into the books. "Perhaps they too would want to come."

"Not with mother's leg. It's too long a journey," father called back.

"Write anyway. The least you can do. My own parents wouldn't budge." Mother turned to Rosa. "You must help me with the packing. Tomorrow we wash and then we pack, to be ready first thing Sunday morning."

"But mother, we know nobody in Bistritsa."

"Hush, child. You heard your father. The Lord will provide."

Next morning was washing day. Mother and the German prepared the sheets for a big washing, done every three months, and two washerwomen joined their German and Tante Sara's German to rub and scrape sheets, pillow cases, table cloths.

At lunchtime, Rosa brought them thick slices of white bread and soup as they sat in the yard at their large pails of spring water.

"Poor little one. I hear you are going away to Bistritsa," said the fat washerwoman, Ioanna, her face glistening greasily in the late summer sun.

"Yes, we are going to golden Bistritsa," Rosa said playfully. "We may even find gold on the street." She hated Ioanna and her wide-jawed disdain for her Jewish employers.

"Send me some, will you?" said the red-faced peasant and the other joined her in a loud, mean laughter. Rosa felt herself blush with anger. "Mock if you please. We are going away from the war, gold or no gold and you must stay here to burn."

"You are laden with gold as it is," said Maria, the thinner washerwoman as she munched on her thickly sliced bread. "All Jews are, everybody knows."

Rosa swallowed and said nothing. She moved aside watching the women's mirth as they put the sheets into the large wooden pail with ashes from the fire in between them, her face paling at the midday sun. They carried the pail between them into the house, chatting and gossiping, apparently oblivious to the raging war. How carefree they seemed, not having to run away from

68

the war, like us Jews.

The following morning they came back, the sheets having been steeped in boiling water overnight. They carried the pail down to the river bank, where they hit the white sheets with sticks until lunchtime came again.

As a child she had asked mother why they always had so much washing. "Only poor people wash every week," mother had said. "Praise God we have enough sheets to go round. No need to wash more than every three months. So naturally we have a lot of it."

As a child she watched the washerwomen and their laughter, their broad shoulders in such contrast to mother's delicate, stern frame. Today she followed them to the river bank, her anger forgotten, watching them rinse the sheets in the river, wring them and hang them to dry in the yard where the late August sun would dry them before dark.

Today the washerwomen were no longer childhood dreams. As she watched, envious of their womanliness, their large strong bodies, their bulging breasts, Rosa marvelled at the speed their thick arms worked, hitting the cloth and wringing, wringing. Today they were women of this land who did not have to run away from war.

Rosa did not want to leave Cirlibaba.

Last Hanukah, at a party given in temple, she had met a young man whose voice rang high above all others singing Ma Oz Tsur. She did not have to make major efforts to attract his attention. David Greifer had already noticed her attractive if slightly plump features and asked her cousin to introduce them.

At fifteen, Rosa was mature and David Greifer, all of eighteen years, did not realise the risk he was taking when he asked her to accompany him for a walk in the snow the following Sunday.

Herr Greifer worked in the local post office until his promised place at the University of Czernowitz became available, he told Rosa as they walked with her two sisters, Hanna and baby Hetti. Alone in Cirlibaba, his parents had died several years ago, he charmed the girls with stories about his lonely childhood and the amusing types he met at the post office.

The Lax girls were not used to meeting young people who made a living. Young people of their acquaintance lived at home. Older, they were safely married. Rosa, Hanna and little Hetti studied each morning with old Herr Gold. In the afternoon they were expected to help around the house.

Young Herr Greifer was different. His life dangerous and exciting. Will he get a place at University? Will he soon leave Cirlibaba forever?

It was six in the winter evening when Rosa, Hanna and Hetti, flushed, returned home. Forever the diplomat, Dora said nothing about the stroll. Rosa congratulated herself for not being found out. She knew her sisters would not give her away. Too many secrets to keep and the reward for telling tales, dipping in a boiling bath or having your hair snipped at night, unthinkable.

That night, Rosa went to bed early, elated. She mumbled her nightly prayer, "Lord God, keep me and save me from the fear of the night," as she prepared to spend the night returning again and again to what was said as they walked and threw snowballs at the edge of the pine forest.

In the morning she had to talk about it. "Wasn't it a nice stroll, girls?" she tried.

"You are lucky," Hetti said, jealous since childhood, when polio had left her with an ugly brace on her leg.

"He is alright," said the more sober Hanna, "but I bet mother and father would not let you marry him."

"Who is talking of marriage? I am only fifteen, you know," Rosa said coyly.

"Well, if you are not thinking of marriage, you'd better not see him again," Hanna said, her severity reminiscent of mother's.

"What nonsense," Rosa protested. "You are too old-fashioned. I had a wonderful time but I have no intention of getting married. To anyone."

It wasn't until Wednesday, when Tante Sara usually came for tea, that Rosa found out that mother had known all along.

"What do I hear, Rosl?" Tante Sara said as the two settled to their usual talk over tea and cheese buchtels, away from the rest of the family. "You had a nice time last Sunday?"

"Last Sunday?" Rosa said slowly, her heartbeat quickening. "Yes, Hanna and Hetti and I had a little walk in the snow."

"With a certain young man, I hear," Tante Sara said sympathetically.

"Yes, there was a young man," Rosa confided, not looking at her aunt. "His name is David Greifer and we met him at the temple. He is very nice. And he has no parents."

"Look at me, Rosl," Tante Sara said and Rosa knew her unfortunate marriage would come up. "I too fell for a charming young man without parents. I made grandfather organise the shidduch for me and you know what happened. I should have let grandfather find me a husband and everything would have been alright. I would not have been where I am now, with Morritz away half the time chasing women. Have you ever heard of a Jew chasing strange women?"

Rosa had heard Tante Sara and Onkel Morritz' story many times. Never understanding why Onkel Morritz cheated on Tante Sara, the most beautiful woman in Cirlibaba. For the time being, she didn't say so. It wouldn't help, she knew. "But Tante Sara," she said instead, "who is thinking of marriage?"

"Well, if you aren't, you shouldn't have been seen with the young man," Sara said, her eyes smiling but her mouth stern. "It doesn't befit the Laxes, you know. Or the Hirsches. You know they all are looking at us, which is why my own shame is so great."

No point telling Tante Sara of Herr Greifer's education and scholarly ambitions. Although it should appeal to her, the only woman in the whole of Cirlibaba who could read Shakespeare in the original.

Instead, she talked of Herr Greifer's poverty. "As a member of the Lax family, I thought we ought to show him some kindness."

"Oh, you are sharp, Rosl," Tante Sara chuckled. "I shall try and talk your mother into inviting young Herr Greifer to tea so we can all meet him."

Tea parties and evening meals followed. David Greifer became a regular visitor, but Dora saw to it that her headstrong daughter was never alone with the young post office clerk. When he came, Hetti or Hanna had to stay in the room. No more strolls in the forest. The tutor, Herr Gold from Czernowitz, was given strict instructions never to let her out of the Hochdeutsch, bible, geography, history, French and English classes.

Rosa spent her days scheming ways of being alone with Herr Greifer, although she was never quite sure whether he came for her company or for mother's cooking. It was an early spring evening when David Greifer ran excitedly to the Laxes, waving the envelope containing the letter he had been waiting for, informing him that his place at the University of Czernowitz was assured for the autumn of 1915. Met at the broad entrance by the German, he could barely control his agitation.

"Fräulein Rosa. Where is Fräulein Rosa?" he snapped.

The German had her orders. "The Fräulein is studying."

"Please interrupt her. This is important. I have important news," he puffed.

"Please take a seat. I shall see if she can be disturbed," the German said officiously.

She went off, her starched black dress rustling. When Rosa appeared, her face a deep embarrassed pink, he started without greeting her. "I've been accepted," he said excitedly.

Rosa could barely hide her disappointment. Had the German not remained in the room as she had been bid by Dora, she might·

even have created a scene.

"So you are leaving us, David?" she said, using his first name deliberately, her voice remaining ice cold.

"Not yet, Fräulein Rosa. Only next autumn. And by then, who knows?"

"Who knows, indeed? We may all be dead."

"But Fräulein Rosa, you talk such stupidities at times," he said, pausing and awaiting a denial. When this did not come, he added playfully, "Are you not glad for me, Fräulein Rosa? You know how long I have been waiting for this letter?"

"It's very nice for some," Rosa could no longer hide her deep resentment that his studies seemed so important to him. For her studies were no more than a chore.

"If you study well with Herr Gold and at the Lyceum, you too can go to University," Herr Greifer said.

It was not what Rosa wanted to hear. "You know Jewish girls are not encouraged to go to University," she blurted out. "Father says only daughters of men who have relinquished their religion study at secular universities. Apart from which, I have very little interest in the Hochdeutsch bible studies Herr Gold seems to think are absolutely vital for the completion of my education."

Herr Greifer shrugged. "Do as you please, Fräulein Rosa. As for me, nothing will stop me from pursuing my education. In six years I shall be a qualified lawyer."

"God willing, David, God willing," Rosa said mechanically, as she had always heard father say.

The rustle of the German's dress cut through the silence which followed. Rosa turned angrily towards her. "I suppose I have to go back to boring old Herr Gold," she sighed. "I hope you have a very good time at university, Herr Greifer. We shall possibly never see you again once you go."

"But of course you will. Czernowitz is only a few hours by train. And when you come of age, you can visit me there too."

The thought of father letting her go to visit a young man on her own. Rosa said nothing.

With the formality born out of his disappointment at what he saw as Rosa's immature reaction to his good fortune, David Greifer took his leave.

During the following months no one talked of anything but the impending war. Everybody knew Romania's only wish was to obtain Bessarabia from Russia and Transylvannia from Hungary. It was all too close to home. As rumours of war kept escalating, the Jews of Cirlibaba, like Jews throughout Bucovina, mulled over the possible repercussions for them.

Later, Rosa would date her deep belief that at times of war

Jews suffer more than most, to these pre-war days when father kept repeating it.

Oma and Opa Hirsch and other family members, congregating each Saturday afternoon at the Lax home for cups of lemon tea, Turkish coffee, home-made cheese cakes and sour cream cakes, argued with pessimistic Anschel.

Years later Rosa will recall Onkel Duvid echoing the popular feeling of the time. "They are all making plans for a short war in which victory would be decisively achieved by an offensive concentration, Anschel," he said one July afternoon. "The Vienna papers call it 'a war without tomorrow'. It will all be over in three weeks."

"You are a great one for the Vienna papers, Duvid," father said with melancholy. "Russia is determined to attack Austria. I feel this time it will last a long winter. And you will not catch me staying here waiting to be slaughtered by the Romanians or the Cossacks."

Rosa sat in on these conversations awed by the unfamiliar words. But while father argued with Onkel Duvid, it was mother who started making plans to move if things got tough.

She was still seeing David Greifer under mother's watchful eye. Dora never discussed Herr Greifer with her daughter, but her cool behaviour implied he was not a suitable match for a Lax.

As for Herr Greifer, he was upset by the prospect that his University studies might be interrupted. Rosa repeated the Saturday conversations to him as they sat in the glass-encased veranda, where the German could keep an eye on them as she plucked chickens, shelled peas or polished silver within earshot.

"You will be taking to the hills long before I go to university," Herr Greifer said one August afternoon, his face pale and his spirit dejected.

"It's beginning to look like it," Rosa said, a certain vengeful joy in her voice which she hurriedly disguised by saying, "I do hope you will be studying very soon. My Onkel Duvid says the war will not last more than three weeks. In which case you will be at university soon and we shall never have to leave this house."

Herr Greifer smiled sadly and said the pit of his stomach tells him this would be a long war. "You are worse than father," Rosa said. "All you worry about is your precious university place." But she was beginning to think that a long war was inevitable.

By September the war was a fact. Father came home with news that the Austrian offensive on Galicia was defeated miserably and that the legendary Brussilov overran Bucovina with its capital Czernowitz, which was to change masters fifteen times during the long war. Russian soldiers were sighted on the hills surrounding Cirlibaba, the Laxes' peasant neighbour gave birth to a daughter and the Laxes prepared for their flight to golden Bistritsa.

The Carpathians appeared through the coach window at dawn. Pale blue, they rose like an echo beyond the sharper hilly outlines. Wooden farmhouses in the distance, sweetly serene. Like a faraway voice, Rosa kept playing back scenes of her immediate past. What was Herr Greifer thinking, all alone in his rooming house? Was he shedding tears over the formal little note she had hurriedly left with his landlady, saying, desperately, that she hoped they might meet again when the war was over?

She slept on and off, her head propped on Hanna's shoulder, waking sharply at dawn. The icy October air, the hills framed with beech trees, did not shut out the silent screams of the previous days. David Greifer faded. And as dawn made way to a blazing autumn sun, something told her she would never see him again.

As the sun shone on approaching Bistritsa, Rosa remembered the rush of the previous days. First the woman giving birth on their kitchen floor. Then packing from lists mother had written in her copious handwriting on long bookkeeping sheets she had brought from the sawmill. Then mother's stomach-aches.

Her confidence in her mother as chief arranger of things waned when she saw Dora weaken with pain as the journey drew closer. Rosa had gathered the family linen, cutlery, crockery and jewellery, packing it all into umpteen packets, some of which were now tightly pushed under the German's feet. One large hamper with some of the linen, tablecloths and crockery, Rosa had brought to the Strattons, the Laxes' next door neighbours, one of the only Romanian bourgeois families living in Cirlibaba, who Dora had always said were decent folk.

"Sorry to see you go, Fräulein Rosa," said Doamna Stratton.

"Don't worry, Fräulein Rosa," Domnul Stratton said, bowing slightly to the serious fifteen-year-old, whose thick brown hair was gathered in braids across her shoulders above the brown lapels of her woollen dress. "We'll look after these for you. It'll all be here when you return, laden with Bistritsa's gold."

Rosa forced a smile. She thanked the neighbours but later told Hanna she didn't trust the man's metallic smile. She did not mention it to mother, who hated to be wrong about anything she made up her mind about.

Then she returned home to hear father, pale and tired, muttering, shamefaced, "They won't pay up." On seeing his eldest daughter, he added, "I told you, Reisale. Jews are the first

74

to suffer when times are bad. My creditors are now using the war as an excuse not to pay their debts."

The children's carriage stopped behind their parents' carriage in front of an imposing-looking building. "King of Hungary Hotel" Rosa read the red lettering on the elaborate plaster front.

"Great," Hetti said. "We are staying in a hotel. Onkel Berl told me hotels are lovely. People make meals for you. They even make your beds."

"Really?" shrieked the German. "What will there be left for me to do, then?"

"You could have stayed behind," Haim, the youngest, said viciously.

"Don't be so silly," Hanna said. "You know mother would go nowhere without her."

The children saw Trajan and father walk stiffly towards the hotel, father's stooped dark-suited figure disappearing into the imposing front door where a liveried doorman held the door open for him.

"Look. People who stay in hotels don't even have to open doors for themselves," Hetti cried excitedly.

"I think I am going to enjoy Bistritsa," Rosa said importantly. "Even though I won't be able to see Herr Greifer for a while."

She closed her eyes, returning to her image of poor Herr Greifer, breaking his heart over her note telling him the family had gone to seek refuge in a glamorous hotel in golden Bistritsa.

Anschel reappeared within minutes, beckoning his wife to leave her seat. Dora exchanged a few words with him, bowed her head in assent and approached the children's carriage, calling them to accompany her into the hotel and bidding Trajan and his nephew, driving the children's carriage, to water and feed the horses in the yard.

There was a lot of red everywhere but the floors were not as clean as Rosa had imagined. The only gold she saw was in the lipstick-framed mouth of the fat owner: her sweet smile revealed a row of golden teeth as she welcomed the Laxes into the hotel.

"Rooms are in short supply," she smiled. "We have had many families just like your honoured family come here in the last few days. I can only give you two rooms and you," she said to the German, "can sleep in the attic, with the houseservants."

It was dawn but they all slept soundly for hours. When they got up, crumpled, having slept in their travelling clothes, it was the German who imparted the news.

"The hotel, Frau Lax," she said with a curtsy to mother, "it is not all that decent."

"What in the name of the Lord are you talking about, girl?" Dora asked crossly, her stomach pains drawing deep lines on her sleep-wrinkled face.

"There are funny things going on here, gnädige Frau," the German said. "Begging your pardon, but there are loose women receiving men all over the place. Not a place for the children, gnädige Frau, if you don't mind me saying so."

Rosa asked her mother what was wrong with receiving men. Had she not been receiving Herr Greifer? But Dora hushed her. She stood up resolutely to leave the room.

"Don't walk out there, Frau Lax. It is not proper," shrieked the German and something in her voice stopped Dora, who turned to father saying, "you should look into things, Anschel."

Father, who had been reading psalms by the light of the large window, looked up, his face serene with the words of the book. "Yes, Dora. Don't you worry yourself. The wish of the Lord will be done," he said, returning to his reading.

Dora shrugged and bid the German bring up a light meal. She forbade the children to run through the hotel while Anschel went out to look things up. That night Rosa went out to use the chamber and saw the dark-haired lipsticked woman who had welcomed them the previous day, pulling a young officer behind her up the stairs.

Older than mother, the woman was wearing the deepest red Rosa had ever seen. On her face there was more red. "Come on, you drunken lump," she said hoarsely. "I don't have the whole night."

Over the uniformed man's shoulder, Rosa thought she saw Trajan with another fat woman, as she fled back to their crowded room.

At breakfast the word prostitute was whispered a number of times in hushed tones between father and mother. "What is a prostitute, mother?" she asked later to be told to mind her own business, as mother looked away.

Mother and the German spent the first day scrubbing the floors of their rooms, making them more habitable. From time to time, Rosa caught a glimpse of mother's face, grimacing with pain, as she heaved hampers and unfolded bed linen. The children, forbidden to leave the rooms, hovered around mother, disquieted, still tired from the journey. Father, having read his daily portion, had gone out to find the nearest temple and "get the feel of things".

By the evening, the rooms looked more home-like. Mother set about making food from what the German had managed to buy in the street market with the help of the pasty-faced landlady when she finally woke at noon.

Father had returned and the family sat down to eat a simple meal, corn meal mamaliga with soured cream and much fresh milk.

"Nu, Anschel?" mother started. "What have you found? We cannot stay here too long."

"I thought a hotel is a place where people make food for you," Hetti piped in before father had a chance to reply.

"Hush, child, your father was about to speak," Dora hissed. "And you know well we could not eat treif in this goyische hotel."

Anschel spoke with effort. "This is a good Jewish town, Dora," he said slowly. "There are two large temples here and many minyans. I have met many God-fearing Jews here."

"But what about business, Anschel?" mother asked impatiently. "And a place to live?"

"All in good time, Dora. The good Lord will provide," Anschel said, almost mechanically, not looking into Dora's angry face.

In the morning, Dora pushed Anschel to go out and try to do business. Despite her own stomach pains, she set out too, leaving Rosa in charge of the others, to get to know the new town. It was a long day. The promise of golden Bistritsa was yet to be fulfilled as Rosa tried to amuse her sisters and brother and prevent them from leaving the room in keeping with mother's instructions. She even found herself missing old Herr Gold and her studies, not to mention David Greifer, by now no more than a distant memory.

Dora and Anschel came back, each with a different story. To Anschel Bistritsa was a good Jewish town. He had found a Talmudic circle and hoped to be allowed to study with its members. And he had discovered the local temple and rejoiced at the prospect of a proper shabbat service in this strange town.

Bistritsa for Dora was full of business possibilities. She had discovered a local money-lender prepared to give Anschel a start and a local sawmill whose bookkeeper was taken to the Kaiser's army and needed replacing.

Rosa looked on as father and mother spoke. Father's soft face, his thin black beard and his luminous eyes, short sighted and staring in the pale evening light, made her want to take him in her arms and comfort him.

Mother's deep blue eyes, her resolute mouth and her sharp tone of voice, on the other hand, brought Rosa back to the peasant bearing her first child some days ago and mother's insistence that a woman's lot is hard. Father, Rosa knew, would try and enjoy his newly-found scholarly friends, while mother would get on with the business of fending for her young, as women should.

The following morning, as mother prepared to set out for her new position as bookkeeper with the Druker sawmills, Rosa prepared to join father in his rounds. "It would be good for you to get out and about, Rosl. You are growing up and it is time for you to find out things," mother had said the night before, not specifying what these things were.

Jews she met on her rounds with father were different from Jews she had known in Cirlibaba where even poorer Jews were the crème de la crème, German-speaking, a cut above the locals.

Here all Jewish men wore black caftans and Jewish women, each surrounded with what seemed like dozens of long-haired boys in short trousers and girls in long dresses, wore head scarves and thick stockings. They spoke Hungarian, a language the strange musicality of which sounded ugly to Rosa, brought up on the pureness of German, spoken well only in Bucovina, as the local saying went.

"Your mother should cover her sheitl and wear thick stockings if we are to succeed in business here," father said after they had been snubbed by a fat woman whose snotty-nosed children looked more impoverished than any Jewish children Rosa had ever seen.

They also found that, contrary to Anschel's first impression, the locals didn't welcome refugees like the Laxes. "We don't need you," the fat woman said. "We have a hard enough time with the anti-semitic Saxons. With more refugees, there is bound to be more trouble."

The following morning Anschel wore his black silk shabbat caftan and fur streiml and business, he swore, took off instantly. Soon he asked Rosa to take some of his rounds while he took others. Some interest money started coming in and they were soon to receive mother's first monthly wages. Yet they were still living in the King of Hungary Hotel amongst bad women, as mother was in the habit of reminding father every night as they sat to their evening meal.

One morning, less than a month after they arrived, when Rosa was on her rounds in a Jewish street, she saw a hand-painted sign, "Rooms for Hire".

Father was struggling to tear himself away from his dusty books to establish a living once again and mother, still suffering from stomach pains, was too tired at night to resume supreme reign over her household. It was up to her to do something about getting them out of that shameful hotel.

She knocked on the peeling door to be met by a broad-shouldered matron, her head covered and her apron tucked into her broad leather belt.

"Yes," said her husky voice in Hungarian, "What do you want?"

"I want to see the rooms you have for rent," Rosa blurted out in Yiddish.

The woman measured her from head to toe and said in Yiddish, "How old are you, child? You won't be able to afford them."

"Yes, I will. Anyway, it is for my family. We have recently arrived from Bucovina and need a place to live."

"Fe, refugees," the woman was about to close the door in Rosa's face.

"My father and I are working, and so is my mother," Rosa said as vigorously as she could.

"There are three rooms and a kitchen," the woman said reluctantly. "And I want seventy florins."

"Let me see the rooms and I will tell you if we want to take them," Rosa said, surprised at her own courage.

"You will tell me what?"

"If we want to take them," Rosa repeated, now more at ease.

"I suppose it will do no harm if you had a look. How many of you are there?"

"Father, mother, four children and our German," Rosa said.

"A servant too? Nu, you might as well look," the woman said and led Rosa to the rooms. There were three large, high-ceilinged rooms, plenty of beds and sideboards, a large dark dining table and some chairs.

Rosa said nothing. It was bare but much better than the hotel. Her natural bargaining talent she dated back to that day, telling herself that it doesn't do to display too much enthusiasm. "Can I see the kitchen?" she asked.

"If you have to," the woman was grumpy but she led Rosa into a stone tiled kitchen with a white china stove and an iron cooking range.

"We shall take it," Rosa said.

"Wait a moment," the woman said. "What about your parents coming to see it? I don't do business with children."

"I said we shall take it," Rosa repeated, cool. "I shall bring my parents in the morning and we shall move in tomorrow afternoon."

"I don't know. There are many refugees in Bistritsa, you know. If another family comes in, with the money, I will not keep the rooms for you."

"Do as you please," Rosa said, adding offhandedly, "we shall pay eighty florins per month."

The woman's mouth dropped open and she said nothing. "We shall see you tomorrow," Rosa said as she walked out.

She walked home through the crowded Jewish streets, the autumn evening starting to crowd in, as the snotty-nosed children pulled each other's side locks, babbling in a strange mixture of Yiddish and Hungarian, which made her feel out of place. Mother and father were not able to get them out of that awful hotel. She was. Little did she know this was to be her pattern in life. Looking after not only mother and father, but after everyone else in the family.

By the time Rosa unpacked the Laxes' feather quilts and linen sheets, embroidered carefully with floral Ds, their silver and copper cooking pots, the rooms began to look habitable. The beds were made, the floors polished by the German, for whom a feather bed had been laid by the china stove in the kitchen, the table laid with the good linen table cloth and the family sat down to have the first real Shabbat meal since they fled Cirlibaba.

The candles were lighting and Anschel made kiddush and passed the silver wine cup to Dora, then to Rosa. He then blessed the bread, cutting the plaited challah into small pieces and giving Dora and each of his children a piece, whispering, as was his habit, "Bless, Kinder, bless the bread." They all mumbled Hamotsi and sang Shabbat songs. "Welcome, angels of peace, angels from up high. The Lord, blessed be he, is King of Kings." As she sang, Rosa met her father's blue eyes, thinking that perhaps she was not a useless girl after all, perhaps even better than the boy she never was.

Golden Bistritsa proved to be hell. Greedy refugees crowding market stalls made it difficult for the Laxes to stock their larder. Although the war intensified, the peasants continued coming into town to sell produce. On Sunday morning they came, dressed in their embroidered waistcoats and white frieze trousers and shirts, thick sheepskins shielding them against the biting winter frost. Much of the food they grew was commandeered by the passing army but there was enough to sell, for a huge profit, to Bistritsa's many refugees.

The Laxes even had fresh milk. Rosa found a peasant who agreed to sell them, at exorbitant prices, four litres a day for the children. Each day she put one litre aside to sour and on the following day, hung it in a muslin to make fresh curd cheese, which, with corn meal mamaliga, made up their daily diet now.

Anschel, whose eyes were giving him trouble, found dealing with the local Saxons and ultra-orthodox Jews harder than he had found dealing with Cirlibaba's peasants and more cosmopolitan Jews.

When she was brushing his black trousers, before he set out on his rounds, Rosa would find pocketfuls of IOUs. When she asked him about them, he would sigh and complain of people's perfidy. Yet he continued his rounds, studying a chapter of Gemarra each night and every so often joining the Talmudic circle in the Jewish quarter.

Rosa continued on her rounds too, never taking no for an answer, not accepting IOUs instead of cash. It was her money and Dora's monthly wages which kept the Laxes going through the first few months of the war.

Letters kept coming from Rosa's maternal grandparents. Cirlibaba had not been taken by the Cossacks who remained a constant threat on the hills surrounding the town. The Russians were to remain in Bucovina undisturbed until the final collapse of their military might in 1917.

Opa Hirsch's letters told of shortages, of fear and of old age. Duvid and Shmuel both declined to leave Cirlibaba and Sara, who had not heard from her husband in months, wanted to wait in case he returned. But Dora thought it was time to try and bring her parents to safety in Bistritsa.

Rosa, who had matured during the family's stay away from childhood and Cirlibaba, was allowed to accompany father to Cirlibaba to arrange bringing her grandparents to Bistritsa. She spent days looking for a coachman willing to make the dangerous journey to Bucovina.

Their own coachman, Trajan, had long left Bistritsa to join the Kaiser's army, taking their horses with him, leaving the two carriage shells standing on their sides, at the back of the landlady's house.

She asked around the sparse market stalls and eventually found a gaunt peasant, whose horse seemed old and hungry, who had come to Bistritsa from the heart of the Hungarian countryside, having lost his family in the early months of the war. Left alone in the world, Janos agreed to drive Rosa and her father in return for a fat fee and a couple of silver coins they had hidden on their arrival. Before they left, Rosa bought fresh produce in the street market, to bring to Cirlibaba. "You could see if there is a business proposition there," were mother's parting words.

They had travelled some hours when they came upon a burning village in the distance. Rosa froze at this, her first sign of real war, while father clutched his psalm book, repeating mumbled prayers to be saved from all their foes.

"I dare not go on," Janos cried in fear. "We'll be slaughtered."

"You are right, my dear man," father said softly, ready to turn back.

Rosa looked ahead at the burning houses. She had been too busy arranging the journey and finding the coachman to remember the possibility of seeing David Greifer once again. For some reason, the sight of the burning buildings reminded her of young Herr Greifer, all alone in the world.

The thought of meeting him spurred her on. "Ride on, man," she ordered. "This village has been burning for a long time. There would be no one here now, they have all fled." And the sheer force in her voice made Janos whip his horse towards the flames.

The charred village was deserted but in front of them, on the main road towards Bucovina, a convoy of peasants walked. Clutching their last belongings, towards the unknown.

"Ask them what happened," Rosa bid Janos, who repeated her question in Hungarian. "They say they have been burned out of their houses by Austrian deserters, may they burn in hell," he repeated in one sentence what the tired villagers mumbled. "We should be careful, Fräulein, they could rob us too. Imagine Austrian soldiers attacking peasants of their own Empire. The days of this Empire are numbered, I tell you, lady."

"May God help us," Anschel whispered. "With all our troubles, this Empire has been the best for the Jews and our Kaiser Franz–Josef, exalted be his name, has been our benefactor."

"You know the story of how I paid my way out of his army, Reisale?" he turned to his daughter, who shook her head, eager to hear again the story of his youth.

Anschel spoke for a long time about the recruiting officer and mother's anxiety as they rode through the burning village. He rarely talked so much of secular matters in one go. The journey and the fear had exhausted him. Rosa looked at him, reflecting on how tired he looked. At 38 he was becoming an old man. Like Opa Hirsch. Both always buried in their dusty books, removed from everyday matters, letting their women make all the arrangements.

They continued despite Janos' protestations. Before nightfall they had found a road inn. There wasn't much food, the landlord said, but they were welcome to beds. On the way in, as Janos unharnessed his old horse, Rosa saw a young girl, her own age, carrying a heavy bundle of firewood she had collected at the nearby forest. She smiled at the girl. The girl didn't smile back. Her face grey with exhaustion, her hands rough, her clothes torn.

They were shown their room and Rosa got out the packed food she had prepared in Bistritsa. Black bread, curd cheese, cold mamaliga slices and milk in an earthenware jug.

She gave Janos his portion and after the appropriate blessings, she and father ate in silence sitting at the edge of their beds. Later they went downstairs to the meagre dining room where several travellers sat drinking locally distilled spirits, discussing the war.

In the corner was a bearded Jew, in black garb and intensive gaze, different from the others.

"Good evening, Reb Jew," Anschel addressed the stranger. "Would you like, perchance, to say a prayer with a fellow Jew?"

"The name is Heller, Yehuda Heller from Frasin and thank you, I would like to say the evening prayer with Reb Jew," said the stranger.

"Anschel Lax, glad to meet you," Anschel shook the man's hand and together, without saying much, they got out their prayer books and spoke the evening prayer at the corner of the dark dining room.

Rosa looked on and the spirit drinkers looked on but the two men were oblivious to the world and its worries. No burning villages or wars could divert father's attention from the words he was now saying so passionately.

When they finished, the two men sat down at the corner table, discussing Talmudic matters. It was late that night before Rosa managed to get father to go to sleep. The following morning, as he dozed on and off, his head jerking to the motion of the carriage wheels, Rosa imagined meeting Herr Greifer. She would queue at the stamp counter and when her turn would come, she would angle her long-lashed gaze at his amazed face.

"Fräulein Lax," he would exclaim. Getting over his surprise very fast, he would ask politely, "and what can I do for the Fräulein?"

And Rosa would say, "Two stamps to Bistritsa, Herr clerk," to see his face blush with the pleasure of hearing her voice.

Cirlibaba approached through the winter haze. Rosa jumped up and down in her seat, careful not to awaken father. When he did wake, asking absentmindedly: "Are we already here?" she could barely contain her excitement. "Look, father, Cirlibaba. And I thought I would never see it again."

The carriage glided through the familiar streets as Anschel directed the bewildered Janos towards his in-laws' home. As they passed the post office on Hauptstrasse, Rosa dared a peep into the darkened office but thought she caught a glimpse of a young severe-looking woman at the stamp counter.

She dismissed the image. Refusing to think about David Greifer as not being at the post office any longer.

There were many hugs and kisses at Oma and Opa Hirsch where Tante Sara was also waiting.

Later she took Rosa to their favourite corner on the glass-encased veranda. "Sit down, Rosl. I have news for you," her voice sad and earnest.

"It's about Herr Greifer," Rosa almost shouted. "What happened to him?"

"He was called into the army just after you left. They took every young man they could lay their hands on for this ugly war. They even took my Morritz," she almost whispered.

Rosa could not talk. Somewhere she had known all along she would never see David Greifer again. "Aren't you surprised," Tante Sara was asking. "About my Morritz, that is? They say he left for a young woman, but I saw the soldiers take him away. They took every man in town not too old or too ill. Or who could pay," she added as an afterthought.

"And he could not pay?" Rosa asked, regretting the question as soon as she uttered it.

"I don't know. He never asked me to get the money. Surprising, no? He was always short of money. Never did a day's work. But I miss him all the same. With all the troubles he has given me, I still love the mamser."

She paused and as Rosa said nothing, continued, "And Herr Greifer too hadn't a penny piece. God knows when we'll see them all again."

Tante Sara lifted her head towards her niece who was trying to fight back her tears.

"Poor little one," she said softly. "I know how you feel."

"You know, do you?" Rosa was crying openly now. "You don't know a thing. It was something which was all mine. No one liked me meeting him, he was not a proper shidduch for a Lax. And he was not serious about me either. More serious about his blessed studies. But I understand him better now that I have been working to help father on his rounds. Our time together was mine and no one can take it away from me."

"I know, Rosl," Tante Sara whispered. "For me too, my time with Morritz was all mine. From the first month he chased other women, but the way I felt and still feel about him was private. You are the only person who will ever know."

Rosa lifted her tearful gaze and looked her beautiful aunt straight in the face. She had heard the family talk of her aunt's contrariness, her independence of spirit. She taught German at the local school and her father gave her money which she gave her idle husband so that he could chase his women, or so the family said.

But Sara never listened. Sitting opposite her sad aunt in the fading evening light on her grandparents' veranda, Rosa vowed to be like her, never to let them break her spirit.

Father and his brothers-in-law were discussing the war endlessly. Onkel Duvid, forever the optimist, kept talking about the Austrian efforts to clear Galicia, now that the Russian troops had been attracted to the Germans. He would not admit that they were less than successful in this aim.

"The Austrian army is suffering from a miserable sense of inferiority," Anschel said to his headstrong brother-in-law. "It will be beaten before it's engaged."

"Anschel, you are such a pessimist," Duvid said. "This war would not last, I tell you. Conrad had marvellous ideas."

"Marvellous ideas perhaps, but he isn't able to carry them through," Anschel said, his information based on talk he heard on his rounds. Rosa had never heard him discuss politics or the war in Bistritsa. Mother was not really interested and he spent every free moment studying his holy books.

"But what about his attack on the Russians from Hungary? He is hoping to push Brussilov from the Carpathians altogether, which means, surely, that we here will remain safe," Onkel Duvid insisted. "He has the battle of Limanova behind him, don't you forget."

"Yes, with the help of the Germans. But his success was confined to Cracow, while the Russian line is stabilised, people are saying," Anschel said angrily. "If you stay here, Duvid, your end is uncertain. Come with us to Transylvannia before it's too late."

While these conversations went on, Rosa went around with the produce she had bought in Bistritsa's markets, to all their Cirlibaba acquaintances. Delighted with the fresh vegetables and cheeses, they offered to pay large sums of money and in some cases, gave her pieces of family silver in return.

That night, she resolved to make this their new business venture and talked to father about it. Father, too preoccupied with what he saw as his wife's relatives' stupid optimism, said he would think about it. "Do you know your uncles are considering moving not to the safety of Bistritsa but to Czernowitz?" he said in wonderment. "Czernowitz is going to become a centre of war. How blind can people be?"

"And what about Tante Sara?" Rosa asked.

"She is going to stay put, waiting for that husband of hers," father said angrily. "Have you ever heard such stupidity?"

Rosa smiled. She would expect Tante Sara to wait for Morritz until he returned. "I wonder where Herr Greifer is right now," she said to father.

"Poor man," father replied. "He is probably somewhere in the mud, preparing to be slaughtered for the Kaiser. What a waste of Jewish lives."

Rosa shuddered at the word slaughtered. "Is this war going to be a long one, father?" she asked.

"Who knows, child? Man asks the questions but only God has the answers. I can see no good coming out of this senseless war. The Romanians may get what they want but the great Empire, our Empire, is bursting at the seams. Now that Stürgkh has been assassinated by the son of that Social Democrat Victor Adler, our beloved Monarch is under severe strain. Only God knows where it will all end."

As preparations were made to move Opa and Oma Hirsch to Bistritsa, Anschel convinced Janos to drive him to his own parents in Putila. The day-long journey was dangerous, but having made the longer journey from Bistritsa, Janos, promised a hefty fee, agreed to take the extra risk.

As they approached her grandparents' home, Rosa remembered all the happy childhood summers she had spent in the village, in Oma Lax's elegant Viennese home. Here she would always be given new outfits, made by famous tailors from Czernowitz and Vienna. Here Onkel Berl gave her little trinkets he kept in his room, bought, he had told her, for his lady friends.

The white-fronted house was as serene as always. Janos' old horse rolled over the pebbles in the yard and Rosa expected Oma Lax to open the door and come to meet them as was her wont. Instead, they were met by a strange silence. Even the yard's dogs didn't bark.

Rosa looked at her father who returned a quizzical look but said nothing. They dismounted and Anschel went to the front door. It was locked and despite repeated knocks, there was no answer. They went to the back of the house, which seemed deserted too. The back door, to their surprise, was not locked and they entered the kitchen.

Greeted by broken glass and ware everywhere, Anschel kept calling for his parents. Rosa ran upstairs but everywhere there was shattered glass, smashed furniture, torn drapes. Her grandparents were nowhere to be seen.

Then she heard faint crying. In the yard a little peasant child stood whimpering.

"They took them away," she said and Rosa hurried to the yard, shook the child and asked, "What happened to Frau Lax? What happened to Frau Lax?"

"They took them away," the child repeated.

Rosa did not see father stand behind her as she shook the waif. "Who? When was it?"

"I don't know." The child sounded frightened.

"What did you see?" father's soft voice enquired.

"The big horses came and the people shouted and took everything away," the child said.

"Where is your mother?" Rosa asked.

The child took Rosa's hand and led her. Her mother, a washerwoman Rosa remembered from her summers here, was standing outside her small wooden house. "Herr Anschel," she cried when she saw father. "Oh, Herr Anschel. Your poor mother and father and your poor brother," she wept.

"What happened?" Anschel's voice was still firm and clear.

"The Cossacks came to the village some days ago and entered your honoured parents' house. We none of us dared say anything when we saw them take everything, all the good silver and linen and furniture," she said. "Your mother had a problem with her leg these last few years, you know, and your father was an old man. We never thought they would take them away too."

"They took them with them?" Rosa asked.

"Yes, Fräulein. Frau Lax shouted at the soldiers, saying they must not touch her silver. One Cossack, I beg your pardon, Herr Anschel, kicked your mother and she fell to the ground and could not get up. I tried to help her up, but the Cossack shouted for me to get away." The woman stopped and looked into father's face. "We could not help your poor mother."

"And what did my brother do all this time?" Anschel asked.

"They took him away too, saying he could serve in their army," the woman said softly. It had been rumoured that when she was younger, she was one of Berl's women and that the little girl was his. There had never been another man in her house. "It was lucky your younger brothers had gone away when they did," she added as an afterthought, referring to Rosa's uncles Faivel and Yossel who had married into families who now lived in Romania, well out of the war for the time being.

"Where are they now?" Rosa asked.

"God alone knows," the woman whispered, crossing herself. "But we could not help them, I assure you, Herr Anschel. We would, you know. Your honoured mother gave me work for many years and was always kind to me and my girl."

"Yes, I know you could not help," Anschel said, his voice still kind. "Which direction did they go?"

"They left the village on their horses this way," the woman pointed. "They tied your mother to the carriages and dragged her along the road. I don't believe, God help me, that she could have survived for long."

"And father?" Anschel whispered.

"Your father and Herr Berl, they made them run by the side of the horses," the woman said, her face contorted with pain. "When I last saw your father and your brother, they were whipping them, shouting in Russian, pushing them to run faster."

"And did my father not offer them money?" Anschel asked. He has been used to everything, including freedom, being bought with money.

"I could not hear," said the woman. "All we could see were the Cossacks carrying sackfuls of silver and ware from the house and your honoured parents trying to reason with them. But I did not hear your father offering to pay. In the end they simply took them away. None of the power and riches remained. Nothing," she added very softly.

Her voice died down. Rosa saw tears roll down her weather-worn cheeks but she could feel nothing. Could not comprehend how her grand Viennese Oma and kind-hearted, bearded Opa could be victims of such crude cruelty. "We must look for them," she heard her voice say. "We cannot let them die like that. Have you any money, father?"

"I have some, but what would we do if they take us too? What would become of your mother and of Opa and Oma Hirsch?"

"Send Janos," Rosa said.

"I will go with him," said the washerwoman.

"I can go," Rosa said, but father stopped her. "You are still a child," he said and to the woman, "We will be thankful if you could find them. Or get a word. We shall wait in the house for news."

"If anything happens to me," the woman said slowly, "will you take care of my girl? She is related," her voice tapered off.

"Yes, I know," father said, quietly too. "We shall bring her up as our own if anything happens, God forbid."

Janos was not given details of his mission. He set off with the washerwoman while Rosa and Anschel tried to clear the debris of the Lax house. Under the wreckage, they found many objects not yet destroyed. Beds to sleep in and some unbroken windows to keep out the cold. That night they slept in Oma and Opa's plundered house, Rosa and Maria, the washerwoman's daughter, on Berl's bed and Anschel on his parents' bed. It was a long night. Maria twisted and turned in the strange bed and Rosa dreamt about David Greifer driving Oma Lax with whips through a wheat field and shouting, "Schnell, schnell, run, you rich Jewish bitch, faster, faster."

She woke up sweating with Maria's hand across her stomach. The pale winter sun drew long shadows on Berl's room, where only the dark desk remained, bare, by the large shuttered window.

As they waited for two days in the Laxes' devastated house, Rosa and Anschel, followed by the shadow of little Maria, worked to clear the rubble and arrange all the unpillaged objects. Anschel spent most of the time telling Rosa of his childhood and his early days with her mother. Young Dora emerged as a hesitant, fragile girl Rosa found hard to equate with the determined woman mother had grown to be. As he looked through old papers, he remembered more about his sister Rosa and talked of her friendship to mother and mother's heartbreak when she died. "You are called after her, you know," he said several times. And all the time he prayed. Fervently murmuring his psalms. Calling to his God for good tidings.

He was talking about the wedding when Janos and the washerwoman returned. Alone.

"We did not meet them, Herr Anschel," the washerwoman answered father's stare. "But we heard."

"Heard what?" Anschel said, impatient for the first time.

"We rode east, beyond Cimpulung," the woman said, with Janos nodding, confirming her story. "And in every village we asked if they were seen. Then, in Gura Humorlui we heard that they were . . ." Her voice broke and she began to sob.

"They were what?" Anschel's voice now resembled a scream.

"They were killed, Herr Lax, killed with Cossack sabres. Without mercy," Janos spoke for the first time since their return.

"Without mercy, Herr Anschel," the woman said. "And Herr Berl, my little girl's father, was killed with them, God rest his soul. And their bodies were thrown on the side of the road, for the ravens to eat."

Rosa could not look at father. The washerwoman sobbed onto Janos' shoulder, gathering her little Maria onto her lap. Her sobs were the only sound cutting through the silence. Anschel said quietly, "Baruch Dayan Emmet," and started praying to himself, while Rosa, her eyes dry, looked ahead of her, numb.

Father spent the rest of the evening praying. Rosa gathered her grandparents' salvable objects and said firmly, as night fell, "We are going to sit Shiva in Cirlibaba, father, not here in this empty house." Father looked up, nodding silently. "We shall go tomorrow morning and we'll take Maria and her mother with us," he said.

Rosa went over to the washerwoman who was sitting in her

house, sobbing by the fire, lit from sticks she had sent Maria to collect in the forest. "Will you come with us to Bistritsa, away from the war?" Rosa said, her youth making room for a maturity she did not know she possessed.

"Thank you, Fräulein, but I shall stay in my own house. It is the only thing I ever had," the woman said.

"But what will you do? How will you rear little Maria?" Rosa asked.

"Janos will come back when he has brought you back to Bistritsa and the Lord Jesus will provide," the woman said, tired.

"We would like to pay you for what you did for us, going to look for my grandparents," Rosa said.

"Thank you, Fräulein. I shall take what you can give. But I did not go for you. I went to find Herr Berl," the woman said. "After all the years, he was still the only man I loved."

Rosa opened her mouth to speak, but the woman stopped her. "Don't say it, Fräulein. I know he had many women," she said. "If he could, he would have had your own mother when she first came to Putila. Everything in skirts was a target."

When she saw Rosa's hurt look, she added, "Have no fear, Fräulein. Your mother, so people were saying, had no eyes for any man but your good father, but this did not prevent Herr Berl from trying his luck." She paused and sighed. "But I had my little Maria by him and he was always very good to me. He bought this house for me and gave me money for my girl. And he came to see us sometimes. When he was not on the road, chasing younger women."

Rosa said nothing. Was there any woman loved in justice by the man she loved, apart, that was, from mother and father? But what they had, she didn't count as love. More a quiet understanding, an acceptance. She looked at the washerwoman sitting by her fire, content in grieving for her plundering uncle and what she saw was passion.

"If this is what you want. But we shall pay you for what you did," she said.

"And I will have Janos," the woman said quietly, but almost triumphantly. "We became close during those two days. He lost his family in the west and he is a good man."

The following morning, Rosa gave the washerwoman Berl's desk, some linen she had salvaged from the house and some of the money they had.

She packed what was left into the carriage and asked the washerwoman to keep an eye on the Lax house. "We shall return after the war," she said. "Look after yourself and little Maria."

It was the first time she had had a real conversation with a peasant beyond household matters. Parting from little Maria and her mother was like saying goodbye to old friends.

The fate of Anschel's parents helped to convince Duvid and Shmuel to join the Laxes in Bistritsa. Sara remained obstinate. She wanted to wait for her Morritz to return from the war. Her parents would not hear of leaving a woman alone in Cirlibaba, still surrounded by Russian troops.

"But if he comes back and does not find me," she kept saying, wide-eyed, "he will have nothing else in the world."

"Apart from his women," her mother said, angry with her headstrong daughter. "And look what happened to the Laxes."

"You cannot stay alone, Sara," Rosa heard father say firmly. He sounded tired, clad in a ripped shirt to denote the seven-day mourning period for his parents and brother.

Sara shrugged. "I am not a child and stay put I will," she said. "You can all run to save your souls. You have no one who needs you here. I do."

These arguments went on through the Shiva. The men prayed three times daily and Anschel and Rosa sat on the floor at the Hirsch house, receiving condolence visits from townspeople and from the Rebbe and his disciples.

Rosa told Tante Sara about the washerwoman and her uncle. "Yes, I remember," Sara said. "How he used to eye every woman. Even your own mother. I was still a child then and very soon I found Morritz. But Berl, he was something else."

"Was he that much different from your Morritz?" Rosa asked.

"Well, at least he never married," her aunt said. "At least there was no adultery involved."

"You know all that and yet you are prepared to risk your life for the slim chance of him returning to reclaim you?" Rosa asked, incredulous.

"Yes, Rosl," her aunt said. "Perhaps one day you will understand."

When they left Cirlibaba, travelling in two carriages, driven by Janos and another coachman they managed to convince to make the dangerous journey, Tante Sara waved to them from her parents' empty house. Rivka was crying bitterly and Shulem shook his head sternly. They all feared they would never see her again.

"When my Morritz and your Herr Greifer return, I shall write immediately," Tante Sara had said to Rosa earlier, as they hugged and kissed, crying.

Now, from her seat on the carriage, Rosa waved to her beloved aunt. "Take care, Tante. And remember."

3

Rosa 1919

Rosa had had enough of travelling.

Throughout the war years, she travelled. Ever since the spring of Oma and Opa's death, she travelled with father and Janos between Bistritsa and Bucovina.

Soon after Romania entered the war in 1916, demanding both Bucovina and Transylvannia, the relative security the Laxes enjoyed as refugees in Bistritsa made room for growing apprehension.

"Romania entered the war only under Russian ultimatum that she would invade it if Romania did not enter the war," Rosa heard father say to Onkel Duvid as fears for their safety mounted.

"If Romania joins forces with Brussilov, our Empire will be lost, Anschel," Onkel Duvid replied. "And then where are we, having fled to this Jew-hating city? When I think that people call this hateful place Golden Bistritsa, I want to scream."

"Calm down, Duvid," father said. "I am the pessimist around here, remember? Romania hasn't got enough trained soldiers to make any difference to this war. Back home in Bucovina they say Romanian soldiers are no more than armed peasants who want to remain on their land. They say their leadership is atrocious. Romanian officers, they say, are strolling around Bucharest soliciting prostitutes instead of leading their men into battle. Compare this with the discipline in the army of our Kaiser."

"Yes, yes, I am sure you are right, Anschel," Duvid said, "But a sudden onslaught into Transylvannia — and you know the Romanians are intent on freeing their brothers from the Hungarian yoke — would shatter the Empire and compel it to fulfil Romania's demands for both Bucovina and Transylvannia. And there is also the fact that there are no fortresses or strategic railways around here to defend us if the Romanians do decide to attack."

The more fears for the safety of Transylvannia grew, the more hostile the local Jewish community became to refugees. Fearing anti-semitism as many more refugees flooded the town, the ultra-orthodox Transylvannian Jews did not welcome refugees into their temples. Anschel Lax and the Hirsches had to organise their own prayer minyans. Refugees even had to bake their own matzo for Pessach. Soon a separate society made up of Bucovinian refugees was formed. Their German, less hard than the Saxon spoken by the local Jews, rang pure and smooth and Bucovinian Jews were even more convinced of their superiority now.

In the circumstances, continuing to do business amongst Bistritsa's Jewish community became more and more difficult.

Duvid and Shmuel took over Anschel's money-lending business as Anschel and Rosa went to and from Bucovina selling fresh Transylvannian produce and later household goods too. An easier way of making a living than money-lending, Rosa believed.

In Bucovina's little towns and villages they did business with their own people. Anschel was able to keep an eye on his parents' house and wind up his late father's financial affairs now that his father and brother were no longer able to do so. Janos was able to spend days with Berl's washerwoman, bringing her and her daughter fresh food. And Rosa saw a lot of Tante Sara who stayed behind to wait for her missing husband.

Rosa did all the marketing. Buying onions, carrots, apples, turnips, even new potatoes in season and as much grain as she could get. On the days before each journey, she bought cow's milk cheese tied in muslin bags and still dripping with moisture. In Bucovina, where Russian, Romanian and Austro-Hungarian troops ransacked farms and storerooms, these products were like gold.

When she could get them, she bought jugs and pans, squares of wool and woven fabrics, made by Transylvannian peasants and welcomed by her customers who could further trade these for food. She and Janos packed the produce into the carriage, disguising it as well as they could, in cane hampers, under woollen blankets. In time, they had regular customers, special orders, all of which meant regular income.

Fearing Russian and Romanian troops, the Kaiser's local representatives in Transylvannia forbade such transactions and confiscated all produce caught by government inspectors. The Laxes were caught only once, bribing their way out of prison. The following week, they were back on the road, despite the inspector's warning.

"At times of war, mein Kind," father said as they evaded the inspector time after time, "if you don't do something extraordinary and put your neck on the line, you starve."

Between trips, father enjoyed studying with Opa Hirsch, who spent most of his days now reading the old books. Rivka cooked for the family while Dora worked at the sawmill which was busy during the war, producing timber for the dying Empire's war efforts. The children improved their Hungarian at the local school and each afternoon, Opa took Hanna and Hetti and his youngest grandchild Haim, for Hebrew lessons. "I don't miss my classes," Rosa told Tante Sara on one of her visits to Cirlibaba. "I am no longer a child."

"Indeed you are not," Tante Sara answered, looking fondly at her seventeen-year-old niece. Dealing successfully with suppliers and customers brought Rosa a maturity that even the horror of losing her grandparents and uncle to the Cossacks had not.

The assassination of Minister President Stürgkh by the son of Victor Adler, "that Social Democrat", as father called him contemptuously, in October 1916, brought more fear to the Jews sheltering from the raging war. Transylvannia had long ceased to be the haven it was when the Laxes first got here. September had seen a Romanian onslaught but by October, with Falkenhayn and Mackensen, commander of the notorious German ninth army ready in counter-attack, the Romanians were standing everywhere in desperate defence.

Now shortages of food, fuel and clothing raised discontent which war-time loyalty had so far restrained and even the Bucovinian Jews were heard grumbling against their beloved Kaiser, dear old Franz–Josef.

"The monarchy is crumbling," Rosa heard father say soon after they had heard the news that their Emperor was suffering from bronchitis. "The Kaiser won't last long now and then where is the monarchy and where are we?"

"Don't fret," Onkel Duvid answered. "I have heard in the town that despite his illness he keeps to his desk reading communiqués from the Romanian and Transylvannian fronts."

When by the end of November the news of the Emperor's death reached the outskirts of his decaying Empire, the Jews were the first to mourn. "The good man reigned for 68 years of unrelieved misery," they said. "Thank providence for showing him the kindness of not having to live to the end of this terrible war."

In Bistritsa, as the local Hungarians were treating Austria as half foreigner, half enemy, the local Jews were growing more and more hostile to the refugees as rumours of the ramshackle Empire committing suicide circulated and seeds of Hungarian independence filled the air.

The new Emperor Charles was young, warm-hearted and devoted to his people, or so the Austrians who happened into Bistritsa from time to time said. The Hungarians and the Transylvannian Jews watched him making peace offers and compromising Hungary with growing resentment.

Early in April 1917 Kaiser Charles was presented with a confidential memorandum outlining the approaching end of the monarchy's military endurance.

"They have no more raw materials, no more munitions," father said on their last trip to Bucovina. "The Austrian people are suffering, there is no one left to fight. The monarchy is at an end."

The Jews accused Kaiser Charles of insincerity. "He came into a terrible inheritance," they said. "But the temptation of peace with dishonour would have broken stronger men."

By the end of 1917 Austria became a federal state and Hungary an autonomous state. The local Hungarian Jews rejoiced. They were now ready to push their refugees back home.

There was not much to sell and business was slow for Anschel and Rosa. Few peasants came into town now to sell fresh produce. People had less and less money and the money-lending business was becoming more of a pawn brokerage, with little prospect of recovering borrowed funds.

With two million dead and almost as many prisoners, the Austrian army was further thinned by desertion. Amongst the deserters was, suddenly, Sara's Morritz.

On their return to Cirlibaba before the end of the war, Rosa was startled to find him in her aunt's house. Just back from the front, Morritz was thin, older and less suave than she had remembered. "It was hell," was all he was prepared to say when she enquired, looking with horror at his greying face. "I kept thinking of home and Sara. The only thing which kept me alive."

Morritz followed Sara everywhere, like a sad, ghost-like shadow. "It was hell," he kept repeating. Rosa watched Morritz's child-like clinging to Sara and thought she understood why her beautiful aunt had waited all those years.

She did not dare ask Morritz if he had seen Herr Greifer anywhere in the great war. Now that Morritz was back, she kept thinking, there was nothing to stop David from returning to her, not daring to complete the thought.

Morritz's return, and apparent attachment to his wife, was the only good news in the midst of the tragic collapse of the Hapsburg Empire which had been so good to its Jews.

By the time the Laxes returned to Cirlibaba, Bucovina was in Romanian hands, the Romanians having again declared war on Germany a few hours before the conclusion of the armistice in November and having won territories in Transylvannia, Bessarabia and Bucovina as they had always wanted, along with a million and a half Magyars and many Jews.

Rosa was back home. The soldiers who went from the area to fight for Kaiser and Empire were either back, reported missing, or dead. David Greifer was not amongst those who returned.

The Hirsch and Lax homes had been ransacked in the last few weeks of the war. Neighbours said it had been the Empire's retreating armies, hungry, tattered, defeated. Dora was not sure. When the Laxes' linen and silver hamper could not be retrieved from their neighbours, who also blamed the soldiers, she smiled bitterly and talked of humiliating wars, compelling decent people to steal and lie.

The sawmill Dora had worked for had also been destroyed by war, burnt by the Russians after the soldiers had used the timber. Anschel had some money he had saved from his war rounds and he began his father-in-law's money-lending busines again.

Rosa's days were empty now. No rounds with Janos, who moved in with Berl's washerwoman in Putila Kaselitsa. With mother at home, there was little to do. Mother filled her suddenly empty days doing housework and cooking. Oma Hirsch was at home and the two women supervised Rosa and her sisters, constantly offering meals, admonishing.

Even her beloved Tante Sara had less time for her now that her Morritz, seemingly a reformed character, was home.

Rosa was lonely. And bored. So when father suggested a trip to Vatra Dornei, she was enthusiastic, although she had had enough of travelling.

It wasn't clear to Rosa what father was seeking in Dorna. He had acquired some forest land which mother intended to turn into a sawmill but his business, money-lending, was around Cirlibaba. After the war people were short of money and required his services.

Dorna was a day away and an unknown business territory. When she asked, father remained enigmatic. "Just a trip, Reisale," he smiled. "You worked hard during the war and Vatra Dornei is an international spa attracting many tourists. Hanna will come too and we shall enjoy ourselves."

Mother provided no answer either. "Just go with your father and enjoy it, child," she said, her severe face relaxing into a rare smile.

Rosa had never been urged to enjoy herself before. Work, duties, prayer, studies had always been much higher on the priority list. Puzzled, she sought Tante Sara's opinion. Sara smiled too, wistfully.

"You are almost twenty now, Rosl. At your age, your mother was already engaged to your father. It took them a while to get married because your father had to report to the recruiting officer in Czernowitz. But girls of twenty are . . ."

Rosa did not let her aunt finish the sentence. "Do you think this is why father is taking me to Dorna?" she almost shouted.

"Everything is possible, Rosl," Sara replied softly. "As you have pointed out yourself, there is no apparent business reason to go."

"But do you know that this is why father is taking me to Dorna?" Rosa's voice sounded stressed.

"No, Rosl. I haven't been told anything, if this is what you are referring to. But it makes sense.'

"I won't be married off, Tante Sara. Not to anyone." Rosa was indignant.

"We have already talked about it," Sara smiled. "Had I listened to Opa I would have been better off, believe me."

"But Morritz is back and seems so devoted," Rosa said.

"It won't last," Sara said seriously, the lines on her face deepening in a bitterness Rosa hadn't seen even during her long wait, along in wartime Cirlibaba.

"But your wait for him, all through the war, in danger to your safety? I was so sure it was worth it when he returned to you."

"It was worth it," Sara sounded tired suddenly. "But in my rational moments, I wonder how different my life would have been had I married Herr Sommer, the silk merchant Opa wanted me to wed. He now lives in Vienna, with his wife and three children, his business even more prosperous than before the war."

This was the first time Rosa heard her aunt mention Herr Sommer but not the first time she heard her voice her regret at having married her beloved unreliable Morritz.

"But you love your Morritz, don't you?" she said, hopeful of a key.

"Yes, I love him and yes, he loves me, in spite of his faithlessness."

"But you could have had an easier life?"

"I suppose so," Sara's eyes closed and she looked serene for a moment. "I could have fled the war in time, not sat here waiting, fearing the Russians and the local peasants. But then I wouldn't have had the thrill of seeing him alive, back with me and not with one of his women."

"Perhaps Berl's washerwoman also kept hoping," Rosa said.

"Perhaps," Sara said. "But Berl was killed and she'll never know. And Morritz is back and I know that my happiness is short-lived."

Rosa was confused. Believing that Sara and the washerwoman had found the key to what she was seeking, a thrill, a throbbing heart, full of the strongest emotions, had been simple. Finding that Sara's love was tainted with bitterness and regret clouded her clear perception of what she thought she had felt for young Herr Greifer, who had not come back.

"What about mother and father?" she asked. "Their marriage was arranged and they seem to live without extreme feelings?"

"I suppose so. But they have a good life, run a good Jewish home, have children."

"But I don't want just to have a good life and run a good Jewish home," Rosa cried. "I want . . ."

"I know," Sara stopped her. "You want excitement, romance, a flutter? This was what your mother yearned for. The famous flutter."

"Mother? She too?" Rosa's excitement rose. "I would never have believed."

"Why?"

"Well, mother is always so sensible. So serious."

"I think you had better go with your father to Dorna," Tante Sara said suddenly. "David Greifer will not come back. He would have returned if he was in a position to do so. He is possibly married now."

"Or lying in a mass grave somewhere," Rosa said, voicing the hateful thought for the first time.

"Yes, I am afraid this too is possible," Sara said sadly. "Dorna is a romantic place, Rosl. And if you meet someone there, it may turn out to be heaven, rather than the hell you imagine it would be. Besides, you haven't got much to lose by going. At least, as far as I know, no shidduch has been fixed, so perhaps your father is hoping to introduce you to a suitable young man, a more modern way of doing these things."

Before the journey, Dora altered several of her pre-war suits, bought in better times from Czernowitz tailors, to fit her somewhat plumper daughter. Rosa's light brown hair and dark blue eyes resembled her mother's when she was her age but her broad gait and tall, erect figure were her father's. Beside her, Hanna's delicate features were less striking but, as they accompanied their bearded father into the carriage, they did not look like two small-town Jewish girls and their orthodox father, more like a bourgeois threesome heading for the big town.

Rosa hadn't been close to Hanna during the war years. She considered herself an adult who dealt and sold, bargained and helped provide for her family. Her sisters, honest Hanna and crippled Hetti, belonged with the children. The prospect of spending a few days with her young sister, three years her junior, was daunting. What will she say to this stern child, so like mother?

As father dozed and read his psalms, the two girls talked of the journey and of what it might bring. Rosa told her sister what Tante Sara had said. Hanna listened seriously.

"You cannot wait too long. Older brides are suspect," she said without a smile. "Besides, they'll never look for a husband for me before they marry you off and I too would like to get married."

Rosa eyed Hanna's serious face as she spoke. Almost seventeen, Hanna still looked like a child, her voice small, her face smooth with that special innocence.

"What is your hurry, Hannele?" she asked. "You are a mere child. You haven't lived."

"The war was life enough for me," Hanna replied. "Running away, then watching you help mother and father and being made to continue my studies as if there wasn't a war on. I want to be useful, but as long as you are at home, they won't let me grow up."

"So you think I should get married to make room for you?" Rosa said, sad at the thought that her family seemed to want to get rid of her.

"It isn't like that, Rosl," Hanna's serious face wrinkled in thought. "It's just that it's time. You'll be twenty soon and had it not been for the war, you might have been married by now."

"If it hadn't been for the war, David Greifer might not have disappeared," Rosa's voice lacked the bitterness she thought she felt. "He would have finished his studies by now and we could have been married."

"David Greifer was not the man for you," her younger sister reminded her, always straight. "Father and mother wouldn't have permitted it. Besides, Herr Greifer himself was not that serious about you."

Rosa knew that what Hanna was saying was true. Herr Greifer had always been keener on his studies than on her. But she couldn't admit it to this child. "You don't know what you are talking about," she feigned anger, but pursued it no further.

In the spring of 1919, the white and yellow Austrian-style buildings of Vatra Dornei glistened in the evening sun as the Laxes' carriage rolled between the Bistritsa river and the railway line, where timber-carrying steam engined trains waited to move off. The carriage stopped outside the ornate casino building at the bottom of the hilly park, as father descended to book them two rooms at the spa pension.

War shortages weren't manifest here, as women in light furs and jewels promenaded along the tree-lined paths accompanied by men in expensive overcoats. Later the girls learnt these were Jewish merchants for whom the war had been a source of wealth. They followed father into the Jewish pension where their rooms overlooked the river.

That evening, dressed in mother's altered clothes and looking beautiful, if somewhat old-fashioned in this elegant resort, Rosa and Hanna accompanied their father into the spacious dining room where a well-cooked kosher meal was served.

Rosa didn't notice a pair of dark brown eyes staring at her from across the dining hall. As she started her main course, stuffed roast veal, a delicacy she hadn't had since before the war, Rosa vaguely saw a bearded young man, accompanied by an older man she had a faded memory of, making their way across the hall.

As Rosa was wiping her plate clean with a slice of rich poppy seed white bread, she became aware that the two men were inching their way from table to table, stopping to talk here, listen there. By the time the dessert, apple and pear compote, was served, Rosa, like everyone else in the crowded dining hall, was aware that the two were making their way towards Anschel Lax's table. Aware of the young man's dark eyes staring at her face, Rosa lowered her lids as the men were approaching their table.

"Welcome, Reb Anschel," the older man was addressing father, using the reverent title Reb, reserved for scholarly Jews. "Do you remember me? We met during the war at a Bucovina inn. You were making your way to your parents' house in Putila Kaselitsa. I am Yehuda Heller, from Frasin."

"Blessed be the present, Reb Yehuda," father replied with the same reverence, his face broadening in a genuinely joyous smile.

"What brings you to Dorna?" Yehuda Heller asked, while the younger man kept staring at Rosa's lowered lids.

"Just a rest, Reb Yehuda," father replied. "We have worked hard during the war, my eldest daughter here, Rosa, and I. We wanted a few days' rest."

"Allow me to present my son Mendel," Yehuda Heller said. Mendel Heller shook hands with father and bowed to the girls, whose hands he did not shake, following the religious custom whereby Jewish men are not allowed to touch women they are not related to, fearing impurity.

Rosa straightened her look as Mendel bowed. What she saw was a handsome, very dark oval face, a bushy black beard and straight, neatly combed black hair. She smiled vaguely, aware of the young man's demanding stare.

"Please sit down with us," father invited the two. As Yehuda Heller embarked on a scholarly conversation with father, the two girls remained seated beside the dark stranger, not participating in the conversation, awkward, aware of his presence but, as he made no attempt to converse, unable to initiate contact. Young girls weren't supposed to take the first step.

The evening wore on and the atmosphere became more stilted. By nine o'clock Rosa announced she was tired and urged her younger sister to accompany her upstairs. As the two girls rose to go, Mendel rose too.

"May I show the young ladies around Dorna tomorrow, Herr Lax?" he asked, still staring at Rosa's face.

"You may ask the young ladies directly," Anschel said. "Would you like to promenade with Herr Mendel while I go about my business?" he asked the girls, astonishing Rosa by his permission to walk with a strange young man — a thing he would never have allowed in the past.

There was no polite way of refusing. A meeting was arranged for the following morning at the pension.

Upstairs, Hanna spoke first. "This young man has designs on you," she said with her usual bluntness.

"I don't like his beard," Rosa said without thinking. "And he makes me feel awkward. I wish father hadn't permitted us to promenade with him. I wonder why he is letting us go with a strange young man. Remember the fuss they made about Herr Greifer?"

"Will you ever stop thinking about Herr Greifer?" Hanna scolded. "We were much younger then and His Eminence David Greifer was not considered a proper shidduch for a Lax, remember?"

"Yes, I know what everyone was thinking," Rosa said. "A young man with no connections, no parents, who had to work for a living. What horror. But after all, what was I doing throughout the war if not working to keep the family afloat?"

She sighed. When Hanna said nothing, she sighed again and said, "Now we have to suffer this boring bluebeard tomorrow."

But the morning turned out to be more amusing than expected. Mendel Heller, clad in a well-cut broad lapelled dark suit, turned up at their pension at the agreed time. After a formal set of greetings, asking the girls if their rest on their first night in Dorna was agreeable, he led the two girls through the small town. Built in a valley, surrounded by wooded hills, Dorna's spas were favourite with merchants from the eastern parts of the deceased Empire, here to take the cure.

Contrary to his silence the night before, Mendel's conversation flowed incessantly. As he took his charges towards the outskirts of the town, he pointed out a fenced area by the Dorna river.

"This is the new Heller sawmill," he announced proudly, staring straight into Rosa's eyes. "When we came back from

Transylvannia after the war, we found our sawmill in Frasin burnt to the ground. Luckily, we had made some money during the war from timber sales to the army and we were able to buy this sawmill cheaply. Father and I are here to supervise the initial stages. Then father goes back to Frasin to rebuild the family sawmill and help mother with the family inn, and I move here."

Mendel Heller, the youngest of Yehuda and Rachel Heller's ten children, Rosa learnt that morning, had spent the war years providing for his family, just like her. With two of his elder brothers serving in the Kaiser's army and several other brothers married and having to provide for their own families, Mendel, still single at twenty-nine, knew it was his responsibility to help the family with the inn and the sawmill.

The Hellers, like the Putila Kaselitsa Laxes, were a well-known Bucovina family. Their scholarship and charity matched their talent for business. Rachel Heller, Mendel's mother, had a Propination for their licensed inn, while Yehuda and his sons ran the timber business.

Unlike Anschel Lax, who had never displayed the same businesslike attitudes as his father, Yehuda Heller's youngest son seemed to inherit his father's business skills. During the war, the two traded army surplus goods and augmented their fortunes. Buying timber from sawmills which remained open to the Kaiser's army kept the Hellers in timber and despite the burning of their Frasin sawmill they had not taken long to reestablish the Heller timber empire.

Rosa was startled by the similarities between the two families. Yehuda Heller, she discovered, belonged to the same Hassidic court as Opa Yacob and Mendel, she found out, had done business with the Drukers, the Cimpulung and Cirlibaba timber company who had employed mother. Mendel's family, she concluded as he spoke, was of the same social standing as her grandparents Helen and Yacob Lax, whom he had known before the war and of whose murder he had been grieved to hear.

Rosa let Mendel talk and then told him of her family's involvement in inns and sawmills and of her own work during the war. She had never told a stranger of her achievements in business. Yet Mendel Heller, far from finding Rosa's independent spirit unbecoming in a young Jewish woman, seemed to admire her all the more for it.

By the time they reached the pension for lunch, Rosa felt she had known Mendel Heller all her life. What she did not know was that Mendel's father, like her own, was intent on finding a spouse for his son. Like Anschel Lax, Yehuda Heller too felt guilty at having used his son to help provide for the family during the war. When, in the weeks after the war ended, another of his sons died in the Spanish influenza epidemic which devastated Bucovina, Yehuda Heller resolved to find a bride for his youngest son.

In their room before lunch, Hanna remarked softly, having listened quietly to the two throughout the morning, "You and that boring bluebeard seem very well suited, Rosl." To which Rosa replied, almost angrily, "I already told you I don't like his beard. He is far too orthodox for me."

"You can always get him to cut it off," Hanna said and the two girls burst out laughing.

The leaves of the beech trees glistened as spring progressed. Rosa and Mendel saw a lot of each other during her short stay, promenading, always accompanied by the silently correct Hanna, up and down the hilly paths surrounding the town.

Rosa strode lightly, feeling truly appreciated for the first time in her young life. Mendel was older, wealthier, more accomplished in business. Yet he drowned her in admiration.

When it was time to go home, Rosa found herself wishing she did not have to go.

"Please call on us," father said to the Hellers as they came to see the Laxes off outside their pension.

"Goodbye, Fräulein Rosa and Fräulein Hanna," Mendel said correctly. "And thank you for your enchanting company."

"Thank you for taking such good care of my daughters," Anschel said, adhering to the required formalities. Rosa smiled, feeling her cheeks redden as Mendel's stare rested on her face, as the Laxes mounted their carriage.

"He is obviously a man of means and mental resources," Rosa concluded her account to Tante Sara on their return. "And Hanna believes we are well suited."

"But do you like him, Rosl?" her aunt asked.

"I like him well enough," Rosa admitted. "But I do believe him to be too orthodox for my taste."

"Do you think you could grow to love him?" Sara persisted.

"You ask such difficult questions," Rosa said, embarrassed. Tante Sara peered into her niece's blushing face and said nothing.

Surprisingly, it was mother and not Tante Sara who clarified things for Rosa. She had just put a batch of challas into the oven. Oma Rivka had gone into town to bathe at the miquva for the approaching shabbat and mother and daughter shared a rare moment alone.

"Nu, what did you make of that young man Heller in Vatra Dornei, Rosl?" mother started.

"He is a clever man and a good man," Rosa said. "During the war he worked to provide for his family, being the only unmarried son to his parents. And I think he has a good business brain."

"Yes, I know all this," mother said, "your father has already told me. But what did you make of him?"

Rosa said nothing. Unsure of her own feelings, she had been thinking of Mendel Heller and wondering if he would propose.

"When my father called me into his study and told me I was to wed your father, I was confused too," mother said and Rosa realised she had never heard mother's side of the story.

"I was looking for something, a thrill, a flutter. This was what our German kept talking about when she told me of her soldier man who had gone to war. But it wasn't there when I met father. He was a good man, a scholar. He even had money in those days. It all looked perfect. Only I wasn't sure. The flutter wasn't there."

Mother stopped and looked at her daughter, whose blue eyes stared at her, amazed, never having heard such a frank account before.

"We were engaged for three long years. You have heard father talk of the recruiting officer. The longer the time, the more eager I became to leave my childhood status and become an adult. I think this was why I married your father."

"And the — flutter?" Rosa blurted out.

"The flutter never came. But there were other things, more important than the flutter. Your father and I live peacefully. We complement each other." Mother paused and then said, "You have known responsibility, I regret to say. Your childhood was cut short by the war. So you won't have to get away from an enforced childhood. But don't think of young Herr Heller only in terms of excitement. Or that elusive thrill some people call love. Love is much more than that initial flutter."

"Do you love father?" Rosa interrupted her mother's measured voice.

"Of course I love him," mother said. "And he loves me. But unlike those novelettes our Germans used to read, those of them who could read, we don't talk about love, though it is always there."

"I thought I loved Herr Greifer, mother," Rosa said, very softly.

"I know, child. I know you thought you did," mother's voice was almost gentle now. "You never had a chance to test your emotions and Herr Greifer never came back."

"But you wouldn't have let me marry him?"

"We didn't think he was the man for you. But if you really wanted to wed him, could we have stopped you? Could anyone have stopped your Tante Sara?"

Mother bent to look at her breads in the oven and Rosa reflected that she had never talked to her like this before. This is probably what the prospect of getting married does, she thought. People start considering you an adult.

When father told her, a few days later, that he had received a letter from Yehuda Heller asking if he and Mendel could come and visit the Laxes, Rosa expected a proposal.

"Mendel Heller is a good man," Anschel said to his daughter, "and he may ask for your hand."

Rosa said nothing but she knew that if he did, she would accept.

Business after the war was brisk and father's rounds frequent. People, however, were short of money and he often came home dejected at their inability to pay. Many had lost their homes to the marauding Russians, who had burnt down houses, after robbing their contents, inns, after drinking them dry and sawmills, after using the timber for their encampments.

The Romanians, now in power in Bucovina, were far less tolerant of their minorities and Bucovina's Jews were uncertain of the future in their new state. No more Propinations for licensed inns were given and with government officials frequenting the area, the Jews soon learnt that bribery was the only way to achieve anything under Romanian rule.

Anschel had to use much of his money, earned during the war and devalued now, to reestablish tenure of his father's property in Putila Kaselitsa. His young brothers, Yossel and Faivel, had moved to Vienna before the war and were now demanding their share, so Anschel was hoping to sell the house and land and divide the proceeds.

It was Yehuda Heller, when he and his son Mendel came for a visit after Pessach, who offered to buy Yacob Lax's house, giving Anschel a fair price and putting him in his favour. Yehuda Heller, like Yacob Lax, was an expansive man, eager not only to distribute charity and good deeds, but to take away people's financial worries.

"God is good," he used to say, "and we, his creatures, can never aspire to even approach his goodness."

As the transaction was being signed and Yehuda and Anschel retired to the study to discuss the Gemarra, Rosa and Mendel strolled around Cirlibaba. They walked to the local market and saw the peasants selling their produce. There were big cow's milk cheeses and glowing spring vegetables just coming in.

Mendel bought Rosa a bunch of red tulips from a hunched woman who mumbled her thanks in Romanian.

They walked towards the forest and Rosa showed Mendel where she and her sisters had been picking wild strawberries as children. She told him of her childhood, of the long days studying at home with the old Czernowitzer Herr Gold, just like her mother before her. She did not tell him of her strolls in the snow with Herr Greifer.

Mendel told her about the teachers his father had hired for his children, teaching them German, English, arithmetic and Hebrew. Rosa was again amazed at the similarity in their backgrounds. Then, suddenly, Mendel stopped.

"Fräulein Rosa," he started, looking into her eyes seriously. "I intend to ask your father for your hand in marriage today. But I wanted to tell you first and get your answer before I do. If you wouldn't have me, I shall go back to Frasin and never bother you again."

"This is highly irregular, Herr Heller," Rosa said, wishing to gain some time before her answer was required.

"I know and I apologise for it," Mendel said. "Since we didn't meet through a shadchan and since I feel we got to know each other rather quickly, I thought I could risk asking you directly."

"Yes, I suppose it is better this way, Herr Heller," Rosa was still hedging.

"So what is your answer, Fräulein Rosa? Will you say yes?" Mendel sounded excited, hanging his eyes on Rosa's face.

We are both adults, both independent people. Father and mother approve, Rosa thought quickly. Aloud she said, "If you ask, Herr Heller, I think I shall say yes."

Mendel's anxious expression broke into a broad smile. "Thank you, Fräulein Rosa. Thank you. I knew you were the one the moment I saw you in that pension and when father said he knew your father, I simply had to make your acquaintance."

"So it was your idea to come over to us, not your father's?" Rosa said, thinking that perhaps there was love here after all.

"Oh, yes, Fräulein Rosa. The moment I saw you across the dining hall."

Rosa looked at Mendel's excited face. His dark eyes burnt under his high forehead and his smile drowned in his bushy beard. This beard will have to come off, she thought, pleased at the proprietary feeling Mendel evoked in her.

By the time the Hellers left the proposal was made and accepted by both the intended and her parents. Rosa and Mendel started using first names and an approximate date was fixed for the engagement party.

Mendel wanted to get married that year and Rosa saw no point in a long delay now that her mind was made up. After a visit to Frasin by Rosa and her parents to meet Mendel's mother, the engagement party was to take place by the end of the summer.

The journey to Frasin, however short, necessitated new clothes. Dora recalled painfully her own journey with her late mother-in-law and her long dead friend Rosa, to Herr Friedmann's tailor shop in Czernowitz, a journey now out of the question for financial reasons and post war shortages.

Again, alterations had to be made. Frau Schuster, the young seamstress who had recently taken up residence in Cirlibaba, worked at the Laxes' house for three days, producing good results with Dora and Sara's old skirts and coats. Rosa looked elegant in a pale cream suit with the skirt just above the ankles in the new fashion and a dark blue blouse to highlight the dark blue of her eyes. Dora, who rarely travelled for pleasure, looked well too in an old grey suit to which Frau Schuster added a new collar.

As soon as their coach ground the gravel inside Yehuda Heller's large court, Mendel ran out to welcome Rosa and his future in-laws. As she watched the darkly elegant figure, Dora could not help comparing this scene with her first visit to Anschel's parents in Putila.

Mendel led his guests first into his parents' apartment which opened into the court, facing a little synagogue and school. On the left was the inn which opened to the street, backing into the court, littered with empty wooden barrels, clay and glass bottles.

From the inn could be heard voices of merry drinking, while in the synagogue, the busy murmur of prayer rose, in complete contrast with the austerity of the Heller apartment. Yehuda Heller was waiting for the Laxes in the heavily furnished yet severe living room on his own. His hearty welcome reminded Dora of her own late father-in-law. He had invited the Laxes to sit down and inquired about their journey when into the room came a small woman with sharp features, her eyes black like Mendel's.

"This is mother," Mendel said to no one in particular and Rosa and her parents rose to greet Rachel Heller, whose head was covered with a tight scarf in the orthodox manner and whose appearance could not be more greatly contrasted to her husband's and son's.

"We are all very pleased our youngest is planning to wed," she said in the manner of one not given to idle talk. "He is nine and twenty and the time has come for him to leave his parents' home."

"He has worked hard to help his sisters-in-law when their husbands were taken into the army," said Yehuda, his tone softer and more appeasing than his wife's.

"So has Rosa," Anschel said. "Her help during the war was vital to the very survival of our family."

"You have chosen well, my son," Rachel's voice rose again. "I can see Fräulein Lax is a hard worker. And an elegant woman, which is much in our post-war circumstances."

As Rosa bowed her head in gratitude, Rachel turned to Dora and in a surprisingly chatty voice, said, "Where did you manage to find this exquisite fabric? You must have sources we don't know of."

Dora, as yet unwilling to tell all, said, "One has to find ways and means, Frau Heller, and do the best one can."

"Indeed," Rachel responded. "You must excuse my own working clothes. I run the family inn, you understand, while Reb Yehuda and our sons run the family timber business. We have many mouths to feed, what with our sons and their families. Mendel is the last to marry, but we won't have to feed him and his bride. He is well able to provide."

"So we understand, Frau Heller," said Anschel, for whom such strong talk was plainly too much.

"Show your bride-to-be the yard, while we here will discuss business," Rachel said, oblivious of her guests' embarrassment.

Dora was horrified at Rachel Heller's lack of discretion. As Mendel escorted Rosa outside, she reflected upon the underhand way her own betrothal was managed, without the word business ever being uttered. Women, in her time, were never party to discussions of dowry or conditions. Theirs had been the domain of meals and clothes.

Rachel seemed to have read her thoughts. "You must think me too direct, Frau Lax," she said. "But I have been a business-woman all my life. Apart from ten brief confinements to have my children, the Lord spare them and give long life to the nine I have left, I have always run my inn. There has never been time for pleasantries."

Dora smiled feebly. There had been something hard about her own mother-in-law too. Perhaps this was history repeating itself, she reflected.

Yehuda did not stop his wife and the negotiations took place between Anschel Lax and Rachel Heller as to Rosa's dowry and Mendel's obligations. With money in short supply, Anschel pledged two forests at Putila Kaselitsa as his eldest daughter's dowry. Mendel was to settle her in a new house in Vatra Dornei where he was to open a new Heller sawmill. The agreement was painless and swift and by the time the young couple returned from the brief tour, not only to the inn and the synagogue, but to the family sawmill, the two fathers had already signed the conditions.

"We shall celebrate the engagement here in Frasin on the last day of August," Rachel said.

"Thank you, mother," Mendel said. "Would that suit you, Rosa?"

Rosa looked to her parents and when she saw her mother nod briefly, she said, "Thank you. The end of August it may well be."

"Would you like to settle the wedding date yet?" Yehuda asked the Laxes.

"What about the very end of the year?" Rosa cried. "It would be wonderful to welcome 1920 with a wedding."

"An excellent idea," Mendel said, looking at her kindly.

"The dead of winter?" Dora said. "It would be difficult to have a large party."

"So much the better, mother," Rosa said. "This isn't the time to be spending large fortunes on feeding people one doesn't think very much of."

"That girl has good sense," Rachel declared and they all laughed, some nervously, some fondly.

Later, after an elaborate kiddush on sweet red wine specially shipped from Palestine, to celebrate the betrothal, the guests were joined by Mendel's brother Shmaya and his family for an evening meal of hot meat broth, pickled ox tongue and bread dumplings cooked in goose schmaltz. There were spirits from Frau Heller's inn and freshly picked fruit from her large garden.

"That seems to have been a satisfactory transaction," Anschel said to Dora as they prepared for bed in an upstairs guest room where large feather blankets covered a large but sloping bed. "I regret father and mother were not given the chance by the enemies of Israel to witness this great day and see their eldest granddaughter being agreed upon for marriage with the son of such a scholarly man and such a righteous woman."

"What a woman she is," Dora said emphatically. "I got the distinct impression she would have been glad to have been made a man."

"You mustn't make such sinful observations on a woman who is clearly a devout Jewess, Dora. Women, let me remind you, are meant to be helpmates to their men."

"Or helpmates against them, as the Torah says," Dora said obstinately. "Rachel Heller did not let her poor husband complete a sentence, never mind express his opinion." Dora paused for a moment. "Perhaps this is the better way," she said very softly. "I only hope she doesn't give Rosa a hard time."

"It will take more than Rachel Heller to bend our Reisale's spirit," Anschel said. "There is, all the same, a certain similarity between the Hellers and my late parents, don't you think?"

Dora agreed but she wasn't going to elaborate. She did think her late mother-in-law a dreadful tyrant and feared Rachel Heller was something of a tyrant herself. But she said no more. She had learnt during her married years not to antagonise Anschel, letting him believe he was getting his own way. She had seen her own mother do it and she hoped her daughter would learn how to do it in her turn.

The summer of 1919 was long and hot. Rosa found herself singing around the house as letters from Mendel arrived regularly. His letters were just short of passionate, declaring his love for Rosa openly. Rosa discussed him with her aunt and came close to saying that she felt in love. Questioned about the flutter, she did not know what to answer.

Meanwhile she was busy embroidering her trousseau like her mother before her. She was still intent on getting Mendel's beard off. On one of his early summer visits to Cirlibaba, she pressed him and he promised to cut the beard down. On the next visit the beard was still there and Rosa spoke to her father who promised to talk to his future son-in-law, but on the next visit the beard was as long as it had ever been.

"I know I promised," he argued with Rosa. "You know I would do anything for you, but I'd feel guilty visiting our Rebbe. By the time we get married, I promise the beard will be trimmed down."

Mendel's shyness and his mother's apparent dominance worried Rosa. Would he be her equal in strength or would he cave in to his family and his Rebbe? Instinctively, she knew he would always give in.

His new sawmill was progressing and after the engagement party in Frasin, he took her to buy their new house in Vatra Dornei. They saw a number of houses and settled on a two storey house in a quiet side street, branching off the main shopping street on the opposite side of the railway from where the spa was situated.

Rosa stood back and admired Mendel's negotiating skills and the ease with which he concluded the deal. It was his business acumen and his confidence coupled with his great charm and endless love for her which made her forget her doubts.

She eyed the large diamond ring and diamond and ruby bracelet he had given her as engagement presents and whispered to herself, once I get his beard off, everything else is going to be right. I shall watch him develop his business and at the same time I shall find some business for myself and together we shall go from strength to strength.

Mendel never seemed to be short of money but in post-war years there was still a shortage of things to buy. After he had signed the sale contract for their new house, he found a dining-room suite and wrote Rosa about it. He did not mention that his mother had said to him when he told her proudly of his purchase, "Why have you bought her furniture? Will she be able to put it on her shoulders? You should have bought her a fur coat."

The winter of 1919 was cold as the summer had been hot. For ease of transportation for the guests, it was decided the wedding would take place in Dorna, where the young couple would settle. Roads were piled high with snow as the guests arrived in town by train and up the hill to the pension by sleighs.

The Chuppa was placed outside the Jewish pension where Rosa first met Mendel at lunchtime on the last day of 1919. As the trim-bearded Mendel smashed the glass under his foot, members of his large family and Rosa's family shouted, Mazel Tov, Mazel Tov.

Rosa, blushing with the gusty winds, hugged herself in her long velvet wedding gown as she walked, leaning for the first time on Mendel's arm, into the restaurant for a family lunch. Much later, the guests welcomed 1920, the first year of post-war economic ease, as people were saying optimistically, in the pension's dance hall, where Yankele Mayer's kleismer band played through the night. There was no segregation between women and men. Perhaps, Rosa reflected, the Hellers were not that orthodox after all.

Watching her daughter waltz with her new husband, Dora remembered her own wedding where dancing was for men only. She remembered Berl's lustful looks and a shudder ran down her spine. Rosa, by comparison, looked much happier today than she had felt during her own wedding. Times must be changing, she thought bitterly.

On her right, her sister Sara was dancing slowly with her Morritz and at the corner of the large hall, she caught a glimpse of her second daughter Hanna talking to a young man whose broad face suggested a Romanian origin. Neither Anschel nor Yehuda Heller were anywhere to be seen. Probably discussing their endless books, she thought as she got up to join Rachel Heller and her sisters, still sitting at the tables, where empty glasses glistened in the shining lights.

At midnight, someone knocked with a silver spoon on a glass and everyone grew silent. Accompanied by church bells from outside the hall, people were greeting each other with Mazel and nachas for 1920.

Dora saw her sister kiss her husband passionately on the lips, her eyes closed as if in a dream. Rosa and Mendel stood holding hands, looking seriously into each other's eyes and Hanna and her young man sat shyly, looking at each other secretively, while Dora forced a smile to fight back the tears she felt welling in her tired eyes.

The hope for better days was in the air as Rosa and Mendel said their farewells after midnight. Rosa kissed her mother lightly on the lips, bidding her a good rest as she and Mendel left the hall to go the room Mendel had reserved upstairs.

"Come my beloved, my bride. Behold thou art fair my love," Mendel recited in Hebrew from the Song of Songs as the two entered their bedroom. He had filled the room with flowers and as Rosa looked into his black eyes, she saw naked passion for the first time. He touched her lips with his fingers, making her shiver. "I waited for this day. How I waited for this day," he whispered. "Ever since I first saw you downstairs that day last spring."

He took her in his arms and kissed her on the mouth, his tongue demanding, searching. Rosa had never before been kissed like this and as she felt his short beard on her smooth cheeks, she observed herself melting in his long arms. "Et dodim kala," Mendel recited again, "Boi Legani."

"Dodi Tsach veadom, dagul merevava," Rosa answered, attempting a smile though her heart was heavy.

"Get undressed," Mendel whispered urgently in her ear. "I will wait here."

Rosa went behind the screen where she found a chamber pot which she was dying to use but did not dare. She unbuttoned her long-sleeved velvet wedding dress and smoothed her full body with her hands, making love to her eager curves, touching her heavy breasts, caressing her long neck. She then got out of her silk combinations and stood in her corset and broderie anglaise bloomers over her suspenders. She undid every last button and hook and, wrapped in a white dressing gown, she walked slowly in the dim light towards the bed where Mendel lay, covered with the fluffy feather blanket, waiting.

"Come," his voice said gently. Rosa turned away from him as she slipped the gown to the floor, sliding in beside him onto the cold starched sheets.

Mendel took her in his arms once again. She was aware of his angular body. He buried himself in her face, kissing and kissing her. She became aware of his erection and recoiled, frightened.

114

Sara had told her how things happen but her passion wasn't sufficient to drown the fear.

"Don't worry, little one, I will not hurt you," Mendel whispered. His hands stroked her body and his gentle mouth covered her body with moist but firm kisses. There was nothing in his love-making to suggest the softness of kissing her mother or aunts, nor the lecherous look in old men's faces, eyeing her as she was growing up. He was touching her, moistening her, preparing her for his penetration and she remained passive, taken by a desire sweeter than anything she had ever known, yet too fearful to participate in what she knew was her rite of passage, her duty, her entry into the world of adults like Sara and Morritz, like Berl and his washerwoman and even, the most impossible of all thoughts, father and mother.

"What do I do?" she heard herself whisper, bewildered at her paralysis.

"You don't have to do anything," Mendel whispered back. "I will not hurt you," he repeated, stroking her between the legs, parting her lips with his fingers, moving her legs apart, heaving himself on top of her, groaning, groaning, groaning. The dull pain between her legs made her wince. She observed herself caressing his head with a hesitant hand as he groaned more, lying with his full weight inside her, still erect, sharp.

When he rolled off, she lay hurt, sad, empty. Mendel, beside her, was lying on his back, breathing heavily, his breaths like sobs. "Did I hurt you, little one?" he groaned. "Did I hurt you, my lovely, my bride?"

"No, you didn't," she soothed his choked breaths, lying for the first, but not last, time to this stranger who became her husband. "This is the way it must be, isn't it?"

"Yes, this is the way it must be. But next time will be better," he said heavily, almost strangely.

The idea of there being a next time frightened her. Give me time to heal, she pleaded in her head and aloud she said, "Next time we do it, your beard must be off, Mendel. It is too rough on my skin. You don't want me to be scratched all over?"

"Not on your face, I don't," Mendel said as he approached her again, starting to stroke her, caressing her body again, preparing for another penetration, another heaving onslaught. He spoke many soft words in her ears that night, softening her rigid body with his long fingers.

Despite herself, Rosa felt her aching insides moisten again and as the sweet, dulled ache filled her, she felt his arched body climb on top of her again and his sharp penetration fill her with a warm liquid as he groaned, groaned.

115

The longing ache did not subside when he rolled off. There was no flutter, no shivering delight. The preliminaries were more thrilling than the act and Rosa, disappointed, murmured again her reassurances in Mendel's ears. No, she wasn't hurt, yes, he was gentle and yes, she loved him too, to find him asleep, his head on her breasts, his breathing regular, loud.

Rosa Heller woke up on the first morning of her married life to welcome 1920 in a strange pension room. Beside her was a bearded man she could barely remember, his dark straight hair clinging to his high forehead. As she stepped off her tossed bed linen, she looked back, stifling a scream at the large bloodstain where she had lain. Like a flash, last night came back to her. She was glad of the fresh bloodstain, less glad of the sharp pain between her legs as she sat on the chamber pot behind the screen. She was now a properly married woman of Israel.

Vienna of early 1920 lost little of its prewar charm, although Mendel assured Rosa that the nervous splendour of the turn of the century, which he could still remember from his childhood visits to his many cousins, had given way to a more sombre outlook.

From Opernring 5, where they stayed with an elegant old Jewish widow whom they only knew as Frau Martine, her name pronounced in the French manner, who let rooms to Jewish gentlefolk, Rosa could see straight across Opera Square to the famous Sirk Ecke, that corner where the upper end of Kärntnerstrasse, Vienna's most elegant shopping street, meets with the 'Ring'.

This wide, tree-lined boulevard shaped like a horseshoe, its two ends resting on the banks of the Danube Canal, was for Rosa the epitome of the true beauty of the old city. The Baroque palaces of the long vanished nobility, the old churches, the wide squares through which Mozart and Haydn, Beethoven and Schubert, of whom she heard talk now for the first time in her short life, strolled. The narrow old lanes of the medieval city as well as the wide streets, with the elaborately ornate buildings from which the Empire had been governed for hundreds of years until its demise only a few years ago.

The Ringstrasse represented both a style and a period, the period when the monarchy had reached its peak under dear old Franz-Josef, now, alas, departed from this world. Mendel showed the apartment blocks of the rich which had shot up in the latter quarter of the nineteenth century as witnesses of that period's growing wealth and past confidence in the everlasting monarchy.

Beardless now, Mendel led his young bride along that

grandest of European boulevards. Vienna, he kept stressing, was as sumptuously endowed as Paris and that, even Rosa knew, was something.

"A house was not fit for the Ring," he said on the day after their arrival as they strolled along the snow-covered Ringstrasse in their thick fur-lined boots, "unless it had all those curlicued figures, garlands, urns. The stonemason's best artistic efforts had to adorn the Ring's houses."

He pointed out official buildings, which vied with private houses for splendour and a variety of styles. They saw the Opera House which, Mendel pointed out, reading from his Baedecker, had been built in the style of an Italian Renaissance palazzo. The university was like a French castle and the Town Hall a virtual neo-gothic cathedral in style. The parliament was the most impressive. Built like a Greek temple, it had the imposing figure of Pallas Athena, the Greek goddess of wisdom, in the front. "But notice how she has her back to the Parliament building," Mendel said. "The builder must have predicted the shameful end of the monarchy even during the secure years of the last century."

It was the first time Rosa had been exposed to so much culture. Any culture, in fact. Father had been interested primarily in his books and mother never talked of anything but her immediate surroundings, her family, her work at the sawmill. Secular books never entered the house and theatre or music were never even mentioned. Once she had heard mother talk of a theatre show she had seen in Czernowitz, with Oma Lax and poor Tante Rosa.

Now Mendel took her to the operettas and Rosa's eyes grew big with astonishment at the costumed players singing songs of love and deceit. A new world was opening. One night they went to the Opera House. Rosa was clad in a new evening gown Mendel had bought for her on Kärntnerstrasse. She had spent some time preparing for the great evening, thinking herself extremely sophisticated in her new gown. But how plain she felt when they stepped towards the main entrance and saw ladies wearing better costumes than she had seen even on the operetta stage. Mendel in his evening suit looked dignified and earnest but Rosa felt like a fish out of water. Throughout the night, her mind was not on the tribulations of the dying Traviata, but on the injustice of having been born a provincial Jew.

Despite her French name, Frau Martine kept a strictly kosher home and fed her guests well. Mendel and Rosa spent their days sightseeing and eating. By day Mendel was considerate, gentle, eager to show his bride Vienna's splendours and its gifts. They

117

spent endless hours searching the stores for clothes for Rosa who, up to now, had only worn garments her mother had altered for her. By night, the generous Mendel became demanding, hungry, his thin body filling her curves with thudded entries, hard, ruthless. Rosa fell asleep exhausted every night, rehearsing the reassurances that she was happy and unhurt but waiting eagerly for morning to break and bring the joy of being led into the elegant streets and stores. The nights, she said to herself, were the price she had to pay for the joy of being not only alive after the great war but also in this magnificent city, already harbouring, under its glossy surface, future doom.

The day before they were leaving, Rosa felt particularly happy. She had had several nights' rest. It was her time of the month and Mendel, a worldly but orthodox Jew, was not touching her. They had just managed to find a winter coat for her. It was black, roomy and fur-trimmed. In her buttoned ankle boots and long woollen skirt, her cheeks flushed against the astrakhan collar, she looked radiant as she waited for Mendel in the entrance hall of Frau Martine's rooming house to join her on their last carriage ride through the streets Rosa had grown to love. She sat, her eyes downcast, thinking of the unwelcome journey home to Bucovina, when she heard a voice above her head.

"Could it be Fräulein Lax?" it said.

She lifted her head. Above stood a moustachioed man in a dark suit, the face vaguely familiar.

"You don't remember me," the man said.

"I am afraid not," she said softly and as she said it, she knew who it was, afraid to believe it.

"David Greifer, of course," the man said loudly. "You must remember me."

Rosa looked around to see if anyone in the little entrance hall was listening. There was no time to feign surprise. She stood and, confused, sat down again. "Herr Greifer, what are you doing in Vienna? We all thought ..."

"You thought I was dead, yes?" The voice was sharp. Rosa looked around again but the hall remained empty.

"Well, I don't know that we actually thought that. But when you didn't return, we didn't know what to think," she said, trying to regain her composure.

"Return? Return to what?" David Greifer sounded almost mocking.

"Well, return to Cirlibaba, of course. We all did after the war, you know," Rosa said.

"Yes. Of course you did."

"Even my uncle Morritz. He returned to his wife, Tante Sara. Do you remember her?"

David Greifer ignored her question. "You had property, buildings, a business to return to," he said, sounding bitter. "What did I have?"

"We thought you had us," Rosa lowered her voice again.

"Yes," David said only, moving closer to her, limping heavily.

"David," Rosa's voice rose in a shout. "What happened?"

"What do you think happened, Fraülein Lax? The war happened. The war." His voice light and cold.

Rosa's stomach contracted. She looked into his eyes, searching. "I am sorry," her voice said. "Was it horrible?"

David looked back, his gaze almost metallic. "It was bad. Yes," he said bluntly. "But I survived."

Rosa didn't see Mendel by her side as she said softly to David Greifer, "We waited for you to return to Cirlibaba, you know. When you didn't come, we feared the worst."

"Well, I didn't return, Fräulein Lax. But I am here. Injured but alive."

"The lady you are talking to is not Fräulein Lax any more," Rosa heard her husband's voice from behind her. The moment, her moment, came to an end.

"How do you do," Mendel was saying now. "My name is Mendel Heller and this is my wife."

"I am sorry," David said in a more formal voice. "I didn't know you got married. Congratulations to you both."

"Thank you," Mendel said, formally too. "You haven't introduced your friend," he turned to Rosa.

"I am sorry," Rosa said, struggling to fight the tears in her throat. "This is Herr David Greifer. An old friend from Cirlibaba," she said, frozen. "When we escaped to Bistritsa, he was taken to the Kaiser's army like my uncle Morritz. But unlike Onkel Morritz, he didn't return to Cirlibaba, so naturally we all expected the worst."

"I am glad to make your acquaintance, Herr Greifer," Mendel shook David's hand. "How come you did not pay your way out of the army?"

"I had no money to pay my way," David said, his voice cool again. "I was an orphan who worked at the Cirlibaba post office for a living. Unusual in Jewish middle-class circles, I believe. I was awaiting a place at the Czernowitz University after the war. The placement had just come through but it was too late and now Czernowitz is in Romanian hands and I don't want to go back. Although my late parents came from Bucovina, Vienna is my home now."

"And what do you do here, may I enquire?" Mendel's gentle voice asked.

"Oh, I deal and I trade," David answered, avoiding Rosa's eyes.

"But your studies, David?" she said, searching his eyes.

"Too late, Frau Heller, too late. I came back from the war and the world as we all knew it disappeared. There is no more room for scholars in my post-war world. Only for money makers."

"You have a point there," Mendel said. "What line of business are you in, if I may ask?"

"I deal," David said obliquely but Mendel's straight stare made him say impetuously, "war surpluses. And women."

Rosa stifled a quick breath. David had not been the right man for her, everybody had said. He stood there, bold, larger than life, measuring her with his cold eyes and behind stood her husband, a good family man. And she felt torn.

"Luft menschen," Mendel murmured.

"Excuse me?" David said.

"Luft menschen all. Jews, who scavenge on other people's wars and misfortunes, wheeling and dealing. That's what they say about us, don't they?"

"Perhaps," David said. "But one has to live, Herr Heller. And when one has no family, no connections, no money and no profession, one has to do what one can."

"But your aspirations to education, to be somebody?" Rosa almost shouted.

"I am somebody now, Frau Heller. I am feared and respected here in post-war Vienna. Perhaps in seedier circles than you two move in, but that is what I have."

"Well, it was nice making your acquaintance," Mendel spoke resolutely, slipping his forearm under Rosa's elbow. "We are leaving tomorrow and there are several things we must do before we go."

"It was nice to meet you too," David said. "May I invite you to dinner this evening?"

Rosa was on the verge of accepting when Mendel said, "No thank you. Our plans are made. But please, when you are in Dorna, call on us. We have just bought a sawmill and a house and will always be glad to entertain you."

"That is most kind," David said, his carefree tone returning. "I shall most certainly avail of the invitation. I have heard wonderful things about Vatra Dornei's famous spa. Could help me with my leg." He caressed his thigh and looked into Rosa's face. "It was good to see you again, Frau Heller. We did have some good times in the prehistory. Before the war."

"Yes. We did," Rosa said, blushing slightly under her husband's gaze. "I do hope you are happy as I am now," she added, Mendel's grip tightening on her elbow.

They took their leave of David Greifer and, biting back her tears as she stepped into the waiting carriage, Rosa bid final farewell to her childhood.

4

Rosa 1930

The house on Hellergasse was let for the whole summer.

"Times are bad," Rosa explained when she arrived with Carla and Herbert at her parent's house in Cirlibaba. "The Heller bank is in trouble."

Dora, who had expected her daughter's arrival for the usual summer holidays, shook her head sternly. Without smiling, she took the children into their room and came back into the kitchen.

"You shouldn't say things like that in front of the children, Rosl. There is time enough for them to get worried."

"You didn't spare me, mother," Rosa said loudly. "Didn't I lend a hand looking after the family during the war?"

"Wonderful as ever," Hetti said from behind the large polished beech table.

Rosa turned to look at her younger sister, who until then had been sitting quietly in the corner, surprised to discover a sneering look in her light brown eyes.

"So you are running to mother when things are not working in the business, big sister?" Hetti said, her malice thinly disguised.

"I suppose so," Rosa said softly, feeling defeated for the first time since it had been decided that she should spend the entire summer in Cirlibaba while the house was let to help meet costs. "We have to economise. Our bank ..."

"Yes, I know. Heller Bank is linked to the Wiener Ost Bank, which is directly linked to the capitalist money centres in America. I am not surprised you are in trouble, big, rich, sister," Hetti said, almost cruelly.

"Where do you get these ideas, Hetti?" Rosa winced.

"It's obvious," Hetti said and Rosa thought she could detect glee in her eyes. "The economy of this country is entirely dependent on international capitalism. We could have been the granary of Europe but look where we are thanks to people like your Mendel and his Firma Gebrüder Heller. Because of property speculators like the Hellers, ordinary people like your own father have no access to the means of production or to financial control. And therefore no say over their destiny."

Rosa looked at her sister, who by now was standing, supporting herself, by the large table. "Mendel and his brothers are not property speculators any more than father is a crooked money-lender," she said vehemently, tears burning the back of her throat.

"Kinder, stop it immediately," Dora said from her place beside the stove stirring the soup, her back to her daughters. "At times like these you must give your sister a hand, Hetti, not one of your political speeches."

Rosa looked at her younger sister quizzically. Hetti's thick body, angled towards her good leg, had gained much weight since she had last seen her. Her face had acquired a line or two around her clear eyes and her beautiful mouth looked bitter.

"Mendel is a good man," she said softly. "You know how he shoulders the responsibilities of both our families."

"If it wasn't for Mendel, father could not have continued his business. You know his eyesight is too weak," Dora said sternly.

"Yes, I know," Hetti sounded tired. "Good old Mendel. Like all capitalists, he is content with charity to his poor relatives but does nothing about changing the whole rotten system from the core."

"Where do you get these ideas?" Rosa asked again.

"In the movement, that's where," Dora said.

Hetti gasped. "Yes, I know, Hetti," Dora said. "I know you have been trying to hide it from father and me, but in a small place like Cirlibaba, things come out sooner or later."

"You may as well know," Hetti said defiantly. "I am tired of pretending. Tired of this life, seeing poor father get blinder and blinder as he makes his rounds, a member of the Jewish lumpen proletariat, pretending to be one of the ruling classes, while Rosa's Mendel waxes fat."

"But he doesn't," Rosa almost shouted. "Didn't you hear me? This is why we are here. We have lost all our money. We have no business. We are leaving Dorna. Selling out."

"Nu, nu," Dora said. "That it should come to this. The good is limitless, but it could have been worse. But you still have one another. And you have us to come to."

Rosa swallowed hard to drown the tears she felt coming to the surface. As a family they were not in the habit of crying and she was not going to let that heartless sister of hers see her start now.

Later, in her old room, looking onto the familiar yard where sawn timber was stacked to dry for the winter, Rosa lay thinking about the irony of her situation. It hadn't taken her long to get used to the life of a lady. In Dorna, the Hellers were the cream. Their two-storey house towered over the wide street, known only as Hellergasse since no one knew its real name. Beside the house, which everyone agreed was the most stylish in the street, Mendel's brother Itzhak lived in a taller, but less graceful house where the family bank operated.

Built with a living storey and a second guest storey, her house was spacious and she ran it with military precision, a large bunch of keys always hanging from her wide belt, presiding over two Saxon maids and a Romanian coachman and always entertaining Mendel's many business guests.

Most of all she loved it when guests came from Palestine. Bringing with them the smell of sun and sea, business associates or Zionist leaders never failed to be impressed by her affluent household.

As she was lying in her old room, Rosa remembered the last visit by Livia and Israel Silberman of Tel Aviv. Israel Silberman was a big orange grove owner but when the Hellers' sleigh came to fetch him from the Dorna railway station, he gasped at the big fur covers Ilie the coachman wrapped around his shoulders and the shoulders of his wife Livia.

Rosa remembered meeting them at the door, ordering die rote Marie to unwrap her guests and serving them hot tea she had waiting by the china stove at the corner of the second living room. They sat by the stove, Marie rubbing their frozen feet with coarse linen towels, sipped their tea and looked around with the admiration Rosa had learnt to cherish.

Hetti, she remembered, was staying with her at the time and as soon as her guests finished their tea and were preparing to be shown to their rooms, she appeared from nowhere.

"Had a good ride in big sister's sleigh?" said her voice, high, petulant.

"Thank you," Livia Silberman said, her German tinged with a slight Hungarian accent.

"You are Hungarian, how wonderful," Hetti exclaimed, launching into Hungarian, which she was the only one of the Laxes to remember after their stay in Bistritsa.

"This is my younger sister, Hetti Lax," Rosa said quickly. "Please excuse her excitement. She may not realise how tired you must be."

"Never mind how tired they are," Hetti said. "I haven't had an opportunity to speak Hungarian for months now."

She chatted with Livia Silberman in Hungarian while Rosa tried to entertain Israel until Mendel returned from the sawmill, where he had to wait until Ilie fetched him, having brought the Silbermans and their luggage to the house first.

It was early 1928 and the visit by Israel and Livia Silberman meant a lot to Mendel, whose business rested mostly on supplying orange box timber to Palestine. Israel Silberman was also a well-known activist in Mendel's own political party, the General Zionists, and his visit, like the visits by other Zionist leaders to the thriving Jewish community of Dorna, was an important lifeline. Having Hetti to contend with was not part of the plan.

"That Hetti," Rosa complained to Mendel before dinner. "She

accosted poor Livia using these awful words of hers: capitalism, marxism, you know. And I could not intervene because they spoke Hungarian. You should have seen poor Israel's face when he heard his wife being made to listen to that diatribe. We ought to do something with that girl. She is twenty-three and no sign of a man yet."

"She has been filling her head with socialist ideas, you know," Mendel said. "I have heard the men in the sawmill say she was seen at the Dorna Hashomer Hatsair meetings. God knows, although they are good Zionists, some of them are too far to the left for my liking."

"What are we going to do, Mendel? I have always looked to you for help with my family. First poor father and his failing eyesight and zero business performance and then sending Haim to school in Czernowitz. But Hetti? I never thought we would have to take drastic steps apart from helping her to find a husband. Women don't usually present the same problems. They get married, don't they? But this Hetti, she shows no interest."

"You know I have tried. But she wouldn't listen to the shadchan," Mendel said. "Perhaps the best thing is to send her to Palestine. There she can join forces with her socialist friends."

"That's an idea, Mendel," Rosa's face lit up. "If she goes, we'd have one less responsibility. Things are tight enough as it is without her, aren't they?"

"You worry too much, Rosl," Mendel tried to sound casual. "Everything will sort itself out. We have a good life here and things can only improve."

Mendel was always like this. An optimist by nature, he would not allow Rosa to get worried on his behalf.

Lying on her old bed, Rosa reflected on the irony of this conversation, held just over a year earlier. How things had changed since then.

She remembered her conversation with Livia Silberman while the men went about their business. Like previous guests from Palestine, Livia was easily impressed. Rosa took her to Dorna's famous mud baths across the river and later, refreshed and glowing, the two women sat by Rosa's china stove sipping hot tea and eating Rosa's famous cheese cakes. "How fortunate you are, Rosa," Livia kept saying. "A cook and a Kindermädchen and a coachman. And someone to carry hot water for your bath and wipe you dry. And this house. And your good clothes. One sees immediately you shop at Europe's best fashion centres."

"Thank you, Livia," Rosa tried to sound humble, although the compliments made her heart sing. "This is nothing but a small provincial town, you know. Nothing as cosmopolitan as Tel Aviv."

"But our life is much rougher than yours, much simpler," Livia said. "My parents hate me living in the sands, as they call it. They would like to see me enjoying the luxuries of their Vienna."

"Mendel is thinking of sending my sister Hetti to Palestine," Rosa confided. "What do you say? She seems to have socialist ideas. Perhaps in Palestine she could find her place."

"Perhaps." Livia did not sound enthusiastic. "She could join a kibbutz or something like that. They are very socialistic. Hard work has never done anyone any harm."

"With her leg I am not sure she could do hard physical work," Rosa started, feeling guilty. "Perhaps she could just go to see if she likes the place. It seems to me that she would never marry anyone here and she isn't getting any younger."

Livia and Israel left having bought most of Mendel's timber and promised to help Hetti settle if she ever came to Palestine.

Rosa remembered broaching the subject with her sister when the Silbermans left and being taken aback by her contempt. "Why should I go to Palestine? I am not a Zionist like you," she said.

"Do you have to be a Zionist to go to Palestine?" Rosa asked naïvely, realising her battle was lost before it started.

"Don't be so naïve, Rosa," Hetti said harshly. "Jews go to Palestine to settle in a land which isn't theirs. Not considering the Arabs." She paused and looked her sister in the eye. "I know why you want to send me to Palestine," she added. "You want me off your backs and you want me to find a man. Admit it."

"What nonsense," Rosa said weakly. "We don't want you off our backs, but yes, it would be nice to see you settled. Married to a good man."

"You think that just because you and Hanna made good matches, this is the only way for a Jewish woman to live, don't you? I look at your comfortable life here in Dorna, pretending to be a lady with all your fineries and at Hanna's country mansion, and you make me sick." Hetti paused for breath. "You will never see me married off like that. No one will find me a man. If I ever marry, I will make the choice and it will not be a marriage of convenience, like yours or Hanna's."

In her childhood bed, Rosa squirmed when she remembered that conversation. She had tried, feebly, to tell Hetti hers had not been a marriage of convenience, that she worked hard to make it work, to make their business work, that her contribution was equally as important as Mendel's. But Hetti would not listen. She reported the conversation to Mendel and suggested they did not try to get a British mandate immigration certificate for her sister. After all, there were many Jews who genuinely wanted to immigrate and who needed those certificates more.

She also remembered Mendel asking her would she like to go to live in Palestine. "As Jews, our days in Europe are numbered," he said that night. "You hear all sorts of rumours from Germany and here in Romania too, anti-semitism is becoming a problem. We have a good business here, but we ought to think about bringing up our children in the land of the forefathers."

"But Mendel, how can we leave everything here and go towards the unknown?" she said. "And Livia Silberman says life there is far rougher than our good life here."

"Yes, I know," Mendel said. "But if we go up to the land, we don't do it in order to get richer or live in greater comfort. We would do it to be amongst our own, where we belong."

"But the British, Mendel? And the Arabs?" Rosa was genuinely alarmed at the thought. "And that awful heat."

"You get used to the heat, Rosa," Mendel said. "And as for the British, they won't be there for long. And we shall learn to live with our Arab neighbours in peace. And one day we shall have a state of our own. You do believe Herzl, I hope?"

All these things passed through her head as she was lying in her room, listening to the children's voices downstairs. If only I had listened to him then, she thought. We could have been safe in Palestine, away from this frightening financial mess, poorer but with no enormous debts to pay.

She got up and wrote Mendel a short note, offering to be with him in Dorna while he cleared his debts and made decisions about their future. "I cannot be here in the relative comfort of my parents' home knowing you are shouldering the burden alone. Let me be by your side. I shall leave the children here with my parents and take the first train and together we shall face our future." She signed and folded the envelope which she carried downstairs.

In the kitchen her father was sitting by the window, his face buried in a manuscript which he looked at through a large magnifying glass. At fifty-three he was an old, spent man, his great scholarship, once admired by rabbis and wise men, suffered now because of his inability to read and his willpower, once strong, weakened by his failure in business. Rosa felt a surge of love for this man, once her business partner, whom she had thought of as a tower of spiritual strength.

"Servus, father," she said softly, thinking, "I love you, father," but not mouthing the words.

Anschel looked at his eldest daughter, his blue eyes clear of expression and Rosa had to remember he was seeing her as a blurred shape of light by the door, not as a person with clear features or expressions.

She tightened her grip on the envelope she was carrying in her hand. Perhaps I ought to stay here and help him, a thought went through her head. Mendel said he did not need me. He can manage without me but father needs me to pull him out of the darkness, she thought, the old feeling of having to carry the family on her shoulders invading her again.

"I hear your Mendel is selling out," father said.

"Yes, our bank collapsed with the collapse of the Wiener Ost," she said, crushing the envelope in her hand and putting the crumpled paper into her skirt pocket. "Mendel is trying to pay our debts but I am afraid he will have to sell the house."

"And what will you do?"

"We shall move on, father. Don't Jews always move on?"

"I am afraid so, Reisale. Whenever there is a war, or a crisis, we Jews always move on. But we survive. Remember the great war? We survived it and you will survive this crisis too."

"How is business, father?"

"Weak, as usual, Reisale. No one is buying property these days. The financial crash has reached Cirlibaba too, you know." He said this almost proudly, Rosa thought.

"I'll see what I can do, father," she said and when she saw Anschel's smile, she knew she had to stay.

Rosa spent the summer putting father on his feet again. Together they went on his rounds, collected rents for the fields and forests he had rented to local farmers and new Romanian land developers who were slow to pay. Rosa reestablished the money-lending business with funds they received from rent. Slowly the colour returned to Anschel's cheeks. At night, he sat with the children, telling them bible stories, teaching nine-year-old Carla and eight-year-old Herbert to read Hebrew, getting them to read him portions of the prayer book. Listening to them, his pale watery eyes smiled.

After the rounds, Rosa spent time with Tante Sara, whose husband Morritz had died the year before. The two women spoke softly about the war, about love and death, Rosa no longer in need of her aunt's guidance, but a wiser woman, whom elders looked up to for support.

From time to time, mother joined them. Never sitting idly as they talked, she knitted or embroidered, using the time, never wasting a moment. Rosa would look at the two sisters, beautiful, sad Sara, whose loneliness deepened with Morritz's death, and serious, wistful Dora, and feel she was becoming them. When occasionally Hetti would sit with them, munching vigorously on mother's yeasty cheese cakes, talking animatedly about her endless politics, Rosa felt a sneaking envy at her sister's unyielding spirit.

She said so to Sara one day. "I feel I have given up on my fighting spirit. Remember how I said I would never yield?"

Sara smiled sadly. "Hate to say I told you so, Rosl. Life smoothes the rough edges as one learns to compromise. Hetti will learn it too, in time."

When Mendel arrived three months later, the children were tanned and rough with the happiness summer brings. When they weren't reading Hebrew, Carla and Herbert spent their time picking wild berries in the forest and running up the hills carefree and abandoned to a wildness Rosa could but envy.

She ran to Mendel as he descended from his carriage, searching his face for signs of what had happened through the long summer. Mendel was looking thinner, more serious, his black hair neatly combed down his long forehead, framing his narrow face and black eyes with a sadness she had not seen before.

"We sold out," were his first words. "Everything."

Rosa hugged him, her full body meeting his angular shape, enveloping him with all the warmth she could feel. "The house?"

"Yes, Rosl. The house was our biggest asset. I got the best price for it."

"But the sawmill? Surely this was the best asset?"

"There were debts on the mill. No debts on the house. All is sold. Hellergasse is no more. They have a name for it now. A regular street name, I forget which, but I saw it on the deeds."

"It always had a name, Mendel," Rosa said softly.

"It always had a name, I suppose, but what you don't know means nothing," Mendel sounded defeated for the first time in their life together. "I shall stay here for some time and then we move to Czernowitz. There is a possibility of starting something there."

"Czernowitz? And what about Eretz Israel?" Rosa asked, her excitement bubbling at the prospect of moving to the big town.

"Not yet, Rosl. Eretz Israel will have to wait until we have a little more to go there with," Mendel sounded tired.

Rosa led her husband into the house and watched him greet his children and his parents-in-law. When Hetti came into the kitchen, Rosa closed her eyes, not wishing to witness the triumphant look on her sister's face.

"So the hero is back from the battlefield," Hetti said. "Have you won the battle but lost the war?"

"Good afternoon, Hetti," Mendel said, his voice patient as ever. "I have not joined the army, so winning or losing is not the issue."

"The battle will be fought one day, Mendel Heller," Hetti's voice was hard. "And you and yours will be amongst the losers, when the proletariat takes over."

"I hope I will not be around to witness that day," Mendel said. "Violence has never been my style."

"But you will, brother, the day of reckoning is not too far," Hetti said.

"Kinder, stop it," Dora said. "Mendel is tired from his journey, Hetti, will you leave him alone?"

"Your father is looking better than I have seen him for a long time," Mendel said to Rosa in her old room later that night.

"Yes, I have been working on it," Rosa said proudly. "We got out together to collect his debts and the money-lending business is afloat once again. We had to, because the property side is more or less dead. Poor father, he should have been a full-time scholar with a prosperous wife to keep him going. He should have lived in a rebbe's court but instead he married a woman poorer than himself and lost much of his father's property through his lack of business acumen. His father could not have known it, otherwise he would never have allowed him to marry mother, whose low dowry provided no security. But why am I babbling on? You know all this already."

"You are a good daughter, Rosl," Mendel said, "and a good wife too," he added proudly.

Yes, I am, Rosa thought as the old thirst started welling up and her throat filled with the tears she had kept down the whole summer. She swallowed hard, determined not to allow the fear of losing herself show and spoke instead of Hetti.

"That Hetti is becoming impossible," she said as she started combing her long hair at the corner of her narrow bed. "I wish she had agreed to go to Palestine when we offered. Between her work at the tailor shop which she calls sweated labour and her evenings with the socialists, she has little to talk about besides politics. She is driving father demented. He does not answer any more, but I can see it is breaking his heart."

"There is not much you can do about it," Mendel said. As his dry soft hands began stroking her body, unbuttoning her clothes, reaching for her full breasts hungrily, Rosa, far from feeling a sense of abandon at the old ritual, grew harder inside, more determined. His angular body, naked now, thrust into hers, his mouth whispering endearments. He was demanding more of her inner softness and Rosa, whose body was submitting to her husband's desire, kept fighting the tears, kept repeating to herself, it's me. It's me who has to see to it. It's me who has to see to father and mother, Hetti, Mendel, Carla, Herbert. It's me, always and ever.

The summer of 1930 was long and hot. At the end of August, Rosa joined Mendel at their house in Dorna, where she stayed to pack up while he went to Czernowitz to find them a place to live.

The first thing Rosa examined was the back garden, her pride and joy. Ilie the coachman had kept her flower beds from weeds but her vegetables were overgrown. She sighed, knowing that from now on she would live in a city and would probably never have a back garden as sweet as this. Sitting at the wooden table by the tall tree, facing the long L-shaped glass veranda surrounding the back of the house, the tears she had fought the whole summer flowed and flowed.

They said it had not been Mendel's fault but his brother Itzhak's. "The Wiener Ost manager called him a financial genius," Mendel told her earlier that week. "Anything he invested in, people lost all their money." They said it had been inevitable. They said the whole world was in a mess and that in America people were standing in lines for charity soups. They said this and they said that but Rosa took no comfort from other people's distress. This was her life, her house, her garden, her family nest.

Unable to start packing, she remained at the wooden table and this was how die rote Marie found her at dusk. "Gnädige Frau, what are you doing sitting here in the garden?" she exclaimed. "I have just been told by Ilie you are back and came to help you pack."

The maid took one look at Rosa's tear-stained face, went into the house and returned with a pitcher of cold water and a little pot of confiture. She poured the water and gave Rosa a silver spoon to put some strawberry confiture into her mouth. Rosa nodded her thanks, unable to speak and drank the cool water which slid through the sweet confiture into her aching throat. I am treated like a guest in my own house, she thought. This was how the Hellers always received their guests, summer or winter.

"Come inside, Frau Heller," said the German. She did not have red hair but was called die rote Marie as part of a family tradition started with their first maid, who had flaming red hair and was called Maria, but preferred to call herself Marie because, she said, she came from France, in Paris.

She led Rosa into the darkened house and sat her gently in the abandoned living room, where the heavy furniture lay under dust covers.

"Tomorrow we pack. Will you stay and help me?" Rosa asked, barely controlling the quiver in her voice.

"Of course I will, Frau Heller," Marie said. "What will I do without you, I don't rightly know."

"I will ask Herr Heller if you can come with us to Czernowitz," Rosa said, her heart lighter with the thought of the efficient Marie sharing her future. "Would you like to?"

"I would, but I will be afraid of the big city," Marie said, her large eyes staring in front of her. "I have never been out of Dorna, apart from the summers I came with you to your honoured parents' house."

"We'll see," Rosa said, her authority returning.

That night she lay awake in their large bed, finally falling into a troubled dawn sleep.

As she woke she found Marie busy in the kitchen, preparing breakfast at the stove. She ate in silence, drinking fresh milk and eating dry cow's cheese in soured milk, perhaps, she thought, for the last time in this beautiful kitchen, where the light bounced off the stove tiles, breaking into a million dust particles dancing on the rays of the late summer sun.

They worked for a week, packing her linen sheets and tableware, silver, pots and pans, vases and trinkets. To her amazement they had filled three tea chests with china alone: a meat and milk set for everyday, a milk and meat set for good use and a milk and meat set for Pessach. Most of all she cherished her good white Rosenthal set with beetroot red flowers and her delicate Rosenthal tea set complete with tiny silver cake forks, which she had received from her mother-in-law when Carla was born.

They rolled the Romanian and Persian rugs and packed the winter clothes, taking particular care over Rosa's two full-length furs. They packed the children's toys, Mendel's Hebrew books, the filigree Menorah Rosa had rescued from her paternal grandparents' house after it had been ransacked by the murderous Cossacks, and the silver candlestick her mother had given her on her wedding day.

When Mendel returned with news of an apartment off Herrengasse in the fashionable centre of Czernowitz, they made a selection of furniture to take with them.

"The apartment is much smaller than this house," he said apologetically. "Some of the furniture will have to be sold."

The day after Mendel's return to Dorna, they strolled along the promenade. "Remember the first day I showed you and Hanna round town?" Mendel said. "How you envied the fur-clad women and now you are one yourself. Fur-clad, but no ready money," he laughed nervously. "Probably like most of those women in those post-war days."

Rosa thought she had grown to like her luxury, fearing she would never get used to the life of lesser comfort, but said nothing.

"I hope you will get used to living in a smaller apartment, with less money and less domestic help," Mendel seemed to have read her thoughts. "I hate to do this to you, but there is no option."

"I know, Mendel," she said lightly. "You have always been a good provider. I have no complaints."

In the afternoon they took the coach to Frasin to visit Mendel's parents. Rachel Heller, older now, sat in the semi-dark apartment in her old armchair, not saying much. Yehuda greeted them warmly, asking after the children. He too had lost money through the family bank. His inn had had to go when the Romanian government did not allow Jews to hold spirit licences, but he still retained his sawmill, selling his timber to big building firms.

Despite his troubles, Mendel fussed over his parents. What a worrier you are, Rosa thought, what worriers we both are. The four sat in the dimly-lit room, enquiring about family relatives, acquaintances, but saying very little. I don't want to end up like her, Rosa thought, not for the first time, looking at the small figure, hunched in her chair, lines of bitterness framing her mouth. I want to be joyous, carefree, cared for, she thought and the tears started welling again.

"It's hard to be a Jew," she heard Rachel say with a deep sigh. "What can we do? We are born to suffer." And Rosa reflected on the many times she had heard Rachel and her own parents say the same thing.

That night she turned to Mendel, pulling him towards her, calling his name softly in the dark. This, at least, was real, she thought, but as his thrusting body invaded hers, the emptiness returned.

5

Hetti 1937

Hetti Lax strained her eyes over the dark suit she was finishing in Herr Schwarz's tailor shop, where she had worked since she moved to Czernowitz.

"Hurry, Fräulein Lax, the customer is arriving in an hour," she heard Frau Schwarz, "you are always so behind with your work, Fräulein Lax. Hurry. You have four more button-holes to do. Good God, girl, what's got into you?"

"I am doing my best, Frau Schwarz," she said nervously. "We are not slaves, you know. And the light here is not too good either."

"Hurry up, Fräulein, and don't be saying all those things to me now," Frau Schwarz said angrily. "The customer is Herr Zimmermann, an important man in this town. He isn't interested in your troubles."

Hetti was angry but said nothing. Her fingers ran over the button-holes, stitching furiously, going round the corners of the hole, pulling the thread through again and again, fastening, re-knotting for the next button hole. Only three more, she thought, and the damned suit will be finished. I wish they'd let me cut the suits instead of merely finishing off someone else's work.

When Herr Zimmermann came for his suit, she could hear Frau Schwarz praise her. "This suit is something special, Herr Zimmermann," she heard her say. "Hand-finished by the best maker in this town. Hetti Lax, sister-in-law of Mendel Heller, who, I believe, you know," her voice sang, flattering, smooth. Sickening, Hetti thought.

Herr Zimmermann looked in the direction Frau Schwarz had pointed and met Hetti's eyes. Smiling, he nodded, tipping his hat to her. "Thank you, Fräulein Lax," his voice rang through the long hall, high above Herrengasse, high above tram bells and car horns.

She lowered her lids, looking at Herr Zimmermann's polished black boots. It was five o'clock, almost time to leave this hated workshop, where she slaved five days each week from early morning, to pay the rent and the food bills.

Too busy thinking about her evening at the movement office, she didn't notice Herr Zimmermann move closer to her sewing machine. Standing over her, he said, "May I talk with you for a moment, Fräulein Lax?"

Hetti lifted her eyes, shrugged and limped after Herr Zimmermann into Herr Schwarz's office.

"Please sit down, Fräulein Lax," Herr Zimmermann said. She had seen him several times at her sister's home not far from the workshop, where she sometimes stopped after work, but his presence here was baffling.

"I hear wonders of your work, Fräulein," Herr Zimmermann said. "And to tell you the truth, this suit, hand-finished by you, is the best I have ever had."

"Thank you, Herr Zimmermann," Hetti said, confused, but guarded.

She fingered her linen blouse nervously as he continued. "Would you like to work for me?" he asked directly.

"Work for you?" she said slowly, her fingers still rubbing her lapels.

"I have noticed that many people come to Czernowitz to buy clothes," Herr Zimmermann said, "now that travelling to Vienna is not what it used to be. I figure there is good money to be made in women's tailoring and I have decided to put some money into building up a business." He paused and looked into Hetti's eyes. "I would need experts as I am far from one myself. Would you come to work for me as supervisor?"

Hetti looked at Herr Zimmermann. His dark blue suit had obviously been bought at a top fashion house and his black kid boots were soft. His winged collar stood arrogantly beneath his shaven face and his eyes hid deeply in his fat face. Yet his gaze was open, honest.

"When would you be opening and where do you intend to situate your business?" she asked.

"You are very straightforward, Fräulein Lax. I like it," he said. "I intend to open before the end of the year in Herr Friedmann's old shop. Remember Herr Friedmann's tailor shop? The one everyone used to come to from the end of the Empire?"

"My mother bought her first real outfits from Herr Friedmann," Hetti said. "What a beautiful cut."

"Yes, and I intend to capitalise on Herr Friedmann's reputation. He has been closed for some years now but if we call the shop Friedmann and Zimmermann, we may prove an attraction, don't you think?"

"It sounds good to me, Herr Zimmermann," Hetti said. It could be an opportunity to shake herself from the tyranny of the Schwarzes' sweatshop, she thought.

"So you agree? I am so happy, Fräulein Lax," Herr Zimmermann sounded genuinely glad.

"Wait a minute," Hetti heard herself say. "I haven't said anything yet. You haven't told me all I want to know."

In the next ten minutes she questioned Herr Zimmermann as to his plans, his capital, the number of people he intended to employ. He offered to double what Herr Schwarz was paying her and this only as a starting offer and she promised to think it over.

"You drive a hard bargain, Fräulein Lax," Herr Zimmermann said. "I must say I like the spirit. You have a real eye for business."

"I wouldn't go so far, Herr Zimmermann," Hetti said cautiously. "My father has been a failed businessman all his llife and my sister Rosa is married to a shrewd man, but I have learnt the hard way that unless you stick your neck out and find out what your rights are, you only stand to lose."

"How right, Fräulein," Herr Zimmermann said as he rose to leave the office. "I shall be back tomorrow for your answer."

That evening Hetti felt lighter than she had felt for a long time. "I have been offered a real job," she told her movement colleagues that evening. "A job with some promotion prospects and a real salary."

"Look out, girl," said the Czernowitz branch secretary Herschel Hertzberg. "If you are not careful, you will soon smell capitalism and want out of here."

"Don't be a fool, Herschel," she said lightly. "But working in sweatshop conditions helps no one towards more social control."

"On the other hand, you are an asset, Hetti," said Bracha, always there, making tea and taking minutes. "You are the only one who has experienced sweatshop conditions first hand here. You know the movement is rather short on real working-class Jews. If you leave and become a high class couturière, we will have lost this precious contact."

"Always the movement," Hetti said angrily. "What about me, sitting there day after day, finishing beautiful suits which I am not allowed to cut or even sew?"

"Leave the girl alone," Sasha said. He was always coming to her rescue when the others pushed her. Sasha came from Poland and he was organising Jewish youth around the socialist flag, a dangerous job. "She has to move out of the exploitative situation one day. What are we struggling for if not to improve the lot of the working class? When one of us makes a step forward, we should not stop her."

"Whatever you say, I am not staying on with the Schwarzes," Hetti said. "They are revisionists and their son goes to Betar, a bloody Brown Shirt, that's what he is. I hate them and their bourgeois exploitation. This is my opportunity, but it won't stop me working for the movement."

As she spoke, her cheeks filled and her eyes sparkled. She could feel her face brighten and could almost forget her ugly limp. Tonight was to be her night, she decided, as the weekly meeting was starting with members drifting into the shabby office, where pamphlets and papers filled every space.

She spoke a lot that evening. The meeting discussed the usual immigration versus work in the diaspora, a subject she felt strongly about. The revisionists were gaining ground and although the movement squabbled with the three other socialist Jewish groups, they had more in common with the communists than with the hated Brown Shirts. Everyone knew what a brown shirt meant those days.

There was little point, she said, in leaving Romania, where they were needed to convert Jewish youths to trust socialism, and go to Palestine, where they would only be taking land away from the Arabs.

"You are talking like a communist," Bracha said. "How do you equate this with working for that Zimmermann of yours?"

"Oh, do leave me alone, Bracha," Hetti said. "I cannot be both a bourgeois and a communist, you know. It simply doesn't make sense. All I can say is that for the time being, it's better to stay here and work with Jewish youth. I am not saying only capitalists go to Palestine although, mind you, with the cost of certificates, I cannot see real working-class Jews being able to afford it."

"You will soon be saying that the Red Army will save your life?" Bracha said mockingly.

"Don't be stupid, Bracha," Hetti said. "I am just talking of things as they stand now."

"I cannot see much future for us here with Goga as premier," Herschel interrupted what was becoming a power struggle between the two women. "He is a fascist and an anti-semite and you know it as well as we do."

"So what do you suggest we do?" Sasha said. "Run away from him?"

"No, I am not suggesting this at all," Herschel said. "I am only thinking aloud. I only know that my father went to Palestine last month and bought some plots of land, just in case."

"Bravo," Hetti said. "And you are accusing me of capitalism when I accept a better job which gets me out of the clutches of those revisionists?"

"Stop it, comrades," branch chairman Dori said. "This is becoming rather personal. I would like to return the discussion to more constructive lines. We must refrain from arguing amongst ourselves when there is so much work to do. It's bad enough that we argue incessantly with Dror, Gordonia and Hanoar Hatzair. As we said we have a lot of work, firstly in fighting Betar and getting as many youngsters as possible away from the personality cult of that revisionist dictator Jabotinsky."

"At least they don't sit idly doing nothing," said Herschel. "At least they are busy starting illegal immigration to Palestine. I have heard Jabotinsky say when he was last in town, 'If you are not going to Palestine, Yiddische Kinderlach, lernt sich schiessen, teach yourself to shoot.'"

"Bravo, Herschel," Hetti said. "First you feather your nest by acquiring land in Palestine and next you idolise that alarmist arch-Brown Shirt Jabotinsky, despite what brown shirts signify these days."

"I said quit the personal arguments, Comrade Hetti," Dori said firmly. "Any more out of you and you would be ruled out of order. As I was saying, our main task is fighting Betar and Jabotinsky and getting Jewish youth away from them. Secondly, we have to discuss seriously, not on personal lines, whether we concentrate on action here or channel our activities towards immigration, which may mean setting up kibbutzim like the Zionist movement and getting involved in illegal immigration. And if any of you feel compelled to continue your personal arguments, please do so later, after the meeting is over."

Hetti felt the blood flooding her cheeks. Dori was branch chairman, but even he could not stop her from airing her views. She started to speak when she heard a new voice.

"I believe the chairman is right," it said. Hetti turned to look at the speaker, a dark-haired man, his face thin and serious.

"Unfortunately," he continued, "having Goga as premier, the discussion is more than academic. King Carol looks after his own Jews, but there is no one to look after Jews in Bucovina or Bessarabia, as we all know. And the difference between Goga and Jabotinsky, while theoretically negligible, is in practice very substantial. The question is whether we turn more left or stay as we are, more or less ineffectual, vacillating between immigration and action here and never making any real decision."

"Would you please introduce yourself?" Dori turned to the speaker. "I don't remember being asked if you could join this branch meeting."

"Sorry," said the stranger. "The name is Menashe König, formerly Bucharest south. My parents live locally and as my mother is ill, I requested temporary transfer to your branch."

"The transfer request has not yet reached me," Dori mumbled, searching through his papers. "Please inform our secretary of your particulars after the meeting so we can check that everything is in order."

"Of course," König said formally. "As I was saying . . ."

"I think comrade König is right," Hetti said somewhat

142

hurriedly, breaking into the stranger's words. "We have been ineffectual for years debating those eternal questions. While the revisionists are gaining force and organising to start illegal immigration and the Khalutzim are setting up training kibbutzim throughout Romania to prepare for immigration, all we hear from Yishuv leaders like Dr Weitzman and Dr Goldman is, 'oh, it's not so bad, you know Jabotinsky'. So we break up their meetings when they sing Betar songs by singing our songs to prove we are socialists and workers and do damn all else. My view is that we ought to turn more militant among the youth, break down parents' objections and make them see that being merely anständig democratic Zionists is not enough any more."

"What do you suggest that we do in practice?" Dori asked the newcomer, ignoring Hetti's contribution.

"It was pretty obvious from what I said that I believe we should turn more left. The Nazi danger is real, believe you me. The comrades in Bucharest have already realised that. We must organise to form a real left wing opposition to all shades of fascism."

"What do you think we are, communists?" Bracha almost shouted towards König. "Soon there will be no real difference between us and them. That should please you, Hetti."

"Kinder, don't start again," Sasha said. "Comrade König may be right. We ought to debate his suggestion seriously."

"We have debated enough," König said. "Not only here, but throughout Europe, young socialist Jews are debating the eternal question of Zion versus the diaspora. If we don't go to Palestine now, we have to act here. As far as I am concerned, true socialism is the only answer to the Nazi danger. The writing is on the wall."

"Your suggestions may mean breaking up Betar meetings, going on demonstrations, putting our necks on the line, just like the communists?" Dori asked cautiously.

"Yes," König said firmly. "That and other things. We ought to show the youth that, as the comrade here to my left said, being anständig Zionists is not the answer, unless we choose to go to Palestine before it's too late."

"What do you mean too late?" someone asked.

"There is reason to believe that at some stage there will not be pogroms, just like in Russia, or even worse. The Nazis mean what they say and the Romanians and Ukranians would not lag far behind," he said confidently.

"In that case," Herschel said, "the answer must be to go to Palestine now."

"That may be one answer," the newcomer said. "For me, going

to Palestine is not the answer as long as the Arab question is not settled. You cannot simply settle on other people's land. Apart from which, the British are not exactly keeping the doors open."

The discussion that evening was the most heated Hetti could remember. From time to time she found herself reiterating the stranger's strong opinions. Here was one person, she felt, who said eloquently what she had been trying to say for months.

No conclusion had been reached when the meeting broke up for the Hora dancing to begin. Hetti remained seated as usual. The Hora was too much for her bad leg.

"Not dancing?" she heard a voice behind her. She turned around and saw Menashe König smiling at her.

"I never dance the Hora," she said. "I have a bad leg. Childhood polio."

"I don't either," he said, coming to sit beside her. "And I don't even have a bad leg. Don't like it."

"I liked what you said at the meeting," Hetti said. "I am Hetti Lax."

"I know. Made some enquiries."

"What else do you know?"

"Not much. Want to tell me?"

"Not much to tell. I work long hours in a sweatshop and go home to a small room in a Jewish rooming house where the landlady is too reactionary to let me bring in guests," she started. Why am I telling him all this, she panicked. Am I saying I would like to invite him to my room?

"Pity," he said. "I would have asked you to invite me in for a cup of tea." He paused and then said fast, "We can of course have tea in my room. The friend I am living with is not at home tonight."

"I don't suppose I dare come with you to an empty place when I don't even know where you come from or why you are really here," she smiled. "I suppose this is a remnant of my good middle-class Jewish upbringing. Do you find it reactionary?"

"Never mind how I find it. We all come from reactionary Jewish households and we all fear that word, reactionary," he smiled back, his eyes hard and dark. "And you are perfectly right not to trust a stranger."

Hetti laughed. "I would like to make you a cup of tea, Hetti Lax," he said. "And I will tell you why I am here while the kettle boils."

Hetti felt confused. This is a comrade, she thought, there should be no question of bourgeois conventions here. If you want to go with someone, go, she told herself. You have always gone with people when you wanted to before.

Aloud she said. "I suppose I'll go with you, Menashe König. After all you are a comrade."

Menashe's dark hair glistened in the dull electric light and his brown eyes danced as he extended his hand to Hetti. "Come, comrade Lax. I have good Russian tea in my room, especially sent from Moscow." He laughed and Hetti laughed with him.

"My room is by the Ringplatz," Menashe said. "Not too far." He slipped his arm under Hetti's elbow and she found walking with him through the snow-laced streets comforting.

Menashe stopped in front of a low apartment house. "This is where my friend Sigi lives, but he is away tonight."

Hetti went up the two flights of stairs slowly, with Menashe one step behind all the time. "You do live in style," she said as she entered the large livingroom, where books were stacked on shelves along the four walls. "So many books. Are they all yours?"

"Some are. Most are Sigi's."

The room was exactly what Hetti had been trying to achieve in her little furnished room, where she stacked books on shelves slung on bricks she got Rosa to get for her from the sawmill. Like Sigi, she had several political posters, but, unlike him, she didn't dare display Marx's bearded face, which, like always, reminded her of the stories grandfather had told her about Moses and the stone tablets.

"May I take your coat?" Menashe said behind her back, startling her, sliding her black coat off her shoulders and inviting her, with a wide gesture, to sit on the velvet-covered armchair. "I see you are mesmerised by Siegmund's unorthodox taste in political posters?"

"Well, I could not have displayed this in my room, my landlady would have thrown me out," she said. "But I do admire the old gentleman, despite the movement's Zionism and despite Bracha jumping every time she thinks someone utters anything which remotely reeks of communism."

She said this lightly, but Menashe was serious when he answered. "Nationalism is the number one enemy of Marxism. That much is clear. And to tell you the truth, I am sick and tired of the movement's soft policy on immigration. The time to act is now, not sometime in an unclear future. Here, not on the shores of some imaginary Kinneret."

"I couldn't agree more," she said. "It's been hard to find supporters in the Czernowitz cell. Perhaps with you here, things will change."

Menashe's face softened into a smile. "I am going to make that famous tea now, Hetti Lax, before we turn this into an extension of the meeting."

"But it's important, don't you think?" She limped after him to the kitchen, where she stood at the door watching him fill the kettle and prepare two cups on a tray. "This business of postponing any serious analysis until we immigrate is hampering the movement's progress. Young Jewish socialists should get involved in the struggle for socialism in this country amongst Jews and non-Jews alike."

"I fully agree, comrade. Which is why I invited you here this evening," Menashe said. "Would madam follow me into the room where her tea will be served?"

"I cannot make out whether you are serious or mocking me," Hetti said. But she couldn't feel angry with this strange man, whose eyes were caressing her face, while his words were concealing more than they revealed.

"I am serious and I am mocking myself," Menashe said. "I have been trying to take myself seriously for years. And one of the things I must do now is decide whether I am staying in this godforsaken town or moving to somewhere big. Like Paris. Or London."

"Oh. We do talk big, don't we?" It was her turn to mock. "What are you doing here, then, if you are considering Paris or London?"

"It's a long story. I'll tell you some other time," Menashe said. "Will you come again?"

"I haven't left yet," Hetti said. "You can start."

"As I said, it's a long story." Menashe sounded tired. Hetti longed to put her arm around his shoulder, shuddering at the thought. "I am tired tonight. It has been a long day."

"A long day doing what?"

"It's part of the story. My family got me back to keep an eye on me and got me a job at a local sawmill."

"It isn't Mendel Heller's sawmill?" Hetti asked.

"No. But we do business with the Hellers. Why? You know them?"

"Mendel is my brother-in-law. What a bourgeois."

"I have met worse," Menashe said.

"Yes. Like the Schwarzes, my employers," Hetti said. " But I was offered a new job today. And I think I am going to accept it."

She told Menashe about Herr Zimmermann's offer. "Take it. Don't hesitate. Never mind what the jealous comrades are saying." His voice was cheerful yet Hetti felt a weariness.

"I think I'll go now," she said. "You are tired and I have to rise early tomorrow morning for another exhausting day at the sweatshop, which, I hope, will be one of my last."

"I shall see you home," Menashe said and rose to meet her plump figure, extending his arms and pulling her fast towards him, kissing her fully on the lips.

Hetti closed her eyes and responded to his probing tongue. He held her tight with one arm while his other hand caressed her hair. Then, as suddenly as he pulled her to him, he let her go. "I'll take you home," said his voice, strained, "I hope you don't consider this an uncomradely gesture."

Hetti said nothing. It's not a bit bourgeois, she kept thinking, to act on desire. Not a bit bourgeois.

Then she swung away. Menashe said again, his voice less strained, "Let me take you home, Hetti Lax."

They walked the short way to her rooming house in silence. When they reached the house, Menashe said, "I can get you a poster of Karl. All you have to do is say the word."

"The word must be please, I suppose."

"Your manners are impeccable, Fräulein," Menashe said, the mockery back in his voice.

"My mother would not entirely agree, but I know what you mean," Hetti laughed.

"When do you finish work tomorrow?"

"At half past five."

"I'll meet you at Feldmann's dairy at six," he said, matter of fact, not asking if she wanted to see him again.

"At six then," she said and turned to go up the stairs to her room.

By the time she saw Rosa on Friday night, Hetti was bursting with news. There was the job offer from Zimmermann, which she accepted and was about to start on the first of the month. And there was Menashe.

But Rosa did not ask for her news. When Hetti arrived after work that Friday, she met with an angry Rosa.

"I must go to Cirlibaba when the snows melt," she said as soon as Hetti set foot in the apartment. "Mother is not feeling well."

"What happened?"

"I don't know," Rosa said, distracted. "I received a strange letter today. She has been feeling poorly for a few months now. She is not getting younger, you know. I must see to her."

"Why can't Hanna go for a change?" Hetti asked. "You are always taking it upon yourself to worry about us all."

"You've noticed, then?" Rosa said bitterly. "I thought you'd never say so."

"Look, Rosa. I know what you have done over the years, looking after father and mother and Mendel and the children and me. Don't you think it's time to stop and look after yourself?

When was the last time you and Mendel took a holiday?"

Rosa stared at her sister. "I must be hearing things," she said harshly. "You know it is the first time you have ever expressed concern?"

"It may be because I feel happy," Hetti said, her voice small, almost shy.

"Hetti, Hetti. Oy my God. Let's sit down," she pulled her plump sister by the arm towards the sofa. "Tell me about about it. What's his name?"

"You are incorrigible, Rosa. Don't you think there is anything in life for women apart from catching an eligible bachelor?"

"Don't tell me that politics make you so happy," Rosa said. "if it is, I don't want to know."

"But everything is political, Rosl," Hetti smiled.

"Oh." Rosa got up to leave the sofa when Hetti pulled her back. "Don't go, Rosl. There is a man. Also."

"Hetti. Hetti, what wonderful news. Tell me. Who is it? Do we know him?" Rosa started towards the adjoining room. "Mendel, come here. Hetti has good news to tell us."

"Wait," Hetti's voice cut the air. "Don't rush me. I am not getting married, or anything like this."

"Excuse me, I was so worried about mother I have forgotten my good sense. Mendel does not seem to have heard me. I suppose he has fallen asleep on the armchair. He is always so tired these days. Do tell me and I promise to keep quiet."

"Well, as I said, everything is political. First of all there is my job. I am leaving Schwarz."

"Leaving Schwarz? Hetti, you have gone mad. It is this man, ! know. He is a dangerous communist and has incited you to leave a perfectly good job and . . ."

"Calm down, Rosa. You know I wouldn't leave just like that. As a matter of fact, I have got an excellent offer from your friend, Herr Zimmermann."

"Manfred Zimmermann? What is this all about?"

"He came the other day when I was finishing his suit. That cow, Schwarz, who never stops chiding me, suddenly praised my work in front of Herr Zimmermann, who seemed well pleased with the suit and offered me a job as a supervisor in a new business he is opening in old Herr Friedmann's tailor shop."

"Old Herr Friedmann's tailor shop? Hetti, how wonderful."

"Remember mother's stories about going there to buy her engagement outfits with grandma Lax aleha ha shalom?"

"Do I remember? And now you are going to work there? Hetti, mother will be so pleased. I shall write to her immediately."

"Maybe this will be sufficient to make her feel better. You know how lonely she gets with only father around now that Haim has gone to Cluj to be apprenticed to Onkel Duvid."

"Maybe you are right. But tell me, when are you starting? And how much is he paying you?"

"I am starting on the first of the month. You should have seen Schwarz's face when he heard. Herr Zimmermann himself came to get my answer and he himself told Schwarz about it. Life became worth living just to see his face. 'But of course, Herr Zimmermann, you are getting a great worker. But, Herr Zimmermann, you are depriving us of our best asset.' The arse-licking pig."

"Hetti," Rosa started, but on meeting Hetti's eyes, they both burst out laughing. "But you haven't yet told me about this man. You don't want to tell me Herr Zimmermann made a pass at you? You know he is married."

"I wouldn't allow him to make a pass at me if he was the last man on earth. Too bourgeois for my liking."

"Nu, tell me who this man is. The suspense is killing me."

"I met him three days ago in the movement."

"In the movement? You know them all for ages."

"I know. But this one is new. One Menashe König. From Gura Humorlui and then Bucharest."

"And?"

"And what? We met, we liked each other. My limp didn't seem to make any difference. The politics match. He is as dissatisfied with the movement as I am ..."

"You are going to quit. I am so happy. Maybe at long last you are beginning to grow up."

"But you don't understand. The movement is too soft for my liking. And Menashe agrees."

"Menashe? Three days and already he is not Herr König?"

"Never was. Comrades are not Herrs, Rosa. It's time you knew this."

It took some time after the Friday night meal and grace to explain to Mendel how she was going to reconcile working for the arch bourgeois Zimmermann with falling for an arch leftist. Mendel asked many questions but Hetti was too happy to mind her upright brother-in-law, whose opinions she regarded as extremely reactionary. He was, she had to admit, charitable. But charity, she often said, did not compensate for political inaction or worse, political action for the wrong cause.

Later that evening the conversation turned to Palestine. "We can get a certificate," Carla said, "but father would not go as yet."

"There is time enough," Mendel said. "For the time being, the

Romanians are letting us live. Even Goga is not as bad as I feared. So what's the rush?"

"I keep hearing about the Iron Guard at school," Carla said. Herbert, who was completely absorbed in his chess board, where he was trying moves by himself, nodded. "In our school some boys were beaten up the other day and someone said it was the Guard," he said. "But then someone else said it was just a personal vendetta. How do you know?"

"There is a lot of work to be done here, with the Guard on one hand and Jabotinsky's revisionists on the other," Hetti said. "This is what I keep saying in the movement. Lots of work before we run to Palestine."

"You know I don't mean it like that, Hetti," Mendel said, his voice kind as always. "I mean that there is no real reason to flee. But I thought I would take Carla for a visit. What do you say, Rosa?"

"Oh, papa, that'd be wonderful," Carla said, her long blond hair glistening in the brightly lit room.

"I say yes," Rosa said. "You need a holiday, Mendel. You have been working too hard."

"And you?" Hetti said sharply. "Don't you need a holiday too?"

"I will go to mother when the snows melt and see how she is and she will make me her famous cheese buchtels and hang milk for me to be made into curd cheese and I shall pick wild flowers and sleep."

"Nonsense, you are just making excuses," Hetti said and the two laughed nervously.

*　　*　　*

Menashe König leaned against the wall in the movement office, listening to the endless discussions about the Purim celebrations. Hetti watched his alert eyes following the discussion in which she did not participate. Suddenly she heard his voice, sharp, confident.

"I have decided, comrades. The movement has no place for me any more."

His words were followed by a stunned silence. No one said anything and Menashe continued, "You are wasting your time and mine with sterile discussions about worthless celebrations which are no more than bourgeois manifestations of traditions which have not brought our nation one step forward from bondage and the inequitable position which we find ourselves in almost thirty years after the great revolution."

"But Menashe," Sacha said. "You have just arrived. You

cannot leave now that we are beginning to get things together, largely thanks to you."

"Getting things together doing what?" Menashe's voice was hard. "Getting youngsters from assimilated homes to identify themselves as Zionists? Socialist Zionists alright, but Zionists all the same. For many years I have failed to understand that our nationalism is as bad as other nations' nationalism, a real obstacle on the road to true internationalism, true socialism. Now I understand and the time has come for me to move out."

"And do what?" Bracha asked.

"I have not yet mapped my political way, but it is certainly turning left, comrade Bracha. I wish you and your Purim celebrations every success."

"So do I," Hetti heard her own voice. "I am leaving too."

"But Hetti," Herschel said. "You cannot change your political path just because of a man you have met only a few weeks ago."

"Don't but Hetti me," she said firmly. "You know I have been unhappy about the movement's policy for a long time. I refer you to the minutes over the past six months. Menashe König just happened to come along at the right moment."

"I knew you would be selling your soul when you took the job with that society tailor," Bracha said.

"What nonsense, Bracha," Hetti said, her contempt thinly disguised.

She limped out after Menashe, whose gait was sure, almost too fast, following him to Sigi's flat.

"You didn't have to do this," he said softly as they were walking up the wintry Herrengasse.

"I know. It was something I wanted to do for a long time now. I needed you to do it first. Where would I have gone had I done it before you came?"

"You could have gone where we are going together, tomorrow."

"And where is that?"

"I have been approached by the Romanian Communist Party."

"You never said."

"I saw no reason to compromise you," he said. "I want you always to make up your own mind."

"Having just told me we are going together to the party tomorrow was not exactly letting me make up my own mind," she teased.

"I am sorry, comrade, you are quite right," he said, his smile a mixture of mockery and softness. "Would you like to come with me to meet the comrades and discuss their offer?"

"I will have to think it over. They are, after all, illegal, aren't they?"

151

"You think it over, Hetti Lax. I won't talk about it with you now, I don't want to influence your choice." He extended his arm to encircle her full waist. "Come. Sigi is coming home tomorrow. It may be our last chance."

"Our last chance?" she whispered but his hand covered her lips as he pulled her towards the bedroom. In the blue street light pouring through the shutters she watched Menashe unbuttoning her sweater and smoothing his large, dry hands over her breasts.

What followed was a confused, yet sharp memory. Under Sigi's feather bed, Menashe's hungry hands caressed every cell of her warm skin. His lips followed the contours of her full body, whispering words of desire in her ears. She followed his touch, abandoning herself to the pleasure, moaning lightly as he touched her hips, her thighs, her inner secrets, covering her with kisses, awakening a burning desire, a painful longing, a heat.

"Give yourself to me, I want your newness, your heat," he whispered very near her ear when she could contain the heat no longer.

"I won't penetrate you," he said softly as her screams weakened and became soft moans again. "Not until you know more. You are so new. So innocent."

"Please," she beseeched him, "please."

"Not yet, Hetti. There is a lot more to come," he said as his white body rose to sit beside her under Sigi's feather cover. He turned to look at her face on the pillow beside him. "You look so vulnerable in the moonlight, comrade. What have you been all my life?" his words slick, those of a womaniser suddenly.

I don't understand this, she thought. Why me? The pleasure was too great, the pain too deep.

"I have been right here," she said, her voice barely audible above her panic. "But you, where have you been? You can start by telling me your story, the whole story. The night is young and if the story is long, I have the time and tomorrow Sigi returns." As she said this, her voice resumed its usual confidence.

"You are right. The time has come to tell you. You may not find it as amazing as all that but before we become a couple, you must know everything," he said, his voice delicately balancing mockery and compassion.

"I was a late arrival," he started, talking softly and rhythmically, as if telling an ancient legend. "Mother, they say, did not show her face in town when she became pregnant with me. After all, my brothers were old enough to be my fathers. I was a mistake, they kept saying. What a start."

School was boring, even in Hungary where they fled during the war. "Just like us," Hetti said. "We too . . ." she started, then stopped when she saw Menashe's face, turned into himself, a world of his own.

"Already in Hungary I knew their world was not mine. Mother called me the leader of the opposition, laughingly, but she was right, even then," his voice trailed.

He would wake up every morning, get ready to go to school but never make it. "The streets were fascinating. Do you remember everyone used to speak of Golden Bistritsa? Well, it wasn't golden, but there were opportunities. I would walk the streets and meet other boys just like me, outcasts in a nation of outcasts, looking for trading possibilities in the streets of this useful place."

After a while, the teachers sent word to his parents asking why the boy was not at school. The Heder teacher too was angry. "Everyone else was studying their Torah apart from me. But I was fascinated with the Torah, learnt to read faster than the others and came to Heder as often as it took to learn to read and write Hebrew. My ambition was to learn Hebrew well so I could go to Palestine as soon as I could."

His father did not take too kindly to the discovery that the boy was not at school. "He used to send my brothers, both young men, big and strong, to school with me. They made sure I was handed over to the teacher. It became complicated to return to the streets. Already then, I knew more than my contemporaries."

One of his pastimes, when he managed to escape school, was the public library, where he devoured books in Hungarian and Romanian and later in French and English. He became a regular scholar, deep in thought, never socialising with boys from good families, preferring the company of street boys, who knew where to find valuables they could trade on street markets. By the time the family returned to Bucovina, Menashe was a ten-year-old drop out.

"From then on, I could not manage school any more, barely passing from one class to the next. Father returned to his prosperous business, spending a large chunk of his money on grinds for his wayward mistake. By that stage, father and mother were pretty sure I was a mistake, a thorn in their flesh, different from anything they had ever come across."

Life in Gura Humorlui was quiet. He was 12 when Hashomer Hatsair recruited him and the movement took most of his free time. "It was here I learnt what jarred in father's way of life.

Selling, buying, dependent on world finance, ups and downs. In a word, I was beginning to realise the evils of capitalism."

Then one year the movement had no place for meetings. "The Jewish community took away our meeting place. And the party, the communists that is, offered us their hall for meetings and from here to becoming members of the Young Communists the road was not long."

"But," Hetti said, "you are not a member now?"

Menashe laughed and continued. "The big crash left father in depression. Just shows you what world capitalism is all about. He never managed to get things off the ground again. What a sight he is, sitting in Gura Humorlui, old before his time, minding mother, who spends her time sitting by the kitchen stove, mumbling to herself about better days. I tried to tell them that money which comes from international sources, tied to the big banks, is no good. But they didn't listen. I was the leader of the opposition, after all, the wayward mistake.

"Yes, they kept reminding me I had been a mistake, a last-minute complication. My brothers could not forget it either. They kept telling me to shut up and stop annoying father. And where do you think they are now when father is all alone? Safe in Palestine, never sparing a thought for father and mother and I, the mistake, am back in Bucovina, to try and help with what little I have."

His first arrest came before his father lost his fortune. "They came for me one evening and searched the house. When they found *Das Kapital*, they decided to arrest me. They had no other proof, but you know the Guard, they don't need proof. I was in the county jail for 24 hours with most of my comrades from the Humora cell. Then father arrived and bailed me out. I suppose he oiled the palm of the commanding officer. I was never tried and that seemed to be the end of that."

That was before the big crash. What came after was even worse. In 1931, very soon after his father suffered the big loss, Menashe was conscripted. "You can imagine the King's army was the last thing I wanted to serve at. The Red Army perhaps, but the idea of fitting in, obeying orders, sleeping in one room with many country yokels, that was not for me."

After the crash, his father did not have the wherewithal to bribe the right people before conscription and Menashe had no option but to enlist. "It was the worst time of my life. It was dirty and they were cruel. More so to Jews. For the first time I felt the severity of what it means to be a Jew in this filthy country of ours. I even joined forces with yeshiva boys. We formed minyans and prayed to escape morning duties and were beaten up for it. Just like the stories one hears about the Czar's army before the revolution when Jewish boys were kidnapped to serve and were tortured for their religious practices."

A rebel since childhood, Menashe planned his desertion very carefully. "It was on our first free weekend. I came to visit father and mother in Gura Humorlui. My brothers had already left for Palestine and were living in Jerusalem, one practising medicine, the other trying his hand in business. Mother felt lonely and looked awful. How is my soldier, she asked, trying to sound humorous, the despair deep in her voice. When I heard her, I decided it was time to leave."

That evening, he told his parents he was going to meet some friends. Instead he took the train to Marmorosh-Siget, to the border with Russia and Czechoslovakia. "The idea was to cross the border into the Soviet Union. They would look after me, I thought, if only I told them my story. After all, the party was proscribed and still is in this godforsaken country and the Russians know how to look after their own."

In Marmorosh he met an old girlfriend who made him change his mind. "It was silly. I should have crossed the border to Russia as planned, but she persuaded me to go to Prague with her." He needed money and telegraphed his parents. "Poor mother, she had some savings which she convinced father to give me. She arrived at the border, looking frail, wrapped in a kerchief like a peasant woman. It was not easy to find the money you wanted, she whispered. You have always been so much trouble, but I persuaded father to let you have this money. After all, we didn't make life easy for you, always talking of you as our big mistake. She shook as she spoke and what could I do but hug her and cry?"

In Prague, living in one room with Miriam, he made a living giving grinds in all the subjects he never wanted to study at school. "It was a good time, Prague is the most beautiful city in Europe. We will go there one day, you and I."

Hetti did not look at his face as he continued, "But it could not last. I had no permit and the police gave me thirty days to leave."

Again it was the family who came to the rescue. His brother managed to arrange for a certificate to emigrate to Palestine. "Another capitalist ploy, I now know. Only the rich can go, it costs one thousand pounds sterling, can you imagine? But big brother, through his Zionist connections, managed to procure one, much to the consternation of the Prague Jewish community, who believed that people who have been working for the cause should get priority."

"And Miriam?" Hetti asked, fearing his answer.

"Miriam had already gone long before I received the certificate. The same way she had run into me, she ran into another old boyfriend in Prague one day and decided to move in with him. I can't say I cried too much."

His brother tried to get him to settle down in Jerusalem. But Jerusalem was restless. There was much unrest between Jews and Arabs and Menashe made his way to the party. That seemed the only thing to do. During the day he worked in a factory and at night he took part in political meetings.

"These were exciting times. You felt the country was on the verge of something. So many idealists and so little practicality, so little reality. Of course, the Zionists were winning and the Arabs were badly organised. We tried to help them get organised and one night, while distributing literature in the old city, I was caught by the British."

The British did not have internment places for people like Menashe. They interned Zionists who were clearly anti-British in one place but were at a loss what to do with Jews who were both anti-British and anti-Zionist. "They decided to deport a group of us. I was the only Romanian citizen and because I had deserted here, I could not return and agreed with a group of friends to meet in Paris. Each travelled separately. It was safer."

The British put him on a ship and he disembarked in Greece. "I ended up in Salonika, where the Jewish community looked after me. Ironically, they were enthusiastic about me having just returned from Palestine." But they too could not organise a permit for him and his plan was to travel via Yugoslavia to Paris.

"Unfortunately, the king of Yugoslavia was due to visit Greece and the border was tightly guarded. There was nothing to do but go through Bulgaria."

He was hungry and exhausted. "I was penniless after months of travelling and I could not see straight for sleeplessness. I hadn't slept for a week when I decided to go to the Romanian embassy and give myself up. I was too tired to think of excuses so I simply said I was a deserter and I wanted to come home."

It was 1935 and the political climate in Romania was bad. As a deserter, Menashe was jailed as soon as he hit Romanian soil. Again, he informed his family and as soon as his mother heard, she persuaded his father to let her go to the Bulgarian border, where he was held. "There was no more money for bribes, but mother arrived, old and ill, to plead with the general. She told me afterwards, I said I was old and sick and needed you to look after me. What irony, you have given us nothing but tsores. The general was apparently moved. Lucky he wasn't an anti-semite like the rest. They allowed me to complete my service, providing

I didn't misbehave and this saved me another jail sentence.

"When I finished the service last year, it was clear I didn't know where I was going. Father's sawmill was going badly, and he had no work for me. The party was proscribed even more arduously now that Goga was in power, so with their approval, I rejoined your movement and was sent to work with youth in Bucharest, all the time liaising with the party."

"You mean to say that all the time you were a party member?" Hetti said.

"Why does that surprise you?"

The grey dawn light stole through the shutters and Hetti knew Menashe was what she had been waiting for through years of obstinate, socially unacceptable spinsterhood.

She stroked Menashe's hair and said determinedly, "Nothing would surprise me after tonight."

"You are an extraordinary woman," Menashe whispered. His hands moved along her body, beginning their journey afresh. "An extraordinary woman," he whispered infinitely softly as he penetrated her, sharp, yet slow.

Hetti felt tears run down her cheeks but could not hear herself cry. Pain and pleasure ran through her spine, intense, as he took her. "Now you know me and I know you," he whispered very close to her ear. "Always."

*   *   *

Hetti collected the finished garments from the two machinists and steamed the seam before she laid them out, ready for fitting in the morning. "Is everything alright, Fräulein Lax?" Frau Lerner asked as she prepared to leave for home.

"Everything is perfect, dear. You go home and I'll lock up," Hetti said. "You too, Martin," she urged the second machinist, who usually delayed for a chat after work. "Off you go. I am in a hurry tonight."

Martin, a sheepish look in his eyes, smiled briefly and moved to button his jacket. "Nice work, Herr Martin," Hetti said. "You are coming along fine. I should soon be able to ask Herr Zimmermann for a rise for you." The boy smiled and backed out of the shop.

Hetti cast a last look around. "Everything is in order," she thought, "as usual." She drew the curtain which covered the changing rooms and looked at herself in the full-length mirror. Then she took off the dark red wool jacket she had made for herself here and put on a light grey silk jacket, which she had copied last week from a French magazine Herr Zimmermann brought from Lyons.

She took a diamond brooch out of her purse and pinned it on her lapel. Her head tilted sideways, she looked at her face in the fitting room mirror. "Mm. Could do with some powder and rouge. Looking a bit pale today, aren't we?"

Menashe said not to get overdressed, but what do men know about these things anyway, she thought as she daubed rouge and lipstick. "Yes. That is decidedly better." She fumbled in her purse again and brought out a crumpled white silk rose which she tried pinning on her lapel. "No. The brooch will have to do," she heard herself say aloud as she stuck the rose absentmindedly back into her purse. She then put on a light grey hat, a tiny creation with a silvery net covering her eyes. "Mm, not bad at all," she smiled.

She peered nervously at the workshop clock. "Four o'clock already. Where is he?" she thought as she heard the doorbell ring.

She curbed an urge to run to the door. "Pull yourself together, comrade," she thought, then started laughing. Still laughing, she opened the door to see Menashe, in his only good suit, handing her a small bouquet of lilies.

"Küss die hand, Fräulein Lax. You are looking lovely this evening," said his lightly mocking voice.

"And you, Herr König," she was still laughing.

"Shall we?" He offered her his arm and they marched arm in arm, to the communal office, where Herr Mutz, rabbinical registrar, performed the ceremony, in the presence of two witnesses, Mendel Heller and Siegmund Apfelbaum and of guests who could not be called upon to witness a marriage, the bride's sister, Rosa Heller, her niece Carla Heller, women, and her nephew Herbert Heller, minor.

When the benedictions were over and Menashe had betrothed Hetti according to the laws of Moses and Israel, he stamped his foot on a wineglass, wrapped with old newspapers, breaking it to commemorate the destruction of the temple.

"Mazel tov," cried Rosa, who throughout the ceremony wiped tears with her linen handkerchief. "Mazel tov," cried Mendel, his hand firmly on his hip, looking tall and benevolent. "Mazel tov," cried Sigi, hiding his sarcasm better than on most occasions. "Mazel tov," said Carla, stealing a look at her plump aunt, who looked so happy and "Mazel tov," her brother Herbert added his voice too.

Menashe kissed Hetti under the makeshift Chuppa, held by four community good-for-nothings, employed by the rabbinical registrar on such occasions. Hetti closed her eyes and opened her lips to feel his warm kiss. "Mazel tov," she thought. "You have got him, despite his objection to stupid bourgeois ceremonies. You are his wife now, girl."

Their guests clapped impatiently. "Nu Menashe, there will be plenty of time for this, now we have the party," she heard Sigi's voice.

"No," said her sister's voice. "First the telegrams."

Menashe and she parted and smiled into each other's eyes. When they had discussed the wedding, they both agreed they weren't going to invite their parents or their large families.

"You know what joy it will bring mother, in her state of health," Rosa argued.

"We'll send them a telegram," was Hetti's reply. "And to Menashe's parents too."

"Oy, what a heartless girl you are, Hetti," Rosa sighed. "Always have been."

Now she urged the little party to the telegram office, which was about to close.

"Married Menashe König, formerly of Gura Humorlui. Very happy," read Hetti's telegram to Anschel and Dora Lax in Cirlibaba.

"Married Hetti Lax, formerly of Cirlibaba. Very happy," read his to his parents in Gura Humorlui.

"Oy kinderlach, you are a heartless lot," Rosa said again as the little party prepared to enter Der Schwarze Adler for their celebratory dinner, paid for by Mendel.

"Stop fretting, Rosl, and enjoy yourself," Hetti said lightly. "This is my first and last wedding."

The following morning, as she helped Frau Dorner try the suits prepared the evening before, she could hear Herr Zimmermann enter the workshop.

"Gnädige Frau," he said cursorily to Frau Lerner. "Good morning, Herr Martin," he said to the youth. "Where is Frau König?"

"Good morning, Herr Zimmermann," she said smilingly, two pins stuck in her lips. "I see you are well briefed."

"I am always well briefed and you had better step into my office." Herr Zimmermann's face did not bear the usual pleasant smile he reserved for his dealings with her.

"Of course, Herr Zimmermann," she said. "As soon as Frau Dorner's fitting is over." Frau Dorner, looking at her youthful figure in the mirror, admiring the slim-skirted suit she had on, said dreamily, "Did I hear him calling you Frau? Now, now, Fräulein Lax, you haven't gone and done something foolish last night?"

Hetti smiled and said nothing. "Really, Fräulein. I would expect better things from you. You know marriage spoils a woman's figure, particularly as soon as she has children. How I wish I had my figure back but that, unfortunately, is not to be." She laughed nervously. "What do you think? I think you have done a wonderful job, as usual. The cut is superb and the cloth sits simply perfectly."

"You look ravishing," Hetti said. "But then you'd look wonderful in anything."

"Now, now, don't be flattering me. That won't do. Don't you think the skirt could do with a tiny bit of lengthening?"

"If you wish, but to me this length is just perfect. Hems are going up a little, I read. And you have got the legs. It's not as if we are talking about a short skirt here."

"Ah, very good," Frau Dorner's lovely face twisted into a reluctant smile. "I'll pick the suits up on Friday morning. I need them for the weekend. We are going out of town."

"Fine," Hetti said, watching Frau Dorner get out of the suit and stand in her silk-stockinged feet in the fitting room.

"Thank you," Frau Dorner said as Hetti saw her to the door, "Frau, what was it, König?"

Hetti nodded, her face, she thought, breaking into a silly smile.

Herr Zimmermann was sitting at her desk when she entered the office. "Congratulations, Frau König," he said, his voice almost threatening.

"Thank you," she said. "Is anything the matter?"

"I am not talking about not being informed. After all your private affairs are your private affairs," Herr Zimmermann started. "But I start to worry when you, my prized supervisor, are getting married to a well-known political agitator."

"Oh, that," Hetti said, suddenly tired, the wine she had had the night before dulling her thoughts.

"Look here, Fräulein, excuse me, Frau König," Herr Zimmermann continued. "It's not that I am conservative, I have had my differences with community leaders in my time. But I do not get into trouble. Political trouble that is. I know Herr König and I am afraid I do not approve of what I know. These are volatile times and the Fascists are on the lookout for people like him. I don't want any trouble here, do you understand?"

"Perfectly," Hetti said. "Do you wish me to quit?"

"God forbid, of course not. Without you the whole business collapses," Herr Zimmermann said. "But please, please be careful."

"I am not sure what you are talking about, but I promise that you will not be involved in anything political, not from my end of things anyway," Hetti said.

"As long as you know what you are doing, Frau König, as long as you don't take unnecessary risks."

Hetti laughed when she told Menashe what Herr Zimmermann had said.

"What do you expect? He has heard I am a communist and he is afraid his precious business will come into disrepute," Menashe laughed.

"What he does not know is that soon the whole thing will collapse. If the Munich painter does half of what he promised, we are all done for, Jew and communist alike. We have only one way out and that is to follow the Soviets."

6

Rosa 1940

"The Russians will look after us," Menashe König said to his sister-in-law, having just mopped up the aspic from his geffülte carp. "I know them. When they come, there will be no more persecution. Everyone who works will be looked after."

"And what about people like me?" Rosa said, serving him her famous beef stew and topping it with a big bread knödel. "Women like me who look after their families but who don't go out to work like I have since the children were born? I hear they send people like me to do factory work. Have you heard such nonsense?"

"It won't come to that," Mendel said, waving his hand to say he didn't want a second knödel. "You know the Russians, Menashe, but I know the Romanians. Since we have been under Romanian rule, I have gradually discovered they all have their price. Even in King Carol's government, every minister has his price, His Eminence included. He is partner to more enterprises than he can count, if you know what I mean. They all take what they can get. And after all, Romania is a neutral country, unlike your Russia."

"Neutral shmeutral," Hetti said, swallowing a particularly big piece of beef and wiping her mouth with one of Rosa's damask napkins. "Neutral here means on the side of the axis. You forget to take into consideration Romania's anti-semitism. In Bucharest, they tell me, there is already a considerable German presence and German agents have settled all over the country, buying grain at double price through the Iron Guard to convince the peasants and the politicians that Germany is on Romania's side. And all the time preparing to take over Romanian oil."

Hetti stopped, looked aside at Menashe and continued. "We are supposed to believe the Guard has been run to ground. But to be perfectly honest, I am not sure I agree with Menashe about good old uncle Stalin looking after us. After all, he is fighting alongside Hitler."

"But Hetti, you know as much as I do that Russia knows what she is doing," Menashe said so determinedly that Rosa had to sit up. "Dialectically, Stalin is simply biding his time."

Hetti shot him a look. Must have had these arguments many times before, those two, Rosa thought. Always having major political debates, using words she didn't even know existed.

Aloud she said, "In Romania, nothing is certain any more. The Romanians don't want to know about us Jews. Such greedy people. And now we live in fear of either a Nazi or a Russian invasion."

"It's always give and take with the Romanians," Mendel said, smiling. "We give, they take. When the Guard was powerful in

1937, the greenshirts came round collecting and Jewish firms were made to give twice or three times more than all the others."

"And what do we get in return?" Rosa said. "Anti-Jewish laws and pogroms. Nice people," she sighed.

"Speaking of Stalin," Herbert said, wiping his plate clean with a thick slice of challah, "our history teacher makes us sing his glory at school. Crazy asking Jews to praise this alliance. But then he has never been enamoured of the semitic race."

"Your teacher or Stalin?" Carla said.

"Both, I suppose. Our history teacher is a real swine. The other day he made poor Bercovich stand in his stockinged feet for three hours just because he did not finish his essay on the Thirty Years' War. The Thirty Years' War, I ask you. Who wants to know when we are in the middle of this one?"

"The punishment is somewhat harsh, but just because there is a war on, it does not mean you can neglect your studies," Mendel said. "The only thing you can be sure of is your education, nothing else is very sure these days."

Herbert shrugged. No point in arguing with his quiet, determined father.

"Anyway," Menashe said quietly, as if to himself, despairing of persuading his wife's reactionary family, "Hitler is helping the fight against capitalism."

"How can you say that?" Rosa burst out. "Just because Stalin is on his side, it does not make him right. What are you waiting for? If he continues to go the way he has gone so far, he will soon occupy the rest of Europe now that he has Czechoslovakia, Poland, not to mention Austria. If only Romania had stayed in the Empire, we would have been far better off."

"Nonsense," Menashe said. "If we had, we'd be part of the Reich by now. Anyway, the days of imperialism are over. Only the British have not heard this as yet. Europe's economy is so out-dated. Look at this country. Only a tenth of the population works, mostly for a pittance. And instead of being able to live off the fat of this rich land, they pay thousands of lei for everything they buy.

"This country could feed the rest of Europe but look at how poor people are. Now if the Russians come here, things will have to improve. Not only will they stop harassing the Jews, they will also improve the general conditions in this country, putting an end to the appalling poverty of the peasants and the urban poor and getting rid of the Boyars."

Rosa looked at her family around the Shabbat table. Mendel in his dark suit. Well groomed as ever, if somewhat tired. No wonder. With his worries. Good job I have managed to persuade him to buy those certificates. He had to sell some shares to buy them, but they may be our only ticket to freedom. There is no knowing what those crazy Romanian fascists will do next.

Carla, now eighteen. Fast becoming a lovely young woman. Pity about that man. She had to attach herself to that most unsuitable medical student. Handsome, yes, but penniless and without any family connections to speak of. Carla spent hours out. Ice skating in the park in the afternoons. Endless cups of black coffee on Herrengasse and at night partying madly with those dark-eyed students. I should have listened to her when she begged me to let her enrol at the university to study languages. She spoke English and French so fluently. And, after her visit to Tel Aviv last summer, her Hebrew seemed good enough to Rosa, whose linguistic talents were, she admitted sadly, somewhat limited.

Next, she cast her maternal eye on Herbert. Too serious for his age. Brilliant at maths and physics. She had high hopes for that boy. Perhaps next year, if the war allows, both children can enrol at the university. Once Herbert sits his Baccalaureat next May.

Hetti too looked worn out. Despite the war, her work for Zimmermann did not seem to ease. Always enough ladies prepared to pay her prices. And in the evenings she was busy with the party. Not that this could be mentioned openly with the Fascists snivelling in every corner. You had to be careful these days. You never knew who was in their pay.

Wherever Menashe went, Hetti went too. You could not wrench them apart. Only God makes such couples. She had to admit that despite her antipathy to their political standpoint, she envied their happiness. She was sure Hetti was not searching for that joy when she was in bed with him. God forgive me for such unholy thoughts at the Shabbat table.

Letting the conversation continue without paying real attention to what was said, that leaves only me. Who am I but wife of, mother of, sister of? Do I exist in my own right?

And if the Russians come, will they really make me work in their factories just because I am not earning money? I work more than many a man who goes out every morning and comes home to be fed and clothed. Look at that Menashe, for instance. Yes, he does make Hetti happy. But what does he do all day while Hetti works? I must say this much for my Mendel — he has always provided. Even in those dicey days of the great crash. When I went home to put father on his feet, Mendel managed to build the business again. Slow at the start, but look at us now. Yes, we were big in Dorna, everybody knew the Hellers. But we are not doing too badly in the big city either. And he organised property in Palestine in case we ever get there. But how he hesitates about going. I always say, if we are going, let us go now. Before we are pushed out by the Nazis or the Russians. But he is an eternal optimist. Always trusting in his God and his good fortune.

And her parents. Anschel almost blind, sitting most days at his books, reading as much as his eyes permitted. He couldn't work any more, his money-lending business was run part-time by Dora, when her own health allowed.

As always, whenever she thought of her parents, a twinge of guilt. I should get to see them as soon as the snows melt. She recalled her visit home just before Hetti's wedding. When she told mother and father about Hetti's young man. Since then, she had managed to drag Hetti and Menashe to see mother and father only once. Dora wrote her a long, somewhat alarmed letter about Hetti's husband. I think he may be a communist, she wrote cautiously. But he treats Hetti well. Always helps her with her coat. Takes her by the arm. Walks slowly keeping up with her limp. I only hope they will soon have children. Hetti is not a spring chicken, mother wrote.

"I tell you," she heard Menashe's voice rise, strong and clear through her jumbled thoughts. "Carol is no longer in control of the Guard, Mendel. No use deluding ourselves. He has spent all his energies checking them after the Calinescu assassination, but they are stronger than apparent. I wouldn't be surprised if he grants them amnesty soon."

"I never heard such nonsense," Mendel said in his assured voice. "Look, after the assassination, he said he was disbanding them. It takes time to eradicate ideas and these people have been aspiring to fascist rule ever since they saw how well the German and the Italian fascists have done. But structurally, they are defeated."

"I would like to believe this no less than you," Menashe said. "Unfortunately, in the context of current European history in the making, they follow the same pattern fascists have followed in Germany, Italy and Spain. First there are struggles with the old-style establishment, rioting, gaining temporary power, rioting against undesirable elements such as Jews, and then access to power. The only difference between Romania and other countries where fascism rose is the amazing greed of all politicians here. The Guardists, believe you me, have endless amounts of money at their disposal, gathered through enforced bribes, so they can bribe on."

"But Menashe," Mendel pleaded patiently. "You are talking as if the Guard is still active. After all, it was dissolved in 1938."

"Oy, Mendel, you are so naïve," Menashe was his usual arrogant know-all self. "There are Guardists galore, they are simply underground. Many are in Germany. They fled there after Codreanu and his legionnaires were shot. We have information that they are being trained in German concentration camps so they can come back and try the same tactics here. And they have their network of spies and informers everywhere. I, for one, am followed wherever I go. I wouldn't be surprised if someone is lurking outside this house even as we eat."

"Really?" Herbert jumped out of his seat and ran to the window to look downstairs into the busy midday street. "How can you tell with all those people walking past the house?"

"Go back to your seat immediately," Mendel said. "Let me never catch you again getting up in the middle of a meal. Anyway, it's nonsense. What do they want with a low-ranking communist like you?" He laughed his short, nervous laugh and looked defiantly around the table.

"You never know who is in their pay," Rosa said. "Doamna Penescu, our washerwoman, told me yesterday that her son, that young good-for-nothing Nico who is always hanging about in the city centre, was recruited by them. Of course she told me he refused, but I wouldn't be too sure. He was doing nothing else and they could do with the money now that her husband has passed away."

"I wouldn't be too worried. Rumours like that have always circulated in Romania ever since I can remember," Mendel, the eternal optimist, said. "The Guardists too have their price. I am sure it's going to be possible to buy them off when the time comes. There is also the question of international guarantees. The Allies, and even Stalin, don't want to see a fascist dictatorship in Romania. They all need Romania with her cheap food and oil supplies, on their side."

"As do the Germans," Hetti said sarcastically.

"You are really naïve, father," Carla said. "After Chamberlain's performance, how can you trust the blasted Allies to protect Romania?"

"Carla, watch your language," Rosa chided. Really that girl will never be a proper young lady if she continues to go around with these students. I must talk to her about it.

"Anyway, father, why don't you make up your mind to go to Palestine?" Carla said, her voice petulant. And, Rosa thought, almost cheeky.

"I have been giving it a lot of thought recently," Mendel said seriously. "I am watching the situation closely and believe you me, I do tend to go along with the Zionists who are saying that leaving is the only way. But, on the other hand, we have property here, we have your grandparents, there are Herbert's studies and, of course, the business. I really don't know what is the right thing to do."

"As long as Stalin is fighting with Hitler, there isn't much to fear," Menashe said confidently. "I know you don't agree, but Stalin really knows what to do. And I must say again that if the Russians do come here, they would look after all workers. I have no doubt of that."

"This is rather irrelevant to me," Mendel said, his voice as gentle as always. "I wish to live neither under Hitler nor under Stalin. The one has declared his plan to finish us off, the other has sent hundreds of thousands to Siberia because they didn't think the right things."

"I don't know how we manage to turn every Shabbat meal into a political debate," Rosa said, collecting the plates. "What's important is to make a decision as to whether we stay and wait to see how the situation develops or make our way to Palestine now. The certificates we already have."

She got up with the plates, handing them to her Saxon maid to take to the kitchen as Carla started serving winter compote, Herbert's favourite dessert.

As usual, the Königs left soon after the meal, leaving Mendel and her to their Shabbat siesta. Carla went out for a walk and Herbert went up to his room to read.

As the apartment became quiet, Rosa, lying beside Mendel, said seriously. "Nu, Mendel, what are we going to do?"

"Do, Rosl? What do you mean?"

"You know the time has come to decide whether to use those certificates," Rosa whispered. "You have been toying with the idea for such a long time now. You even liked it in Tel Aviv. Carla certainly had a wonderful time, surrounded by all those adoring young men. Not that she told me much about what she did, but I gathered from cousin Mitzi's letters. Apparently when you weren't looking, she was having a great time."

"She was," Mendel smiled to himself. He was not going to volunteer too much information to his wife. She was so fussy about Carla. You'd think the girl was misbehaving, when all she did was go out to two or three dances with her young cousins. "But what has all that got to do with it? Tel Aviv is a rough place. We shall never have the same standard of living we enjoy here."

"I know that," Rosa sighed. "But what good will that do us if the king declares an amnesty for the Iron Guard? Did you see the daubings on the walls near the butcher? Death to all enemies of the fatherland. You spend most of the week in Dorna but I have to go to the butcher and the laundry and see the signs. This is how it started in Germany, Mendel."

"Sha, Rosl," Mendel said sleepily. "There is time enough to discuss all that. The war has been on only six months now and not much has happened. I've heard it called a Sitzkrieg. Everyone says it won't last long."

"I remember Onkel Duvid arguing with father saying the first war wouldn't last," Rosa said.

"Hitler is such a meshugenner, the allies won't let him carry out his crazy plans," Mendel said impatiently.

"Oy, Mendel, you do make me angry," her voice rose. "I am scared. Do we have to wait until it is too late? You and me, we both got through the first war by running away here and there. Then it was our parents who made the decisions, now it's up to us. There has never been anything like this before. Hitler wants to destroy us all and the Romanians are waiting for the right moment to join in the fun with their Totul pentru Tara. You know where you have heard the word fatherland before, don't you?"

"What do you want me to do, Rosa? Leave everything here and run?"

"No, Mendel, but I want you to start making arrangements and get ready. There is also the matter of our parents. I don't want us all to sit here until it's too late."

When the snows melted and the big muddy thaw filled Bucovina's rivers just before Pessach, Rosa made the journey to Cirlibaba. As always in the last few years, she was alarmed at how old they had grown. Dora's hair, tied tightly back, was all white now and her gait, once sure and broad, was slowing down. She ushered her daughter into the house which, Rosa found herself thinking, needed a fresh coat of paint.

They sat in the kitchen by the china stove, still lighting despite the longer days. Rosa spoke to her parents about the family, about Carla's new boyfriend, about how well Herbert was doing with his studies, about Hetti and Menashe. Anything but her fears about their future in Romania.

After lunch Anschel withdrew to his study. Rosa saw him struggle with the small print through a strong magnifying glass.

"Let me read to you, father," she said. "I know this is not woman's business, but your eyes are too weak to read this small stuff."

Anschel smiled. He handed her the book, finger-marked and grey with wear.

"There was a stone in Jerusalem," she read. "Whoever lost an article repaired thither; whoever found an article did likewise."

She read and Anschel explained the Talmudic problems as they arose, elaborating on interpretations by scholars and rabbis of the past. And from time to time, by his own Rebbe. He was enjoying himself and Rosa, herself not very interested in the complex world of Talmudic interpretations, took pleasure in his childlike joy.

They got to the end of the passage and he stopped her with a wave of his hand. "You should take that Mendel of yours and leave, Reisale," he said suddenly, his voice firm.

"What?"

"Now that the king has signed the amnesty for the Guardists, there would be no stopping them. With Horia Sima in the cabinet, I wouldn't be surprised if we enter the war soon on Germany's side. The only reason the King has signed that amnesty was German insistence. He was also afraid that if the Russians advance on the north of the country, the Allies wouldn't defend Romania," Anschel said. "The amnesty was all the Guardists needed. Only a few days ago a Jew from Timisoara came to the Rebbe and told an awful story of destruction of temples, Jewish shops and businesses by Guardists. Already they hold Nazi-like rallies and then loot and kill Jews, just like the Nazis, cursed be their name."

"Yes," Rosa said, her voice not much above a whisper. Reduced to the young girl she was when mother first said they were leaving Cirlibaba for Golden Bistritsa. "I know. And one hears terrifying tales from the refugees. Czernowitz is full of Jewish refugees from Poland, all desperate to get south to Bucharest. But Mendel reassures me that the King has the Guardists under control. He says there is plenty of time."

"There is no more time, Reisale, believe your old father." Using her childhood name which she had always hated but which now seemed protective. Caressing. "Do you remember your grandparents? Slaughtered by the Cossacks, cursed be their name and their memory for ever? If you stay, the Cossacks will be back. Only this time the danger comes from all directions. The Nazis yimach shemam, the Garda del Fier and the Cossacks themselves."

"If you are so sure, father, what about you and mother? And Tante Sara?" Panic rising in her stomach.

"We are too old to travel. Too old to start again."

"Nonsense. I won't leave you behind. If we go, you come too," she said, thinking we have been here before, this is not the first time we are running.

171

"If, shmif," Anschel said. "If you start taking everyone with you, you will never go. There are also Rachel and Yehuda Heller, no? They are certainly too old and sick to travel. And there is Hanna and there is Haim and his medical practice in Cluj and there is Hetti and her meshugenne communist, God keep us from such tsores." Big sigh. "No, Reisale. You and Mendel and the children must make the first move. You have the certificates. You are the only ones who can get out now, before it's too late."

"You think we should head for Palestine, then?" Rosa wished her father would take her in his soft, large hand and lead her to safety. She wished she did not have to cajole Mendel into believing the whole idea was his. She wanted to be taken care of yet she knew no one was going to. She knew it was up to her.

"How do I know? Palestine is not the safest place on earth either. All I know is that I want to see you out of harm's way here. You have always been the one who took it upon herself to look after everyone. Now it's your turn to look after your own."

"I don't know, father," she said, her voice one level above a whine. "Mendel is now talking about going as far as Bucharest and . . ."

"Bucharest is no good, child. Now that the Guard is in the cabinet, there will be no stopping them."

"Mendel says the King would not let them go wild in the capital, not with his Lupescu woman around. He says she'll make him look after her own, the Bucharest Jews at least," she said, repeating mechanically what she had heard Mendel say reassuringly so many times.

"I think your Mendel is looking for excuses, if you don't mind me saying so. Tell him the time has come. He has to make up his mind soon."

"I have told him, but he is still hedging. There is so much property and money tied up here, it's hard to let go. And then there are you and mother. I don't see how I can leave without you."

"I have already told you we are too old to start again. I have my studies and my Rebbe and your mother has her rounds. She is making a little money and with what you and Mendel send us, we don't need much."

Rosa went back to her childhood room and put her head on the pillow to cry. It isn't the first time, she kept saying in her head. We have been at this crossroads before. The first war, then losing David Greifer, then Oma and Opa Lax, then losing all during the crash and now this. If only someone would take her in his arms to lead her to safety. If only someone . . .

Later that evening, when father retired to bed, Rosa sat with

Dora in the kitchen, nibbling at her mother's cinnamon cookies. She wished she could lay her head on mother's broad shoulders and be rocked to sleep. But Dora had never rocked her children to sleep. Too busy. Too preoccupied with her own feelings. Stern. Remote. All she had ever instilled in Rosa were guilt and an eternal sense of duty.

"Mother," she started hesitantly.

"Yes, Rosl," Dora said, barely raising her head from her sewing.

"Father thinks we should move out, Mendel and the children and I."

"Yes. He has been saying this for a while," Dora said.

"And what do you think?"

"I don't know the answer, Rosl. You should do what you think best."

"But mother," Rosa raised her voice slightly, trying to shake mother into emotion. "I don't know what to do, mother."

Help me, she wanted to cry, her head bursting with indecision. You have always been so determined. You always knew what to do. Help me now.

Aloud she said, "I cannot go and leave you and father here. And Tante Sara. What will happen to you?" And the moment passed.

"Don't worry about us. We shall manage. We have always managed. Thanks to your generosity. And you know your aunt's obstinacy. She has survived the first war, she'll survive this one too, she says."

"But what if the anti-semites strike? What then? You remember Opa and Oma?"

"These are different times. We are too old, Rosl. No one will want to hurt old Jews like us." And for a moment Rosa believed her.

But she persisted. "You must tell me what to do, mother," she said at last.

"You must make up your own mind. For Mendel too," Dora said. "When the Russians came to Cirlibaba, I told your father it was time to move. I had to tell him. He would not have deserted his books."

"Yes," Rosa said. "Remember that peasant woman whom you helped to give birth here on the kitchen floor? And all the while the peasants screaming. And Trajan the coachman told me three women had been raped and I thought rape meant having your period."

Dora looked on at this outburst impassively. "I can't say I do," she said, her voice implying she thought Rosa's reminiscences trivial. "But I do remember that I had to get your father and you children out of here," she said evenly. "Now it's your turn. If you leave it to Mendel, you may never go."

Rosa returned from Cirlibaba determined to prepare for their flight. Every Friday as Mendel came home from the sawmill in Dorna, she asked how much timber was left. As the war progressed, Mendel was selling off timber and not buying new stock.

Immediately after Pessach, Rosa took down the curtains for washing and did not hang them back again. The apartment looked naked as the spring evenings lengthened.

Gradually more things got packed. Silver, cutlery, china, Czech crystal got packed into large hampers between bed and table linen. So we have something to put our heads on, Rosa kept saying with every additional packed item.

Whenever Hetti came for a meal, she remarked on the changes in the apartment.

"You are living like gypsies, when are you off?"

"I don't know. I only know we are going soon."

Hanna came into town from her country estate. Dressed in earthy colours, in country gear, completing her sensible manner. She too could not fathom the changes. "What's your hurry? Now is the best time to sell timber. War is the best time to do business. Let me get hold of your Mendel and tell him."

"Do me a favour and don't. All he needs is someone to persuade him there is money to be made out of this war," Rosa sighed.

Not that Mendel needed much prodding. Now he too was ready to go. In April his sawmill in Dorna was daubed mysteriously. Alle Juden Raus in big white letters on the wall outside the gate. On the bottom, in smaller letters the name of the Iron Guard newspaper, Totul pentu Tara, all for the fatherland.

The Friday after the incident, he was paler than usual. "It won't be long now, Rosa," he said, using her name ceremoniously. "I promise."

As the town's well proportioned streets filled with ragged-looking Polish refugees, Ostjuden if ever she saw any, trying to haggle over food prices, selling their few belongings, reminding Rosa of the Laxes' days in hostile Bistritsa, she was watching Herbert get lower grades at school. He was angry and confused, but Rosa felt powerless. The end of the year and his Baccalaureat were approaching but he could not concentrate and she could not blame him. She too wandered aimlessly across the apartment, trying to fill her days, waiting. She no longer talked about the University of Czernowitz. She just kept putting food in front of him as he sat for hours at his desk, daydreaming.

Carla went out less and less. Her friends were living in fear of conscription as rumours of Romania joining the war abounded. She wasn't seeing that boyfriend of hers any more. Like some of their friends, he had joined a Zionist group and moved south to Bucharest to prepare for emigration. Once or twice she mooted the idea that she too might join them only to be met by utter panic from Rosa. "We stay together now, Carla," she said briefly one afternoon as the sun was struggling to peep out of the clouds, a reminder of the post-snow rains which flooded the country, washing the stucco rococo Austrian architecture of their streets, remnants of better days as far as she was concerned. "The Heller family stays together in these uncertain times," she repeated. "Soon we will all emigrate and then you can join whatever movement you like. In Eretz Israel."

As her friends were clearing out, Carla helped Rosa to pack. They filled suitcase after suitcase as rumours of an imminent invasion escalated.

May of that year was warm and clammy after the big thaws. Rosa met with her friend Ada Merdinger for their weekly coffee at Friedlander's milk bar and told her they were planning to leave.

"You are crazy," Ada said, stretching her long hands and contemplating her long, red nails. "This will soon blow over. If you go now, you will be sorry later. Nowhere in the world can Jews have such a comfortable life. It's the ideal place for Jews like you and us who can pay their way. I keep saying to Martin how lucky we are."

"Lucky?" Rosa could not believe her ears. "Living in fear of either a Nazi or a Bolshevik invasion you call lucky? Having a Guardist in the cabinet you call lucky?"

"You are panicking, Rosa," Ada said, pursing her crimson lips. "Nothing much can happen here. Martin says that the Germans won't be able to break through the Carpathians. Anyway, why do they need to invade now that Romania is so friendly towards them? They can have all the grain and oil they like." She paused, looking at her friend. "I don't know if you know, but many Jewish bankers are involved in German finance. They need us Jews here and they need to leave us in peace."

"And what about the Russians?" Rosa said.

"Oh, I don't know. I just cannot see any trouble from that quarter," Ada said lightly. "Didn't you tell me that your communist brother-in-law says we'll all be alright if we can work?"

"If we can work. But can you see you and me working in a factory?" Rosa looked at her delicate hands which hadn't known real work for years, not even housework. She met her friend's eyes and they both laughed nervously.

"You can always buy your way out," Ada said confidently. "Haven't we always?"

"You may be right, Ada. But my father used to say that at times of war it is the Jews who suffer, always the Jews who are forced to move on. I don't trust the Romanians to protect us from either a German or a Russian invasion. They'll make us pay and they'll turn us over."

"If they turn us over, they lose their income, silly," Ada said as if scoring a point.

"I don't want to have to pay them forever, the greedy, lazy Romanians. All they ever do is eat, drink, sleep and fornicate," Rosa said. "All I know is that I want out of this uncertainty. We have had enough in our lifetime."

"I still think you are crazy," Ada said. "And so does everyone else. They talked about you in Temple last week, Martin was telling me. They think you are panic-mongers."

The friends parted feeling less charitable towards each other, each thinking the other crazy, wrong. Time will tell, was all Rosa managed to say to herself as she walked slowly along Herrengasse.

She didn't bother to look at the shop windows, crowded with goods as if there wasn't a war on. As Germany was advancing on the western front, Romania was luxuriating in affluence while the rest of Europe was pouring its all into the war effort. Garments from hard-hit France adorned the Czernowitz clothes stores. And all the while Germany, Rosa remembered Menashe saying, was making ever-increasing demands for food from Romania, where not enough grain was grown to meet all those demands.

Ada's words kept playing back in her head all day. What if we are wrong. Look at these riches. What if I am dragging Mendel away from his lucrative business and us all from our comfortable way of life where everything, including freedom, can be bought and sold.

The day Paris fell was not a good day for Rosa. Herbert had just got his Baccalaureat results which were mediocre, to say the least. Rosa felt a sharp pain reading the large headline in the Czernowitzer Allgemeine Zeitung bemoaning the fall of a city much admired by a country, the capital of which had always been called the Paris of the East.

Rosa looked at her son and said quietly, "At least you did better than Paris."

He looked up and said nothing. Later she heard him cry silently in his room and did not have the heart to comfort her tall, blond, bright son, whose young manhood was to be remembered by disappointments.

The sun was stiflingly hot early in the morning during the last week of June as Mendel was preparing to travel to Dorna as usual. Rosa packed him a small suitcase with underwear and some sandwiches for the train. He was to come home tomorrow. Now that the business was winding down, there was more work to get through in the Hellers' Czernowitz office than at the sawmill.

He kissed Rosa goodbye lightly and promised to see her the following day. "Don't delay," she said for some reason. Mendel laughed and said she was becoming a right old woman. "Everything will be alright," he smiled. "Don't fret. We are doing what has to be done and soon we'll be on our way."

The news of the ultimatum came as a surprise despite her preparations over the past few weeks. The collapse of France, the Allgemeine said later that day, means Carol will now have to reorientate his foreign policy and become openly a "neutral ally" of the Axis.

"The Soviet Government," said the Allgemeine, "has made official demands for control over half of pre-war Poland and for the cessation of Northern Bucovina and all of Bessarabia."

Rosa took the newspaper to Hetti's salon. "Read this," she said, her hands shaking. "What does it mean?"

Hetti took her eyes off the suit she was cutting on the large cutting table. "Wait a moment until I finish that jacket. I am almost there."

She continued cutting silently, then looked at the end product, muttering, "Good". She took the paper from Rosa and read in silence. "It means the Russians will be here any minute," she said, a small smile on her plump face. "Romania will have to accede to their demands, otherwise the front will move here and this is the last thing the Germans would let Romania get them into."

"Are you quite sure?" Rosa said fearfully.

"How can I be quite sure?" Hetti laughed. "I am not a prophetess. But it stands to reason, doesn't it?"

She looked at Rosa's pale face. "Why are you fretting? This is, after all, what you have been preparing for, isn't it? If you want to avoid the Russians, although I, for one, think you are wrong, now is the time to make your move."

"But Mendel is still in Dorna," the panic rising.

"When do you expect him?"

"Tomorrow."

"Don't be a hysterical fool, Rosa. These things don't happen overnight. I am sure tomorrow will be alright. Book your train tickets," Hetti said.

"Won't you and Menashe come with us?" Rosa pleaded, knowing the answer.

"No, thank you. There is no point in wasting your time on us. Menashe is actually looking forward to the day when Soviet troops will sweep through Czernowitz and the party can march openly through the streets with the red flag flying and him in the ranks. And me too, of course," she added, as an afterthought.

"You'll look after father and mother and Tante Sara for me, won't you?" Rosa asked, although she knew the answer.

"I suppose so," Hetti sighed. "I wish they were going too. This responsibility is too much for me what with the business, the party and Menashe. Or if they move to Czernowitz." She paused, looking Rosa in the face. "You are leaving your apartment?" she asked hopefully.

"The lease runs until the new year. You are welcome to move in after we have gone, but perhaps you can try and persuade father and mother and Tante Sara to join you here. Perhaps if they are not alone in Cirlibaba," her voice tried.

"I'll do my best," Hetti said, unconvincingly, Rosa thought.

She walked towards the Ringplatz. The perfect proportions of the Austrian architecture instilled a certainty for a moment, counteracting the fear she felt for her family, for her parents, for herself.

That evening she telephoned Mendel in Dorna and gave him the news. "Don't delay," she said again.

"I can only come as fast as the train will take me," he said.

The morning of the thirtieth of June brought news of an impending Russian invasion. Rosa was reminded of the day, during the last war, when the Cirlibaba peasants screamed with fear as Brussilov's troops were approaching.

"Go to the Allgemeine," she told Carla, "and find out whether it is today."

She sat in the apartment awaiting Carla's return. Herbert was pacing up and down the apartment where furniture with dust covers and suitcases made a past tense of the present.

"Stop it, Herbert," she said. "You are making me nervous."

"And what do you think I am?" he retorted.

"I wish your father was back," she said. "When does that train arrive again?"

"Three," Herbert said. "Nothing has changed since you last asked me this." He continued pacing.

Carla came back panting. "Nu?" Rosa accosted her before she could set foot inside the apartment.

"Tomorrow," Carla said, out of breath. "They said the invasion is planned for tomorrow." She looked up at her mother's face, searching for assurance.

Instead, Rosa gave her money and said, "Go find a cart and take these crates to the station and send them to Dorna."

To Herbert she said, "You go to Tante Hetti and say we are leaving for Dorna tonight. Give her the keys and tell her to tell the rest of the family."

"At last, something to do," Herbert sighed and left the apartment, almost running, not without his mother's warning to be careful echoing in his ears.

By the time they returned, Mendel was already at home. "You know who I met on the way to the station?" Carla said, out of breath.

"You are going to tell us anyway, so why ask?" Herbert said.

"Count Teodorescu, you know, that Ruthenian count from the big house by the park."

"What was he doing at the station?" Herbert asked.

"He was also taking some crates to be sent on the train, stupid. He is also clearing out," Carla said triumphantly. "In fact, he saw me trying to hire a cart and invited me to put my crates on his cart. He too wasn't taking much, he said. Travelling light, my dear girl, he said to me, helps you get to your destination faster. I asked him what his destination was, but he was pretty vague. Possibly Istanbul, or perhaps even further afield.

"I asked him about his family. He has seven daughters, I knew them at school. Such anti-semitic snobs they were. Now they are in the same boat. He said they had all already gone. Several were in Switzerland and one was married to a Syrian, imagine. His wife had gone a while ago and was waiting for him in Istanbul. She wouldn't be too pleased if she knew about the young female he had on that cart with him."

"Enough with that nonsense," Rosa stopped her. "Time to move now."

She cast a last look at her apartment where she had known a good life for the past ten years. The heavy oak furniture that was all the rage at the time. Her sofas and armchairs, all covered in white dust covers. The carpets, those too big to travel, rolled up, waiting for Hetti to unroll them. I am not going to brood, she reminded herself. Life must go on.

Aloud she said. "We have to walk to the station. Let us go now."

Mendel hugged her shoulders and urged the children to pick up their personal cases. His case, a leather hold-all, was heavy with well-cut suits, expensive shirts and starched nightshirts. He put on his winter coat which, in the June heat, looked out of place and said, somewhat sadly, "So, off we go."

"On our way again," Rosa sighed, echoing his sadness, carrying her black suitcase where she had packed her elegant costumes, her summer and winter frocks, her Viennese-style suits, matching shoes and silk underwear and nightwear. She put her case down for a moment to put on her Persian lamb, took her crocodile handbag in her arm and started moving towards the door.

The sad little party moved as fast as they could towards the station. Walking through Herrengasse, they called to say goodbye to friends in various shops on the street. Martin Merdinger, Ada's husband, looked up from the counter of his leather goods shop.

"You will be sorry," he said emphatically. "You are leaving at the wrong moment. Things can only improve."

Doctor Hecht, their physician, rolled his eyes to the ceiling when they entered his clinic. He too could not fathom their flight.

Rumours of their leaving had reached members of the Czernowitz Jewish bourgeoisie, many of whom now came out of their businesses and homes to plead with the Hellers not to be fools and wait for the Russians and the good life their arrival heralded. "I am sure there will be no anti-semitism, no persecution," Herr Amster, the accountant, said. "Look at me, I would have left long ago if there was real danger. I am usually quite good at predicting political disasters." The Hellers did not argue with their friends. They shrugged and continued.

By six they reached the station, a gold and white Austrian delicacy, where Menashe and Hetti were waiting to say goodbye.

"Look, our crates are in the same place I left them this morning," Carla cried, incensed. "I paid good money for them to travel."

Mendel went to the counter and money changed hands. The crates, he announced on his return, would travel with them on the next train, a cattle train, to Dorna.

"A cattle train?" Rosa was horrified.

"There is no passenger train until morning. We cannot delay any longer," Mendel said firmly.

"At least you will be sure of somewhere to sit," Menashe said.

"They all tried to persuade us to stay," Rosa said to Hetti. "All the good bourgeois are waiting breathlessly for your Bolsheviks."

Menashe laughed. "I don't know about them. All I know is that Hetti and I will be well looked after. Our work for the party, illegal as it was, risking our lives for the red flag. We shall be alright."

Rosa searched his face. "I only hope you know what you are doing. I hope you can look after Hetti."

"The train leaves in five minutes, time for goodbyes," Mendel announced.

Rosa's eyes filled with tears. She might never see that rebel sister of hers again, she thought. Then the thought hit her. She might never see mother and father and Tante Sara again. She clutched Hetti to her ample bosom and wept loudly. "Watch mama and papa and Sara for me," she cried. "Don't let them down."

As the train chugged slowly out of Czernowitz, going south to Dorna, Rosa's tears rolled silently down her rouged cheeks.

For years the thought of abandoning mother, father and Tante Sara will populate her dreams. To the end of her days, her silent crying will wake her up several times a night.

Rosa took off her Persian lamb and spread it over the crates, making room for the four of them. She took out of her case a carefully-packed parcel, wurst sandwiches wrapped in greaseproof paper, and offered them to her family. She then produced a large wine bottle which she had filled with hot tea. "It's gone cold, I am afraid, but it's better than nothing," she said.

Mendel smiled at her reassuringly. "We have done the right thing, Rosl. We are on our way to freedom."

As he said this, the train started slowing down. Rosa looked out, barely deciphering the name Gura Humorlui on the billboard.

"All out," she heard a shout. Clutching her coat close to her body and straightening her skirt to conceal the sterling she had earlier concealed in her garter, she stepped off the train, following Mendel and making sure the children were immediately behind her.

In the small station, darkly lit and ghostly, a small group of people gathered. Carla recognised Count Teodorescu and whispered wildly to Herbert, pointing to him and his "female".

"Jidans, here," said the young officer. Behind him was a group of soldiers, their rifles at the ready.

The count pulled his young woman aside, relieved. Doing this, he smiled at Carla apologetically and shrugged.

The small group of Jews was brought into the station master's office.

"Names, addresses," barked the officer. He made a list in a slow, unsure hand. Mendel gave their names and a Dorna address.

"We have reason to believe," the officer addressed them ceremoniously, "that you are carrying foreign currency. Travelling with foreign currency is not allowed according to his Majesty's regulations. Anyone wants to volunteer foreign currency?"

There was a small movement amongst the group but no one volunteered. The greedy bastards, Rosa thought, surprised at her own vehemence.

"We'll have to search," the officer said, coarse. "Men here, women here."

Rosa tightened her knees and resolute, approached the officer when her turn came for interrogation.

"Any foreign currency?" he asked, his voice almost a shout.

"Of course not," Rosa said calmly, pulling the hem of her summer frock up a bit. "If you don't believe me, go ahead and search."

The officer looked her up and down and recoiled. Her elegant assurance threw him. "Next," he barked. "Any foreign currency?" Rosa moved away slowly, her movements not betraying her trembling relief.

They were to be held at the station until further instructions as to what to do with them came. Rosa was prepared to settle her family on her Persian lamb on the station bench, but Mendel said quietly through his teeth, "This is impossible, I'll see what I can arrange."

He went to the officer, whispering in his ear. From where she sat in the dimly lit station, Rosa could see some notes change hands. Mendel approached her quickly, saying, "It's all organised. Come," leading his family into the sleepy town. "I know a small pension here where we can spend the night."

The following morning, the Romanian proprietor of the pension served them coarse bread and eggs for breakfast. "The Russians have entered Czernowitz at dawn," he said cheerfully.

"So I understand," Mendel said. He slipped the proprietor, a small moustachioed man, a note and said that if the soldiers asked for him, that he would be down shortly. To Rosa he whispered. 'I am going to find a way out of detention. You and the children wait here'."

Fortunately, the officer did not call before Mendel's return at noon with a young man who clicked his heels and bowed lightly at Rosa, saying the customary "Gnädige Frau", when Mendel introduced him as Domnul Ionescu, of the City Hall.

"We have just returned from meeting with the officer," Mendel said to Rosa. "Domnul Ionescu here has persuaded him that we come from southern Bucovina and need not be returned to the north. There is a train for Dorna in an hour. Our crates have already been transferred. It's a passenger train."

Rosa smiled at Ionescu. "Thank you so much, Domnul Ionescu, you may have saved our lives." As she said this, she saw Mendel slip Ionescu an envelope thick with notes. The young man left the room, walking backwards, smiling.

* * *

Rosa heard loud shouts from her sister-in-law's room. "Do you think we can live like this forever?" Mara was saying, her voice carrying over the rooms which separated them. "It's all very well for you, you are not at home. Mendel is not at home either, for that matter, but I am not able for it any longer."

"Keep your voice down," Rosa heard her brother-in-law say. "They can hear you."

"I don't care who can hear," Mara said and stormed out of her bedroom. Rosa left her seat by the window and went towards the door and her angry sister-in-law.

The two women met on the landing. Mara's expression froze. "I heard," Rosa said. "Don't worry. We'll be gone soon. I am sorry this is taking so long. Now that Carla has gone to Bucharest with her doctor's certificate, I hope we too will soon be allowed to leave."

Mara lowered her eyelids. "I am sorry, Rosl," she started.

"Don't say anything," Rosa said. "I know how you feel. I feel the same about not having my own home. And having our house down the road with strangers looking out the window isn't easy either. God knows when we shall have our own home again." She sighed and ran back to her room. Mara ran after her as Rosa collapsed on the double bed, sobbing. "Don't cry, Rosl. You know I didn't mean it," she said, patting her sister-in-law's shaking back.

"But you did, you did," Rosa cried. "We are refugees. Nowhere to go. And we are such a nuisance."

"No, you are not," Mara was desperate now to comfort her distraught sister-in-law. "It's just that I am under such pressure."

"Oh, I know under what pressure you are, Mara," Rosa sat up, still shaking, the tears streaming down her face. "Why don't you come with us too?"

Mara's pretty face lost its sympathy on hearing Rosa's last sentence. "Don't start again, Rosl. This is partly what I mean by pressure. I have a houseful of Hellers who never stop trying to persuade us to go to Palestine. I don't want to go to Palestine. I never wanted to go and I never shall go. Dorna is my birthplace, it has been good to me. I have a good life, a nice house, and many friends. Why should I go?"

Rosa had stopped crying by now. "I don't understand you. What are you all waiting for? My sisters mock me. My parents and my aunt say they are too old and reassure me nothing would happen to them. And you and Itzhak talk about your good life. Soon he won't be able to do business. What will you do then?"

"Oh, do stop it," Mara sounded irritated. "I am sorry you have heard me complain, but at times I do wish you'd shut up about the future. The present is enough for me to cope with."

"You may be right," Rosa said, her face dry by now. "I sometimes think we have been too hasty. But it's too late by now. Now that we have organised that doctor's certificate for Carla and sent her to Bucharest, there is no way back. I hope Mendel will be able to go next and then Herbert and I. It's a matter of a couple of weeks."

"Is there no way back, then?" Mara said. "Perhaps you can get Carla back, say you are not well, or something?"

"No, Mara. We have made up our minds, there is no way back," Rosa said. "I only hope it won't be long now."

That afternoon, as she walked towards Mendel's sawmill at the edge of the town, where the rivers Dorna and Bistritsa meet, Rosa decided they would leave within the week.

"She said she could not stand us being there any more," she told Mendel when he met her outside the sawmill gates. "We have to go now, Mendel. This is unbearable."

"I shall go right to the commandant and get our permits," Mendel said and Rosa knew it wouldn't be long. She took in the beauty of the valley and the hills, as they passed by the park on their way to his brother's house. They didn't talk and Rosa knew Mendel too was thinking of their first walk along the same paths when they first met.

"I didn't plan to stay here that long," Mendel said, as they approached the house. "What if we did not go in to eat and went to the casino instead to have a cognac?"

"You know what the casino is like these days," Rosa said. "Full of drunken Guardists. No, let's go and eat and retire early. I am tired. And perhaps we shall soon leave. We need all our energies for the journey. It's a long way to Eretz Israel."

There was no feeling of September in the air as the train started moving slowly out of the station. Rosa felt the sweat pouring from her armpits under her navy silk dress as she waved lethargically to Mara and Itzhak. At her side Mendel, in a light suit, the last to be cut by Hetti before they left Czernowitz, waved too until Mara's summer dress became a tiny yellow blob against the parched green of the mountain, all dry after the big heat of the summer.

"On our way again," she sighed. "There is nothing stopping us now. In a few weeks we'll be in Tel Aviv."

"I don't know about a few weeks. It may take a bit more. Have to organise passage. It all takes time. And money," Mendel said, sounding tired. In his dark eyes Rosa saw a new look, at look of fear. They were bidding farewell to twenty years which had started one snowy Tuesday at the town they were now leaving. She smiled at him and took his soft palm in her hand.

"I hope we have taken the right decision," he said, withdrawing his hand, his voice not at all the voice of her optimistic Mendel. "Everyone was so doubtful."

"I know we are taking the right decision," Rosa said, "even though none of our families was confident enough to join us. We were right about the Russians too. I have heard that Jews are not allowed to go to Heder any more and that speaking Yiddish in the streets has become dangerous in Czernowitz. What should we have waited for? To be rounded up and packed off to Siberia?"

"No one is sending people to Siberia, mother," Herbert said from his seat on the bottom bunk, already laid out for the night's journey. "I wish you didn't always expect the worst."

Rosa sighed again. Perhaps she was expecting the worst. But after all, her life had been full of disasters. She had always had to journey away from one danger into another. "Never mind," she smiled at her son. "A Jew is born to suffer, you know, there is not much we can do about it."

"What nonsense, mother," Herbert said, his face grimaced in disgust. "I really don't want to hear you say such rubbish again. It rubs off, you know. Look at it from the positive side and you'll see that we have taken the only positive course of action, considering our options. Not like some silly Jews who prefer to stick their tiny heads in the sand."

Rosa looked at the hills chasing one another as the train sped by. Past many names she had known as a child and others which became stepping-stones in her adult life. She tried not to think of her mother and father sitting silently by their china stove or her aunt Sara or her sisters. Time enough to think of it tomorrow, she told herself. Aloud she said, "Why don't we prepare for bed? It's going to be a long night."

Mendel nodded assent and they lowered their bunks and prepared to get into night clothes. Rosa looked at his big body, thinking about love. She had grown to love him in their twenty years together, as mother had predicted. Without flutters, without excitement. But there was a certainty about this man.

"If I die tomorrow, will you miss me?" she asked suddenly, her voice soft so Herbert, who now stood outside their compartment, would not hear.

"What a question," Mendel said and she could see him blush in the evening light.

"But really, I would like to know," she insisted.

"I would miss you very much," he said solemnly. "I have loved you from the moment I laid eyes on you in Dorna so many years ago." He stopped talking and looked at her. "And you? Would you miss me?" he asked, not daring to ask about love.

"I would miss you very much too," she said very softly and touched his hand lightly.

She did not say anything else and he did not ask. Their night train climbed one rolling hill after another as she thought, why can't I say I love him? What am I still looking for?

The morning light woke them from a heavy sleep. The train had slowed down and as Rosa drew open the calico curtain, she could see the greyness of the big city suburbs approaching. It was seven in the morning and they were in Bucharest, a city she hadn't frequented much in the past, preferring Vienna or Prague.

Carla was waiting on the platform at the Gara de Nord with a porter in tow. "Come quick," she said excitedly. "I've managed to get a trăsură. It's not easy these days. There are such crowds in town. It's simply full of refugees."

She pulled her mother's arm, letting Mendel and Herbert manage the luggage, leading them to what she thought was her waiting trăsură but what turned out to be a long queue of people who, like themselves, had just stepped off the train looking for a carriage.

"The dirty swine," she said, her voice more mature than Rosa had remembered. "I paid him to wait. You cannot trust those city drivers. I should have stayed with him."

"Never mind," Mendel said. "We'll get another. It's only a matter of time."

"This is not Bucovina, father," Carla said. "In Bucovina they are greedy but honest. Here they are greedy and dishonest."

"How is the pension?" Rosa changed the subject.

"It's just about clean," Carla said. "I got the landlady to scrub your rooms, but I wouldn't say it's perfect. But it's Jewish and they serve a kosher breakfast."

"Well done," Mendel said and patted his grown daughter on her head. Rosa nodded but said nothing. She could see Carla was now able to help provide, as she had done so many years ago in what now seemed another world. And she resented her daughter's newly-found independence.

The city heat was rising as the station emptied. The Hellers had queued for nearly an hour when Carla suddenly saw a trăsură approaching the station.

"It's him," she jumped excitedly as the open trăsură approached. "The dirty swine. Come here," she shouted in Romanian, a language Rosa had never mastered.

The trăsură, pulled by an ancient-looking horse which, Rosa thought, should have been put to pasture long ago, approached them as Carla shook her fist at the driver. "Come here, you," she ordered, her voice achieving an authority Rosa was beginning to appreciate and envy at the same time.

What followed was a fierce argument between Carla and the driver who clearly wanted to shirk responsibility, both speaking Romanian fast, using strong language Rosa shuddered at.

At the end it was Carla who won the argument. The driver dismounted his old carriage and helped load the Hellers' hamper and suitcases. The now much shortened queue looked on as the Hellers followed their luggage onto the old trăsură which, Rosa noted, stank of horse and sweat.

Carla gave the address of their pension and so began their slow drive along the Calea Victoriei, Bucharest's main shopping street, which at this hour of the morning was beginning to fill up with shoppers and strollers. The trams, packed with people hurrying to work, hanging onto the open doors, competed with trăsurăs, taxis and cars and the pavements were full of dark, small people rushing and pushing each other, all attempting to avoid the many beggars who, Rosa made a mental note, started work early in this busy city.

The shops were opening and city life, so different from Czernowitz, where everything was small and concentrated around the elegant Herrengasse, was bubbling and foaming in the rising autumn heat. At the end of the broad street, at a large square of what were obviously public buildings, Carla directed the driver to turn left.

"The pension is just off the Calea Victoriei," she said. "It's convenient for everything. If one could still go for a drink at the English Bar at the Athénée Palace, you could stroll there in no time."

"What do you mean, if one could still go for a drink?" Herbert said.

"I suggest we go to the pension and you take a rest, you all look exhausted," Carla said. "When you get up, I'll fill you in on what's been happening here. Things have been very unsettled, I am afraid. Being a Jew is not comfortable any longer. The Athénée Palace, once the haven of the British in Bucharest, is now full of Germans and more and more Germans are coming every day."

"You seem to have made yourself quite at home here," Rosa said, trying not to sound too negative.

"Well, I have been here almost two months," Carla said. "It hasn't been easy." Suddenly she looked like the vulnerable child she used to be until recent years and Rosa regretted her envy and censure.

"Poor girl," she said, hugging her tightly. "It must have been tough for you alone in this crazy city. I never liked Bucharest, you know. Not half as much culture as Vienna."

"It was pretty frightening at first," Carla said. "First of all, women and particularly young women cannot go out alone here. It's simply not done. Particularly since most Romanians are so dark and blonds like me are immediately identified as Jews and therefore a target."

"What about cousin Helena? Was she any help at all?" Rosa asked.

"She was wonderful. Without her I don't know what I would have done," Carla said. "She introduced me to some nice people and I met some of my old friends from Czernowitz, the ones who were planning to go to Palestine but got stuck here without certificates or papers. No, don't worry," she added seeing her mother's quizzical look. "He is not among them. He has since got to Palestine. One of the lucky ones. Then there are the ones involved in illegal immigration," she said this softly, looking at the back of their driver who didn't show any sign of having heard a thing. "It's very secret. Particularly now with Guardists everywhere."

"We'll have a lot to do here," Mendel said. "We still have to organise our passage and get the right papers. It will take some time. And a lot of money."

"Things have been dicey here for Jews recently, what with rumours of the King abdicating," Carla said. "You'll see for yourselves. Every day brings new rumours and new scares. The mood of the people is always reflected in the streets. The people of Bucharest seem to express their feelings so publicly, it is simply frightening at times."

They were now driving along a wide avenue where lime and chestnut trees shaded the cobblestones. There was little movement here, only a few people walking to the tram station and the horse's hooves clicked rhythmically in the silence.

Outside what looked like a large dwelling house, painted white, Carla ordered the driver to stop.

"That's it," she said. "A quiet place and full to the brim. I had to pay her handsomely to keep your rooms. There are simply too many Jewish refugees in town. Some live in the Jewish quarter, but frankly, I couldn't stand the stench. And besides, I was advised not to go there, in case of pogroms. There is a bad smell in the air."

As Rosa entered Doamna Bercovici's pension, she remembered the Hungarian whorehouse she and her parents stopped at on their arrival in Bistritsa. This is miles better, she thought with relief and aloud she said, "Looks quite nice," looking up to Mendel for his approval.

Mendel was not thinking about his physical surroundings. After a short nap, he went out to the Jewish community offices to see about organising papers. He would be back in the evening, he said, leaving Rosa to find out all she could about her new abode.

That was an eventful autumn in Bucharest. The king, who had been well disposed towards his Jews, perhaps because of his Jewish mistress, the infamous Madame Lupescu, had disappointed his people, having caused vast territorial losses, with Bucovina going to Russia, Transylvannia to Hungary and southern Dobruja to Bulgaria. Day after day during the month of September, the Hellers' first in the capital, people gathered in front of the palace shouting and demanding Carol's abdication. When they listened carefully, the Hellers could hear them call for death to the king, his mistress and advisers.

After the relatively abundant Czernowitz, where the shops had been well stocked until her last days there, Rosa was appalled at having to queue and almost beg for fresh vegetables to bring to their landlady so that she could make them one meal a day. The Jewish butchers laughed in her face when she asked for meat on meatless days, which now numbered up to four days each week.

"Who do you think you are," they shouted in Yiddish once they realised she spoke virtually no Romanian, "a lady? We have no meat for regular customers and you think you can barge in here and buy just about anything you feel like?"

Some days, the butchers in the Jewish quarter would offer her a piece of beef, for an inflated price. Rosa felt humiliated but she paid just to put something in front of Mendel and the children, whose mainstay now was mamaliga and badly baked bread, made with more cornmeal than wheat flour.

She would walk, tired and defeated, through the filthy streets of the Dambovita, where men in black caftans and women in headdresses reminded her of the Bistritsa of her youth, and tried not to think. But the inner voice would not keep quiet as letters from her parents started arriving, giving her news of Hetti and Menashe, both apparently settling well under the Russians.

Did we do the right thing, the voice would say, shrill and high-pitched in her head. Where is all this going to lead to?

Bucharest was full of people who, like her, did not know what the future would bring. These were Polish Jews who had managed to get out before the Germans occupied Poland, and Hungarian Jews who had left early enough to settle in Bucharest. Now, with more and more Germans arriving daily as part of the infiltration to control Romanian food and oil production, these Jews felt uneasy, fearing the rumours, which increased daily, of Romania joining the war on the axis side.

When the coup against the king came, it was bloodless and in contrast to the mounting fears, paradoxically silent. Carol and his fortunes were still in the palace as his young son, Crown Prince Michael, became king and general Ion Antonescu, a close associate of the dreaded Iron Guard, came to power, governing a cabinet mostly of Guardists.

The news on the radio indicted Carol and glorified Antonescu as the great hope for a greater Romania.

"I don't trust that man," Carla said and Rosa had to agree despite Mendel's reassurances.

"I have heard him promise there will be no bloodshed, which must mean he will protect his own Jews from Muntenia and Modavia," he said. "They all do. They can all be bought."

"This doesn't include Bucovina and I wouldn't like to stay here and try him," Rosa said. "How are we getting on with the papers?"

"You know I have been going every day to the Turkish consulate, but no luck yet," Mendel said. "For one thing, no one speaks any language I know there."

"Why didn't you say so," Carla said. "I'll come with you tomorrow. They are bound to speak French."

And so, Carla started going to the Turkish consulate daily

trying to obtain a Turkish transit visa which the British would not let the Turks issue. Rosa was always nervous when Carla went out on her own. She was also very unhappy when she was out with her friends.

"You don't have to sit in the Doi Tandifiri," she said time and time again. "The Guardists know it as an intellectual café and they are sure to raid it one of these days."

"But mother," Carla argued time and time again. "I never go there on my own. There is always a large group of us."

Rosa sighed. How long would she be able to keep her daughter wrapped in maternal cotton wool, the voice nagged. "Whatever you do, never come home with one young man only," she said. "It's a well-known fact that they are in the habit of picking up young Jewish boys and taking them to the station for interrogation and then, where would you be?"

"Yes, mother," Carla said, resigned to living under her mother's watchful eye.

"Your mother is right," Mendel said. "This isn't an issue of maternal control or hysteria, as you would have it. These are real dangers. You know Jews aren't safe after dark."

"Who is staying after dark anyway?" Carla said. "Yes, I know there are real dangers. But I wish you would stop treating me like a schoolgirl. A generation ago, I would probably already be married."

"This isn't the issue and you know it," Mendel said. "I would like you to convince your friends to move to another café and I would like you to come home in a group of people. This is not too much to ask. Hopefully, we shall soon be out of here."

"Sitting on half-packed suitcases is going to kill us all," Rosa said. "It isn't fair on you, children, but soon we shall be in Eretz Israel, safely away from all this."

When Carla was invited to her first ever New Year's Eve party, Rosa would not let her go. "You'd never know where she'd end up," she said to Mendel, who tried to convince her that if Carla spent the night in the house where the party was held, she would be perfectly safe.

"And what if they decide to raid this house?" she said.

"They could just as easily raid this pension," Mendel argued. "Let her go and enjoy herself. Life doesn't offer her an abundance of joy these days."

Carla was allowed to go to her Silvester party but Rosa didn't sleep the whole night. At midnight, as the city's bells were heard ringing, Mendel hugged her and wished her a happy 1941. Twenty-one years ago, on her wedding night just after the first war, things seemed more hopeful, she thought.

191

Mendel pressed his face into hers, whispering endearments in her ears. "Don't press me now, Mendel," she said, her voice on the edge of tears. "I am too frightened and confused."

"It was you who were so certain we had to go," he said softly. "Come now, drown your worries," said his voice as his hands pulled her to him. Her body resisted his advances but he was stronger. As she lay under his heaving body, her voice kept going. He was hard, demanding as always but there was a new flicker of cruelty in his rhythm, not heeding her fears which slowly became sobs, with warm tears rolling down her cheeks and onto his hard, bony shoulders.

Spent, Mendel did not console her as was his wont. Instead, he rolled onto his side of the bed, staring into the ceiling. "You withhold yourself from me," he said. "There is never an inch of give. Your worries always come first. When will you learn to trust me, to trust anyone?"

Rosa reflected. Possibly never, said her inner, lonely voice. Aloud he said, "I am frightened, Mendel."

"It's time to stop being frightened," he said. "Time to hope and time to give yourself to me." As she did not answer, he said, his voice registering despondency, "Now go to sleep," turning onto his side.

The first few mornings in January were icy as the snow piled high in the streets. Rosa and Mendel walked together in the snow, enjoying the ghost-like city. Once, as they approached the Athénée Palace, Mendel suggested they have a tuică in the English Bar.

Rosa hung on to his arm, her face buried in her astrakhan collar. She had said very little since New Year's night. She followed him into the lobby where, to their horror, a large Swastika welcomed them. The hall was crowded with young men, all speaking brittle German, different from their soft Bucovinian version of the familiar tongue. Rosa looked at Mendel and he nodded lightly as he turned towards the exit.

Outside, a convoy of black motorbikes carrying newly-recruited Guardists in brand new leather jackets and fur caps revved up to make room for a shiny black limousine which stopped outside the hotel.

"Come," Mendel said softly into her curls. "Let us away before they notice us."

It was only when they reached their pension that she started breathing easily again. "What a silly idea," Mendel said, "Having a drink at the English Bar. I am sure there are no English left at the hotel."

"Whatever gave you that idea?" Carla said when they told her.

"The town is littered with Germans. We've all known that for weeks. My friends never go out any more. We meet at their flats and make coffee in a pot instead of sitting in cafés now."

"I am glad to hear that," Rosa said. "Any chance those lazy Turks will give you the visas?"

"I'll go again tomorrow," Carla said. "Have we got the Romanian exit visas?"

"Not much point in getting those before we have the Turkish permits," Mendel said. "We'll get the exit visas alright. All you have to do is fold a couple of thousands into the application form."

That night Rosa, who could never forgo point scoring, said to Mendel, "Well, I knew there was something to worry about. Did you see those Germans? Not much different from the Germans in the newsreels. Our time is getting short, Mendel, I don't care what you say about me not trusting you. I want out of here. And soon."

Mendel turned to touch her shoulder. "Don't worry, Rosl," using her nickname for the first time since New Year. "I will do my utmost to get us out."

The following morning Carla and Herbert went to the Turkish embassy. "Don't wait for lunch for us," Carla said cheerfully. "We are going to meet a group who are departing for Palestine tomorrow. There is a sort of lunch farewell party as no one can have night parties any more. We'll see you late afternoon."

"Don't forget, demand those visas today," Rosa said. "And be careful where you walk, do me a favour."

Mendel said they might as well eat out at the Jewish restaurant, the only one which remained open since the Germans arrived. "I love Appelbaum's geffültes," he said.

Rosa shrugged and put on her Persian lamb, pursing her lips as she painted them redder than red. They walked out together along the Calea Victoriei where well-wrapped Romanians edged along the snow-covered pavements, fighting the icy winds, anything but sit at home, where heating fuel was in short supply and food reduced to grain and curd cheese.

At Appelbaum's they met Herr Gartenlaub, an old Bucovina acquaintance, whom they invited to join their table.

Herr Gartenlaub, who had just come to Bucharest a few days before, told of Guardist intimidation. "On the whole, however," he said, his cheerful grin lighting his otherwise dull expression, "things haven't been too bad. People are awaiting the bad times, which haven't yet come, thank God. Everyone is talking about the Russians in Czernowitz and saying how easy they have been on the Jews so far."

"And what are your plans?" Mendel asked cautiously.

"I intend to stay here until things calm down at home and then return," Gartenlaub said. "The children are settled, the eldest in Palestine, the youngest here, thank God. Now that Eva has passed away, what do I have to worry myself? Nothing much can happen to me now. I have enough money to last me a few months and by then, things should calm down, don't you think?"

He looked at Mendel when he asked this, not at Rosa, who thought, more fool you, why don't you up and go to your son in Palestine, but said nothing.

Mendel said something general about the need for caution these days but did not offer advice. "We have decided we have to move to Palestine, but who knows, if the situation in north Bucovina improves, perhaps we needn't have left?"

Rosa shot him a sideways glance. Can he still be wavering, she thought, but said nothing.

Appelbaum's geffülte was as succulent as ever and his soup smooth and tasty. The three chatted at length about mutual acquaintances and as the Hellers rose to go, Herr Gartenlaub promised to call on them the next day.

"Don't forget, we may not be here very much longer," Mendel called as they departed.

It was five before Carla and Herbert returned. Rosa, as worried as she always was when her children were out of sight, accosted them. "Nu? where were you?"

Carla did not say anything and dragged herself towards her mother, falling, exhausted, into a chair by the pension door.

"Let's go upstairs," she said and something in her voice made Rosa and Mendel obey in silence. Carla and Herbert entered their parent's bedroom and sat on the bed. "Sit down, mother," Carla said, her voice almost a whisper.

Rosa looked up. "But Carla," she started, silenced by her daughter's look.

"There has been a round-up of Jews today," Carla started. "We are lucky not to have been picked up."

"The Guardists have had some fun this afternoon," Herbert continued. "They drove through the streets in their motorcycles, picking up anybody who looked Jewish."

"Did you see this?" Mendel asked.

"We saw some of it and walked purposefully, not looking back," Carla said. "We saw them dragging some poor unfortunates by the arms as they drove their motorcycles. People were screaming and there was blood on the snow."

"They were beating them up with thick sticks and there were

some shots," Herbert said, his face pale, almost white. Rosa gathered both children in her arms, whispering, "My poor darlings, were you frightened?"

"Of course we were frightened, mother," Carla's voice started with a hiss and ended with a sob. "They were ... they were ... murdering Jews on the streets," she sobbed. And her voice trailed softly, a long wail, into the evening light which enclosed the four of them in the little room, enfolding them, away from the day's harshness.

"Where were you until now?" Rosa remembered to ask.

"We hid in some coffee house, speaking our best German and looking very confident," Herbert said. "It was Carla's idea," he added, shooting his sobbing sister a soft look. "We didn't want to run, they would have suspected. And being so blonde, sticking out like sore thumbs amongst the dark little Romanians. But Germans are also blonde, I figured, so we spoke our best German, pacing ourselves not to talk too fast. Then Carla said, into that café, Herbert, and in we went, facing the street and eating chocolate Torte with Schlagsane while Jews were being murdered. What irony."

"And then?" Mendel asked.

"And then they passed off," Carla said, wiping her eyes. "And we walked, still not too fast, over here. I hope no one suspected and followed us. It was all done so openly and not one Romanian said one word."

"What time was all that happening?" Mendel asked.

"After lunch," Carla said. "We had such a nice party and then our friends stayed and we decided it was time to come back. I know how worried you get, mother. And by the way, we have those damn visas."

"Oh, my God," Mendel said suddenly.

"What is it, Mendel? Didn't you hear what she said about the visas?" Rosa said.

"Gartenlaub," Mendel said. " I hope he didn't get caught up in this."

The following day they learnt the horrible truth. Their Buvocina friend, Martin Gartenlaub, was amongst the victims of the fighting between the Iron Guard and Antonescu's army supporters. In all 170 Jews were massacred that day. Gartenlaub, they learnt from his son, had been hung from a meat hook in the municipal abattoir and slashed across his face and his body until he expired and his body was thrown in the street outside the abattoir until his worried son was told where to get him.

That week was the saddest Bucharest Jews had ever known.

Funerals were carried out hurriedly so as not to vex the raging Guard, which lost its fight against Antonescu's troops. Guardists were still seen clandestinely roaming the now deserted snow-covered streets, like wolves looking for prey. But not many Jews were seen on the streets outside the Jewish quarter, where only few ventured from the outside to shop for food.

Mendel said a private Kaddish for Gartenlaub and when things calmed down, he made for the Romanian emigration office and, after due payment, returned to the pension with exit visas for the four of them.

Moving away again was a great joy for Rosa. Now we are really on our way, she kept saying to the children as they packed once again their few suitcases and linen hamper. We'll soon be home, our real home. As she was saying this, she caught Mendel's gaze and smiled. We are in this together, she was thinking. Away at last.

She wrote a final letter to her parents and sisters outlining the financial arrangements Mendel had made for her parents, as he had for his.

For themselves, he had arranged to transfer money via a local acquaintance — as taking money out was not permitted. "We are to receive this money in Istanbul," he said to the three of them. "I want you to know the address of the man who is supposed to have it for us, just in case something happens to me."

Carla and Herbert exchanged glances. "It's all becoming too much," Carla said. "Let's have our supper and go to sleep. It's going to be a long journey."

Their last supper in Bucharest was the usual mamaliga and bad bread to which their landlady, in an unusual fit of generosity, added two eggs made into a watery omelette. She sat with them as they ate, making her farewells, overstated and sentimental.

"What will you do now, Doamna Bercovici?" Carla said. "Now that your best guests are leaving?"

"New will come, Fräulein Heller," said the woman. "There is never any shortage of refugees in times like these, thank God. But I will never get such good, generous guests like your good parents."

Carla smiled and, moving her head towards Herbert, made a face so vile, he could not help giggling.

The morning train to Constanza was packed with refugees like them. People trying to leave this cursed land. When they finally reached the Black Sea, dazzling in the white winter sun, Rosa felt a heavy load lift off her chest. "God sei dank," she said to Mendel. "Baruch Ha Shem," he smiled back, squeezing her hand in his, the first gentle gesture since New Year.

As Mendel helped her into the old liner taking them to Istanbul, she heard Carla whisper, "They are here too. The Turkish embassy staff. I have seen them all, even the ambassador. Must have read the writing on the wall. Romania will be joining the Axis any day now."

7

Hetti 1975

Hetti wakes. Like every morning, five thirty sharp. Swollen hand wipes greasy forehead. Sweating. Why is my face always greasy in the morning. Haven't started the day and it's already greasy. One thick leg descends onto the cool floor tiles. The other, heavy even without the brace, gropes slowly. Finding the tile and touching the coolness. Alarmed. Small eyes peering at the grey-blue morning. Already shines, this pale Asian sun, so early in the morning. Too early.

Hetti limps to the lavatory. Every morning the same story. Constipation so early. It will take half the day for it to go. It will be hard today. God knows where I'll be able to find a clean lavatory in the cemetery. Must remember to take an old newspaper and scissors. To put on the seat. I am not prepared to sit on their filth.

The kitchen is always dark in the morning. The sun rises in the east but the kitchen opens to the sea. To the harbour and the tall tower of the grain silo. Hetti rolls up the new plastic shutter, seeing, like every day, the grey flag of the grain silo. Why don't they wash that flag.

On the grey work top a small aluminium coffee pot with two teaspoons of coffee and one of sugar, ready since last night, after the late news. Like every morning she regrets not having gone to bed earlier. But it is becoming harder and harder to sleep.

There is nothing like a good cup of coffee in the morning. They grind it for her twice a week in Jaffa street. This luxury I can still afford but who knows for how long. They say the Americans have given up drinking coffee since it became dearer. But they also say that the reparations money is going up. She read it in the paper last week.

The coffee is boiling. Boil it once and no more, Menashe used to say, if you don't want to kill it. Hetti is still in her nightgown. A coarse yellow cotton gown with puffed sleeves like a girl's gown which she makes for herself every six months. Like that gown sent to the camp by those stupid Bucharest Jews. We needed food but they sent nighties. Only that one was made from broderie anglaise and we had to sell it for food.

Hetti lets the coffee stand for four minutes, exactly, to let the grains go down. Pours coffee from the pot into a thick pyrex glass. She has seven pyrex glasses but only four saucers. I must complete the set one of these days. She never bothered buying a proper china service. Nothing could be as good as the Rosenthal we had in Czernowitz. She sighs.

She drinks the coffee and its heat awakens her, burning her innards. I always take my coffee too hot and my tongue burns the whole day afterwards.

The news isn't on yet. Not yet six. Hetti remembers the strong mother of her childhood as an old woman sitting for hours on Rosa's veranda hiccupping continuously and asking every so often, is it already six? Is it already seven? Thus, the entire day. She would sit, older than her years, a tortured woman whose time passed hellishly slowly, between the geraniums in black tin cans on Rosa and Mendel's veranda and the lizards running amok on the hot pebble wall. We shall visit her grave too today, after Mendel's.

After all these years she lived in Downtown Haifa amongst the Arabs. How Menashe spoke about the Arabs and their right to this land, which has become hers. Downtown Haifa didn't sound that bad. Independence Road. Independence for whom, she could hear Menashe laugh.

Houses corroded by the eternal presence of the sea. Tin roofs. Condominiums with patchy apartments and dusty shutters and bits of pale blue paint around doors and windows. Against the evil eye.

Opposite her window a dome which could be either a mosque or a church. There is a rusty cross on top but with all the Arabs it could be a mosque. Clay flower pots above her head and big glass pickle jars, turnips, gherkins, peppers. Dust everywhere. Grey, pale, so Asian. Hard to bear.

She rinses the pyrex glass and limps slowly to the bathroom, her legs swollen in the morning heat. She showers, splashing warm water on her thick body. An ugly scar crosses her stomach where they had cut away her womb. What luck I had Yossi first. What would I have done without that child, without that golden child, even if he is in Vienna. What would I have done without him? Again the back aches. It was never right since the camp. What can I do? I stayed alive. They say this is the main thing.

In the flowery housecoat, without underwear or shoes, she starts cleaning the little dark apartment. Dust everywhere. How it accumulates. Since yesterday morning. Hard to keep clean but I must clean up before I go to Tel Aviv, before half past six. Hetti sweeps, dusts, wiping the sweat off her greasy brow, blinking her small eyes towards the pale light.

The news at six o'clock. Another soldier shot. Lucky Yossi isn't here for reserve army duty, thirty days each year. Not like Carla's Avner. Poor Carla, she must be so worried, particularly now that she too is a widow. After the news, morning music which Hetti barely hears. Working fast, shaking sheets and pillows, folding sheets, covering the bed with the bedspread she crocheted several years ago.

In Yossi's room, she passes a fat-fingered hand on his tidy bed.

The bed which awaits him for when he wants to come home. She says aloud, "for when he wants to come home," knowing he won't.

When the radio announces six twenty-seven, she places the broom in the kitchen veranda by two giant glass jars with gherkins in brine, garlic and dill. She rinses her hands in cold water and looks at them, swollen, red, the nails cut short. She has no rings. Her wedding ring was bartered for food in Transnistria and Menashe didn't believe in engagement rings.

Hetti takes off her housecoat in front of the bedroom mirror. Her body thick, the scar ugly, the breasts thin, dwindling. I wasn't always like this. I was always plump, yes, but not fat. My breasts full, my nipples big, dark. How Menashe loved to play with them. How he whispered, close to my ear, his hands running all over my body. Hetti passes her hand along her body. What am I any more, only a ruin. That's all. But my face is alright. Small eyes, but my face is still nice. She looks straight into a trusting face, that of a girl, in the long mirror. She cups one thin breast in her hand to make it look round, full, like once.

What to wear. Tel Aviv in May is already so humid. And the dirt. And you are not supposed to wear gay colours. It's an anniversary after all. She decides on a round neck blue dress with half sleeves. She hasn't worn sleeveless dresses for a while now. My arms are ugly. Old. She places two white cotton pads in the armpits to prevent sweat stains.

Hetti packs her handbag carefully. A transparent blue head scarf. Matches the dress. A clean handkerchief. She counts five blue notes, slowly, twice, and puts them in her purse. Her key. Lipstick. She paints her beautiful lips and returns it to the bag. A small bottle of Ricci's L'Air du Temps which Yossi sends every year for her birthday from Vienna. His letter which arrived last week to read to Rosa and Hanna. Three chocolate wafers wrapped in foil and two purple plums, for the bus ride.

Hetti casts a last look at the darkened apartment. Everything in order. She bolts the new plastic shutter and shuts the kitchen window. She locks the kitchen door and hides the key in her sewing drawer.

Ten to seven. If I go down to the bus station now, I'll arrive exactly on time. Eight fifteen, eight thirty. Rosa will make me a cup of tea with milk and give me two of her cheese buchtels and we'll leave exactly at nine.

After all the years in the camp Hetti König found herself in downtown Haifa. When she arrived she lived first in a wooden shack in the transit camp in Tira with Yossi, who was ten when they arrived and skinny. Luckily two families from Bucovina

202

lived nearby and she could speak German to them. Other than them, everyone else had been a schwarzer.

She had to live in the transit camp for almost three years. There had been no question of reparation money then and she earned a little money by making alterations to people's clothes and charging as much as she could get away with.

When mother died, she moved with Rosa and Mendel to their two-bedroom apartment in Tel Aviv. They gave her a bed and Yossi a bed and Yossi went to school with Tel Aviv kids whose fathers dealt on the black market after the war and who always had money to spend at the corner kiosk. Every day he would return from school in tears. The other children would beat him and shout eshte romaneshte after him.

Hetti looked after the children of Doctor Mayer who had come from Bucovina in 'thirty-six when you could take all your money with you. They were very nice to her and after two years of a bed for her and a bed for Yossi in a room which also held the Hellers' wardrobe and into which Rosa came several times each day to get clothes or put clothes back, Doctor Mayer offered Hetti a loan, until the reparation money was fixed. By that time everyone knew it would be possible to get some money out of the Germans, cursed be their name. Not out of the Romanians. On the contrary. Rosa, Hanna and Hetti had to go to the Romanian embassy and sign away any claim to family property.

"Buy yourself a lease on something, Frau König," Doctor Mayer said. "It isn't fair on you or your sister to go on living like that."

Rosa and particularly Mendel had been very generous although Rosa would lose her temper occasionally but, Hetti figured, it was primarily because the apartment was too small. When Herbert came to stay, he had to sleep on the couch, which wasn't exactly fair. So she decided, after much discussion with Mendel, to accept the doctor's offer.

She chose Haifa because it was quieter and more beautiful. And because Hanna and Carla lived there with their husbands and children. Hanna suggested that Hetti should not look for a place on Mount Carmel. Property was too expensive and she wouldn't find anything large enough for the two of them for the money she had. Look at us, she said, living in a one-bedroom apartment, driving each other and little Anschel crazy. Try downtown. There are lovely old Arab houses, where the British used to live. High ceilings, large rooms and, most importantly, really cheap.

Hetti found the apartment on Independence Road and reflected on the ironic name, thinking how Menashe would have laughed. Surrounded by Arabs, Moroccans and stairs. Metal frames which dust and rust competed to corrode, like ants. The colours of death: yellow, dirty white, grey. Peeling plaster in small houses, faced in stone. And the relentless humidity of the sea.

Before she leaves, she puts the hated brace on her swollen leg. Then, handbag on her rounded arm, she locks her door. From the apartment opposite Arab music is heard. "Dalia," someone screams, "turn off that radio, do you hear? You are driving me crazy."

And Dalia's familiar voice shouting back, trying to drown the wailing music, "Leave me alone. Go to work and leave me alone."

Hetti shrugs. They are always screaming, her neighbours. Near the exit she remembers she had forgotten to take an old newspaper and scissors for the lavatory. She climbs the stairs, breathing heavily, opens the door and enters the shadowy darkness. She fishes the weekend supplement out of the paper basket. Haven't read it yet, perhaps I can read it on the way to Tel Aviv. Her short hand gropes in her sewing drawer taking out a small pair of scissors. With the newspaper and the scissors she sets out again on her way.

Above her head in the bus-stop colourful wool is blowing in the morning breeze. Raw material for tomorrow's rugs. Little workshops, grocery stores, carpentry shops, cobblers. Corrugated metal shutters rolled over dark holes where business starts early. And opposite, a row of houses amongst which her house too, a life lived on balconies. Women banging eternal dust out of eternal rugs. Pickle jars. Colourful washing hanging and blowing in the lazy morning wind. A couple of rusty wheels above a stone wall with various layers, like an archaeological excavation. Just like me. Layer upon layer of forgotten history.

Menashe would have enjoyed interpreting all this dialectically, she thinks and the pain cuts through her. When she came she joined the downtown Haifa cadre of the Communist Party but she could never quite understand what they were about. And without Menashe it didn't make much sense. She, a recipient of German reparation money and they, a motley crowd of Arabs and Jews, fighting for aims so alien. She stuck it out until Czechoslovakia, when Nadia, a strong-willed Arab woman who has since moved to Gaza, got up and said she could not stay in a party which agreed with tanks in Prague. Sit down, the branch chairman shouted, what do you know about tanks? Tanks are crushing us here too, Nadia shouted back, looking around and finding Hetti's bewildered gaze. We too are under occupation and the time is not long before we too will be crushed.

There was a big fight. Staunch party members sided with Moscow at all costs. Later Nadia said it was understandable. Some of their sons and daughters were studying in the Soviet Union and Romania at the expense of the party, so how could you expect them to criticize the hand that fed.

Nadia left and some of the Jews left and suddenly Hetti König found herself the only Jew in the downtown cadre. She met Nadia for coffee in Escander, an Arab restaurant down the road from her house and Nadia talked at length about her reasons for leaving. Hetti listened quietly. The time will come, Hetti, Nadia was saying, when Jews and Arabs will no longer be able to be brothers in a common political cause in this country. You mark my words.

Hetti went home and thought about what Nadia had said. What am I doing in the party, she kept thinking. When she was young, socialism was a rebellion against home, against the drudgery her parents represented. Against orthodox Judaism. She had never been able to see her mother as a woman who had tried to rebel against her own upbringing in her own way. Her father she thought indulgent, all studies and no action. And as for Rosa and Mendel she grew to resent what she chose to call their empire building and lack of social commitment. But was it envy, she found herself wondering now. Was it merely a way out of a miserable youth, when, lame and plump, she felt she had to hide behind mockery and squabbling to conceal her hurt from them all?

There was no one she could talk to about the crisis. Rosa would not have understood. To her getting out of the party was a wise decision, whatever the reasons. She still went on about verfluchte Kommunisten whenever the party got involved in political debates. She wouldn't have a clue. Party members would not want to see Hetti's point of view. What would you have done, Menashe, she cried night after night. Tell me what to do. But no voice came in reply and Hetti didn't go to the next meeting. She allowed herself to drift out of the party without making a stand, without a dramatic exit like Nadia's. Now she continued to live among Arabs, making their clothes and keeping her mouth shut whenever the horrors of the occupation bothered her. There were no more political arguments with Carla, who had her own family, or Herbert, who had left for South America. And even Rosa didn't bother to argue with her younger sister much since Mendel's death.

Communism had gradually become a pale memory, part of a distant past. Something to do with love.

Half-way to Tel Aviv Hetti gets the plastic bag with the plums and wafers out of her bag. She eats one plum gingerly and its red juice trickles down her chin. Her chin is covered with black hairs which she has to pluck every few days. Her skin is bumpy, greasy, full of black pores. I wasn't always like this. My skin was smooth, pink. Menashe used to say my skin was that of a young girl.

When the bus stops at Netanya she eats the second plum, remembering she wanted to read the weekend supplement. No point reading now. It's hard reading on the bus. I'd have to put on my glasses and anyway, it gives me nausea. Especially after eating the plums. Instead of reading she eats a wafer and looks out the dusty window. They never clean these buses, it's as dirty here as it was in the camp.

The dark-haired girl soldier in the next seat gets off in Herzlia. Hetti spaces herself, hoping no one will come to sit next to her. I am too fat for these bus trips.

At the entry to Tel Aviv the heat envelops her, black, noisy, steaming, like stinking steel wool. How could I have lived in Tel Aviv. The noise at seven in the morning, the buses driving through every small street. I am lucky to have my dark silence. Even though it is only downtown Haifa.

She gets off before the bus reaches the centre. Number 12 takes her almost to Rosa's front door. She limps slowly on swollen feet. Today would never end. How I hate anniversaries. At our age it's only a date.

Every year she has two dates: Mendel's anniversary and Hanna's husband's anniversary. Mendel was a good man. Despite our early arguments he always helped me. If only I had listened to Rosa and kept in touch with mother and father. Menashe could have been alive now.

Rosa and Mendel went and I didn't bother about mother and father and Menashe would not go with them to Mogilev when they pleaded with us to join them. It was all Transnistria, all camp territory, but they were better off with the money Mendel managed to get through to them. We had to go with the comrades, believing the Russians would save us. What a joke.

And now Menashe is dead. I don't know even where he died. Or when. Which is why I don't even have a day. And it's Mendel we all remember. Mendel with the soft voice and the large brown eyes. Even in his last few years, when he suffered so much with his digestion, he had a glint in his eye.

Hetti smiles to herself. I didn't know I had such thoughts. I had never before thought of him this way. But he was like a big child, always smiling. Even when things were bad in the Israel he had dreamt of. How Yossi loved him. He used to bring him little brown paper bags with chocolate sweets and sugared almonds when he returned from his business meetings, selling, dealing. There wasn't much business but he kept himself busy so he didn't have to sit on the veranda the whole day hiccupping, like poor mother.

Hetti takes a deep breath before she rings the bell. She smoothes her blue dress, passes a thick hand on her extended stomach. One has to make an effort for Rosa, she is always so correct, so perfect.

Rosa opens the door before Hetti rings the bell. She doesn't smile, never wasting anything. "Servus," she says, her voice low. "Come in, Hetti. Don't stand outside. You always stand by the door as if you have to prepare yourself to come in. Hanna is already here."

Hetti enters, her gait heavy, dragging her brace. She is already tired. How will I last through this day? Hanna sits on the sofa in the darkened room and sips tea with milk. On the table before her a plate of cheese cakes. Rosa's forte. They all bake them to mother's recipe, but Rosa's are the best. Hanna too doesn't smile. "Servus," she mumbles. "Did you have a good journey?" Then, without awaiting an answer, "I came last night. I cannot get up so early. I slept here." She points an arthritic finger to bedlinen heaped on the blue armchair.

The rules of the game are familiar to all three. Hetti is always tired and the prospect of spending a whole day with her sisters does not fill her with joy. Everything is always the same. Nothing changes. Why are our celebrations only anniversaries?

Rosa had been a lady once. A whole street was named after the Heller family in Dorna where the family owned banks, sawmills, hotels, even a car when no one else had one. No one knew what the street's real name was. She was used to giving orders to gardeners, servants, cooks. Hanna too had been a lady. She had acres upon acres of land and her husband's family, all gone in Transnistria, thought themselves too grand for the likes of the Laxes.

Now Rosa goes to the market on varicosed legs, buying half a kilo of aubergines, a kilo of onions, bargaining with the schwarzers, cursing under her breath. And Hanna sits in a kiosk selling sweets and newspapers, her back becoming less straight as the years go by.

And they are all widows, never remarried, clutching to the memory of their dead husbands and feeding on the lives of their children. Where are the spirited, lively Lax girls? What has become of us, Hetti reflects bitterly. Then, looking at Rosa who

207

enters with a fresh glass of tea for her and seeing the radiant, beautiful face and at Hanna, whose features are still delicate, despite the wrinkles, she knows they are still here, in this small Tel Aviv apartment. Her powerful sisters. It is only I who had died a little on Menashe's unknown death day. Only I whose rebellion had been quashed between the rivers Dniester and Bug, along the muddy, slushy roads to this promised land from Transnistria.

Rosa and Hanna had been good to Hetti when Yossi was a sad little boy. Now, far away from her, he writes three times each year: her birthday, Pessach and New Year, his handwriting large, round, saying nothing very much. Rosa always tries to find out from Hetti what he is up to and especially why he isn't married yet, but Hetti doesn't know so she cannot say. Rosa is sure, Hetti knows, that Yossi, how can she put it, is a bit strange. But she says nothing, not to hurt her sister.

Tel Aviv is beginning to get on Hetti's nerves. They are standing in a crowded bus and no one gets up to give them a seat. Her big body sways, like a sail in the wind, with the bus travelling fast, taking the bends sharply. Shrill music fills the air and the mad young driver — a schwarzer if she ever saw one — even smokes under the sign saying No Smoking, No Spitting. One day I'll spit in a bus, Hetti thinks and smiles rebelliously. I'll show them.

At the entry to the cemetery Carla waits for them. She has come straight from Haifa. A widow too, since last year. Last year she brought Ruth with her. All the way from London. It was just after her father died. Ruth clung to her mother's arm, her voice almost weepy. But how well-dressed she was, Hetti remembers and a sharp pain cuts her stomach in two. Yossi has nice clothes too, she says to herself. She finds herself saying these things to herself. Otherwise she feels uglier, poorer. Why do I always want to be like Rosa, she thinks and a bitter smile stretches her beautiful lips.

Rosa had always been luckier. She hadn't been in the camp. She left on time. Not that she didn't implore us to join her. And mother and father. But Menashe wouldn't hear of it.

The Russians will look after us, he used to say. Anybody prepared to work will be looked after. He said it so often that Hetti believed him. And mother and father wouldn't go because they believed no one would touch the old people. Little did they know. Mother never said much but Hetti managed to get Hanna to talk about father's death. Completely blind, he simply gave in one evening. Everyone came back from the field and he had stayed behind in the wooden barn which was their home in

Mogilev. He waited for them to come back and pointed to his Gemarra which he couldn't read any more. Give this to Mendel, he said faintly. Then his head dropped on his chest.

Mother, Hanna said, didn't cry. She called the leader of their group and asked if she could have some young men to remove father's skeletal body. There was a small burial ground outside their encampment. Someone said Kaddish in the failing evening light very fast and very softly and two men dug a small rectangle. His body was no larger than a child's. That night mother tried to get father's bread ration before his death was reported the following morning, but someone had already reported it and all she got was her own ration.

Rosa and Carla kiss and the traditional drama begins. Rosa takes out her black chiffon head scarf and wraps her beautiful greying hair. Dark glasses complete the picture. Carla wraps her perfect blond bun with a silk scarf and the two walk, holding each other, towards Mendel's white grave. Hetti and Hanna, also wrapped in dark transparent head scarves, walk behind them. Rosa, who hadn't said very much since morning, swallows little sobs. Hetti knows she is making an effort to cry, because this is the done thing. She hears the word Herbert mentioned and knows Rosa is also crying for her son, far away in South America, who cannot be with her today.

Mendel died at seventy-five. Sudden coronary. He had suffered with his digestion for years but who doesn't suffer with bad digestion in this country with sprayed fruit and cockroaches in the kitchen. When he died, it took no longer than five minutes. He didn't suffer but Rosa said it was harder this way. It would have been easier for her, she said, had he died slowly. Had she had more time to talk about everything. Plan. Get directions.

Not that she needed directions. She knew exactly what to do with the little money he had left, what to invest in, what to buy, when to sell. She knew exactly how to bargain five agorot off the price of strawberries and how to tell the glazier that his work on the kitchen windows wasn't worth even twenty piasters. She still called agorot piasters. She had never become used to this sudden independence. She still lives at the time of the British Mandate when Mendel had property. When he was somebody.

By the grave Rosa turns to Hetti. She hugs her sister and says, through heavy nasal tears, "Hetti, Hetti. My poor Hetti."

Hetti knows that Rosa says what she says because she knows how envious she is. Envious even of this miserable anniversary in this giant arid Tel Aviv cemetery, in this grey hot spring day, in the new state of the Jews who came from all over to this Asian country to crowd together in stinking noisy buses, to hide in dark apartments and to be alone.

She knows that Rosa wants to say to her that there is nothing to be envious about. That she too has difficult hours in her Tel Aviv apartment. That her aloneness is like Hetti's. And that she knows how hard it is for Hetti who hasn't even got an anniversary. Hasn't even got a day.

Rosa blows her nose noisily into a large white handkerchief. "I suppose we can move to mother's grave now," she says, her voice strangled. Carla puts her arm around her mother's shoulders and the two start moving slowly away from Mendel's grave.

Hetti and Hanna move close to Mendel's grave and put a small grey stone on the tombstone reading "Mendel Heller, Frasin 1890 — Tel Aviv 1965."

It isn't eleven yet but the heat is beating down. There is no spring here, summer comes directly after Pessach through exhausting hamsins. Not like the Bucovina of their childhood when new shiny leaves started budding on bare winter branches, when snowdrops and daffodils filled the fields around their house in Cirlibaba. This is Palestine, also called Israel, where you have to travel two hours by bus to meet your sister.

Hetti limps towards her mother's grave. The tombstone is more modest and father's name is engraved in black near mother's. Reb Anschel Lax, it says, died Transnistria at the hand of the enemy of Israel.

A sharp pang of hunger cuts through Hetti. Since Transnistria she is always hungry. After they sold all her well-cut suits which Menashe made her pack when it became clear they had to go with the others, there wasn't much left to eat. Coarse bread and, if there were turnips and potatoes, ciorba, and that was that. She was lucky, she kept some English wool lengths to wrap her freezing body and later, Yossi's thin body too. She had to sleep on her good woollen rags so they wouldn't steal them. She wouldn't part with them to the end, not even to buy food.

Poor father, she hears Hanna's voice, faint, through her aching thoughts. Didn't have the luck to be buried in the holy land. And Tante Sara and Itzhak and Mara and poor Ada Merdinger, Rosa says, nodding in agreement.

Hetti had never grasped the holiness. For her, life here was anything but holy. Life without choice. Because she couldn't return to the Czernowitz of her happiness with Menashe. Because Czernowitz wasn't in Romania any more but in the Ukraine and she knew that Jews, even communist Jews, found nothing but hate there. And because she couldn't go to Vienna.

Yossi didn't invite her even for a visit. Because she had nowhere else to go.

The four widows position small dusty stones on Dora's and Anschel's graves. A bare tombstone visited by no one but them. And they too visit it only when they visit Mendel's grave because Dora's anniversary is in August and who can get here in the heart of summer.

They don't shed tears at Dora's grave. Rosa takes off her dark glasses saying authoritatively, "You are coming to lunch, aren't you?" Carla explains, as always, that she has no time. She had to go back to Haifa and her work. Rosa argues and as always Carla wins. At the exit she kisses the three sisters and rushes to her bus. They return to being three tired old women waiting for a crowded bus on a white spring day in the dirty city.

Good job Menashe cannot see me now. Sweaty, even smelly. Worse than the peasant women who used to come to market to sell eggs or look for work in Jewish homes. Menashe said that one day the peasants would rise and stop being slaves, but I always felt I was better than them, even when I joined the party.

Then the fascists came to power and the peasants showed us very fast who was boss. Their children joined the Guard and they laughed at us. And being a party member did not make any difference. Our egalitarian politics didn't help. Our love of justice stood for very little. If only I had learnt to love the peasants, really love them and believe in their redemption like Menashe did. But Menashe too was not saved by his love of justice. Like everyone else, we too were led, like sheep to the slaughter, as they say. Like everyone else we had to go north to Transnistria, today part of the Soviet Union which Menashe dreamt of belonging to and which she cannot even visit.

They get on the bus, sit down, silent. The cemetery always makes them pensive. Rosa and Hanna think of their husbands and sink into their silence, saying nothing. Hetti too sinks, wondering why they are saying nothing. Leaving the cemetery is always a descent into the heart of sorrow.

When they reach Rosa's apartment Hetti remembers she hadn't gone to the lavatory. She must go now. In the last few years she finds it hard. A bitter problem. She doesn't need the paper and scissors she had carefully packed this morning but she wipes the seat with a piece of toilet paper. Her life moves between a desperate need to run to the lavatory and chronic constipation. She leaves the lavatory disappointed. Perhaps after lunch. It's only half past eleven. Since the camp nothing comes easily. She has all sorts of pains, some real pains which doctors can name and give her pills for and other imaginary pains she had invented so as not to let go of the camp and of Menashe in the hard years at the transit camp and later.

There were very few easy years. Perhaps only the years when Yossi served in the army. He was a weak, sad adolescent and when he enlisted, they made him a clerk and he served not far from home. They were reasonably good years. He would come home every evening, tanned, healthy and somewhat less sad. Then he went to the university to study philosophy but after a year gave it up. Hetti, who had worked hard before the German reparations to enable him to finish school and have everything the tall, strong sabras had, was broken-hearted when he told her he wanted to go to Vienna to study medicine. He went and times were hard again. She would save food from her mouth to send him money. She made clothes in her downtown Haifa apartment for her poor neighbours, cutting, sewing and finishing on her dining table. Slowly, her reputation spread and she became popular. She put aside all her earnings and once a month sent Yossi all the dollars she could buy on the black market.

And then he decided to stop studying once again. Hetti couldn't understand him at all. She had never understood her sad, silent child in spite of their years together, crowded into small spaces, thrown together in the years of transit from Ukraine southwards to Dorna, then to Bucharest and then in the shanty town near Haifa. He stayed in Vienna, worked in some business and Hetti knew that Menashe was not the only one for whom she didn't have an anniversary.

Hetti sits motionless in Rosa's room, livingroom by day and bedroom by night, trying, like always after the cemetery, to conjure Menashe's face. He had, she says to herself, dark hair and a thin, serious face. This she registered the first time she saw him when he barged into the chairman's words at the movement meeting. But what nose did he have, what chin. This she cannot remember now. She shuts her eyes, squeezing her lids tightly, trying to position him in front of her, trying to feel his smooth hands on her arm, on her forehead which has since wrinkled so.

But all she can conjure are bright, shining colours, dancing and swirling in front of her tightly shut eyes. The sun, the heat and tiredness can conjure only meaningless shapes, not her beautiful, wise Menashe.

She cannot remember him any more. This is the painful truth. She has no photographs, they didn't take any to the camp and no one took pictures in Transnistria. Hetti pulls her eyebrows and feels her hands clench into tense fists, like they always do when failure hits.

She hears Rosa and Hanna's voices speaking soft German in the kitchen and unclenches her fists slowly, deliberately. She limps slowly to join her sisters in the kitchen. The kitchen is small but she pushes her thick body in, standing by the sink, listening to their conversation. They aren't saying much but their quiet voices calm the void burning inside her like a white midday sun.

Although they always try to avoid speaking of it, Rosa and Hanna speak, like always, of their grandchildren. They are involved in bringing them up, just like in the old house, in the family tribe of their childhood when all were one big family.

Hetti half listens and as they speak she suddenly has an awful feeling of loss. As if she has missed the most important train of her life. She remembers Rosa's nervous flight from Czernowitz and her fear they might not have time to cross the border, bribe the officials, catch the train, get transit visas. She, who missed all this, knows now that she had missed many other things. The things which constitute, how can she put it, a normal life.

Her life had never been normal. Not by comparison with her sisters'. First there was the movement and then Menashe and the party. She could hear his voice now, suddenly, lecturing over hot, tasteless ciorba in the long summer evenings in the camp. There was no salt in their encampment and it didn't take long to get used to eating saltless ciorba. Gradually, their Jewish party comrades became ill or died. They were not as strong as the others, not used to physical existence, more used to words. Menashe and Hetti were left alone. Some nights they were allowed to sleep together on the dirty straw, which sometimes, when the weather got wet, had white maggots crawling underneath their bodies. Menashe made love to her on the infested straw, not whispering endearments but telling her, as he approached his climax, to be strong and survive because they had much work to do. Much work, he whispered as loudly as he dared, much work to do, my Hetti.

When the new commander came to Bogdanova, Menashe was not allowed to sleep with her any more. Strict segregation between women and men and regular morning calls to count heads were enforced. The new commander, a red-faced Romanian whose whip was not as fast as his tongue, made war on lice and typhoid. He gave them mattresses and made them burn the maggotted hay in the farmyard. Then he sent the men on work parties. Menashe would go chopping timber in the forest and one day he did not return. There were various versions but Hetti could only ascertain that he got into an argument with the sergeant about communism and the sergeant sent him deeper into the wood on his own. The work party was made to return without him after only a short hour of searching.

It was midsummer 1944 and by early 1945 Yossi was born. Someone said she should call him Menashe but Hetti cried out, how can I when I don't even know if he is dead. She gave birth quickly on the dirty frozen floor of her hut. No wonder he was always so skinny. Who needs grandchildren when I have this golden child, she thinks, and the fear invades her deeper and deeper in her sister's steamy kitchen. May he just come home to me, may he come home to me. She sings the words in her head and she knows he will never come.

Lunch at Rosa's always calms her stomach. The waves of fear abate and the storm becomes a light ripple of customary digestive pains. She reads to her sisters, no longer lucky ladies but two old Bucovina women sucking mamaliga with yogurt through false teeth, Yossi's latest letter. A letter like all his letters. "Nu, when will he get married, that Yossele of yours?" Rosa asks as always.

Hetti ignores the question. Lucky they took my uterus out. It's enough to have one such child who lives far away and who writes letters saying nothing. She passes a secret hand on her scar, smiling to herself.

Fruit compote and coffee and a long afternoon nap, an endless dive into the black. She is always tired but when she sleeps in the afternoon she cannot sleep at night. Never mind, I can always watch television tonight.

Evenings in downtown Haifa are always more beautiful than the days. The sea is dark blue and the stars shine golden over all the churches and all the mosques and all the small dark holes. In the evening you cannot see the rust or the pickle jars. All you can see are the lights on the verandas, all you can hear are the television sets.

It wasn't pleasant during the '73 war. Her party friends ignored her and her neighbours were tense. She thought of moving somewhere else but then she remembered Menashe and stayed put. Where could I have gone, I am like these houses, full of holes, full of broken parts, half church, half mosque, something God forgot to finish. Yossi didn't come home for the war, never mentioning it in his letters. When Rosa or Hanna asked her about it, she didn't answer.

She limps slowly towards her house. Eight thirty and the street is full of life. Suddenly she feels love for all these people, the schwarzers and the Arabs she despises during the day who only by night, in the dark blue hours, she can love quietly, without having to admit it even to herself.

In the letter box a sudden postcard from Yossi. The Spanish Steps, Rome. Dear mother, I am on holiday in Rome with friends. Having a wonderful time. Y. Fourteen words excluding the Y. What friends. Holiday from what. What do you do, my golden child? Why aren't you talking to me? She says all this to herself, mechanically, used to meaningless complaints.

She enters the dark apartment. Dusty smell again. I have cleaned only this morning. You can spend the whole day cleaning, sewing, shopping in Jaffa street and speaking to the neighbours using meaningless words. What a life. Nothing happens, nothing moves, just like the stagnant summer air by the grain silo.

Suddenly she sees Menashe. Without concentrating or closing her eyes. Hands in his pockets, snooty like a child. Sees them both after they first met. She shy, awkward. He confident, knowing where he was going. What love, she aches. Nobody understood. Her family thought she was crazy to marry a communist and his friends thought he was crazy to marry a limping bourgeois couturière. What love.

But then the war and the lists for the camp. They went north like everyone else. They starved like everyone else and haggled and bartered like everyone else. Menashe tried to organise a cadre in Transnistria but the people had no time for him after the comrades died one by one. Not used to physical labour, the comrades, who talked about work as if it was a religion, died like flies. Typhoid, gangrene, cold, hunger. Hetti and Menashe lasted longer than most but then he was taken away and she never saw him again. What love.

Rosa and Mendel got away. Hanna and Marcus went with father and mother to Mogilev and had an easier time. But Hetti didn't regret Menashe's obstinacy. They had their love.

After the war the men who survived were taken to the Red Army. Many didn't return. She took Yossi and as soon as the Russians allowed, started travelling south. Near a river she met a man who told her he saw Menashe up north. Lecturing on Leninism in the freezing cold.

Sometimes in the early morning, when she cannot sleep, she imagines Menashe hadn't died. That he is alive somewhere in Russia or Romania with another family. That he was told that it was she who died.

But it makes no difference which of them died. And so she continues to live with his fading features and with Yossi's short letters from Vienna and with a scar across her stomach and a brace. And that, as they say, is it.

She decides not to watch television. Perhaps I'll be able to sleep tonight. The cemetery tires me so. I am too fat, too heavy for this long journey. A journey from which I return less and less each time. There are still people who tell her, how lucky you are to have such a wonderful family, such wonderful sisters, such a successful son. But they say it less and less and she listens less and less.

She prepares a glass of lemon tea and sits, feet up, on the armchair in the dark room. She can hear a blond singer from a neighbour's television set, her head bobbing up and down and her voice plaintive, singing a throaty Hebrew song. Maybe I'll watch some television after all. It'll help me sleep. Anyway, what else have I to do.

The night is getting blacker and the smell of the sea fills the air. There are little lights at the edge of the water. Little stars, gold paper confetti in the heart of darkness.

Ruth 1984

Where did the journey begin?

Was there ever a day when you didn't know you would be travelling? Was there ever a day when you didn't know that love was a word of duty, a word of need? For the people saved from there, love was a different word.

You grew up arrogant but not confident. As long as you remember you were searching for the place from which you wouldn't have to journey. You have lived your adult life away from Mount Carmel. Every moment you have journeyed further towards a centre you have not yet reached.

Early in the morning, the town hall in Dorna starts chiming Porombescu's eternal jingle. Some mornings you go down to the market, where Rosa's German maids shopped, to buy Helena flowers. Or tomatoes. Or wild mushrooms. At lunchtime you celebrate with what she makes out of the treasures she has bartered that day. You talk and you eat and you stroll and every day that passes makes it more difficult to leave.

When you do leave, Helena and Siegmund and their neighbours and friends come to say goodbye at the station with flowers and cakes. This night journey is the easiest. You sleep through the night as the train speeds towards Bucharest. You sleep and you don't moan. Not like Rosa who shouted every night for the parents she had left behind. Not like Carla, golden, beautiful Carla who also cries in her sleep. For Rosa? For there?

Marshall has found his wife. A local beauty called Letti whose English rolls heavy on her tongue. She tells the most astonishing stories about being imprisoned in a psychiatric hospital and not being allowed to see her child because of her Jewish background. You celebrate your last day in Romania with them: Letti has just been given a passport and a hope for freedom.

You invite them to dinner in an open air restaurant by the Athénée Palace. You order beef and wine. Don't order champagne, Letti pleads, it's immoral. I can live for a week on what you are spending here tonight. You have got to get used to spending money, Marshall tells her. In America you will have plenty. Letti looks at him, not understanding a word. The band plays on and you want them to dance, but Letti is too bewildered. The bill comes to less than ten pounds. Will you be able to get rid of these damned lei before you go?

By now Bucharest is familiar territory. After years of hiding the fact that your people came from Romania you feel proud to belong here. It has taken this journey for the sabra arrogance to thaw. You are an exile like the rest. You are there now.

*　　*　　*

Where did the journey begin?

Did it begin here, on the tarmac before boarding the Tarom plane leaving Bucharest? Up until now you have been travelling one way — the journey back will take the rest of your days.

Books from Cleis Press

Night Train To Mother by Ronit Lentin. ISBN: 0-939416-29-8 24.95 cloth; ISBN: 0-939416-28-X 9.95 paper.

Beyond the Border: A New Age in Latin American Women's Fiction edited by Nora Erro-Peralta and Caridad Silva-Núñez. ISBN: 0-939416-42-5 24.95 cloth; ISBN: 0-939416-43-3 9.95 paper.

Peggy Deery: An Irish Family at War by Nell McCafferty. ISBN: 0-939416-29-8 21.95 cloth; ISBN: 0-939416-28-X 9.95 paper.

The Little School: Tales of Disappearance and Survival in Argentina by Alicia Partnoy. ISBN: 0-939416-08-5 21.95 cloth; ISBN: 0-939416-07-7 8.95 paper.

Cosmopolis: Urban Stories by Women edited by Ines Rieder. ISBN: 0-939416-36-0 24.95 cloth; ISBN: 0-939416-37-9 9.95 paper.

The One You Call Sister: New Women's Fiction edited by Paula Martinac. ISBN: 0-939416-30-1 24.95 cloth; ISBN: 0-939416031-X 9.95 paper.

Unholy Alliances: New Women's Fiction edited by Louise Rafkin. ISBN: 0-939416-14-X 21.95 cloth; ISBN: 0-939416-15-8 9.95 paper.

You Can't Drown the Fire: Latin American Women Writing in Exile edited by Alicia Partnoy. ISBN: 0-939416-16-6 24.95 cloth; ISBN: 0-939416-17-4 9.95 paper.

With a Fly's Eye, Whale's Wit and Woman's Heart: Relationships Between Animals and Women edited by Theresa Corrigan and Stephanie T. Hoppe. ISBN: 0-939416-24-7 24.95 cloth; ISBN: 0-939416-25-5 9.95 paper.

And a Deer's Ear, Eagle's Song and Bear's Grace: Relationships Between Animals and Women edited by Theresa Corrigan and Stephanie T. Hoppe. ISBN: 0-939416-38-7 24.95 cloth; ISBN: 0-939416-39-5 9.95 paper.

The Absence of the Dead Is Their Way of Appearing by Mary Winfrey Trautmann. ISBN: 0-939416-04-2 8.95 paper.

The Shape of Red: Insider/Outsider Reflections by Ruth Hubbard and Margaret Randall. ISBN: 0-939416-19-0 24.95 cloth; ISBN: 0-939416-18-2 9.95 paper.

AIDS: The Women edited by Ines Rieder and Patricia Ruppelt. ISBN: 0-939416-20-4 24.95 cloth; ISBN: 0-939416-21-2 9.95 paper

With the Power of Each Breath: A Disabled Women's Anthology edited by Susan Browne, Debra Connors and Nanci Stern. ISBN: 0-939416-09-3 24.95 cloth; ISBN: 0-939416-06-9 10.95 paper.

Woman-Centered Pregnancy and Birth by the Federation of Feminist Women's Health Centers. ISBN: 0-939416-03-4 11.95 paper.

Susie Sexpert's Lesbian Sex World by Susie Bright. ISBN: 0-939416-34-4 24.95 cloth; ISBN: 0-939416-35-2 9.95 paper.

A Lesbian Love Advisor by Celeste West. ISBN: 0-939416-27-1 24.95 cloth; ISBN: 0-939416-26-3 9.95 paper.

Different Daughters: A Book by Mothers of Lesbians edited by Louise Rafkin. ISBN: 0-939416-12-3 21.95 cloth; ISBN: 0-939416-13-1 8.95 paper.

Different Mothers: A Book by Sons and Daughters of Lesbians edited by Louise Rafkin. ISBN: 0-939416-40-9 24.95 cloth; ISBN: 0-939416-41-7 9.95 paper.

Long Way Home: The Odyssey of a Lesbian Mother and Her Children by Jeanne Jullion. ISBN: 0-939416-05-0 8.95 paper.

Fight Back! Feminist Resistance to Male Violence edited by Frédérique Delacoste and Felice Newman. ISBN: 0-939416-01-8 13.95 paper.

On Women Artists: Poems 1975-1980 by Alexandra Grilikhes. ISBN: 0-939416-00-X 4.95 paper.

Since 1980, Cleis Press has published progressive books by women. We welcome your order and will ship your books as quickly as possible. Order from: Cleis Press, PO Box 8933, Pittsburgh PA 15221. Individual orders must be prepaid. Please add shipping (1.50 for the first book; .75 for each additional book). PA residents add sales tax. MasterCard and Visa orders welcome—include account number, exp. date, and signature. Payment in US dollars only.